I0674936

The Englische Voice

Book 6 in The Amish Singer Series

by Bob Nailor

I thank and praise You,
God of my ancestors.
You have given me wisdom and power,
You have Made known to me
what we asked of You,
You have made known to us
the dream of the king.

Daniel 2:23

ISBN: Book: 978-1-61877-181-0
ISBN: Ebook: 978-1-61877-180-3

This Page Left Blank

The Englische Voice

Discover other titles by Bob Nailor at
www.bobnailor.com

Dedication

This book is dedicated to
the ladies of The Bryan Alliance Church
and my fans nationwide
who, when finished reading prior books would ask:
What happens next?
Thank you, ladies, for pushing me beyond book one.
This is the finale.

Cover collage by Bob Nailor.

This Page Left Blank

Table of Contents

PRELUDE

Daniel sat on the edge of the bed. He listened to Martha sleep and he smiled, yet the dream was vivid. He gazed off into the corner of the room where a shadow danced as the moonlight cast a cool blue-white light of the wind blowing branches outside the window into the room.

The dream. He sat in a room with several people and watched a young lady... an Amish lady sing as she sat on a ladder at the edge of the stage. It was not really a ladder, Daniel thought. It was more of a make-shift golden staircase with white billowy stuff to look like clouds.

Daniel smiled at the memory. He knew the young woman; she was a granddaughter, but there was a man with her. She gazed at the man with loving eyes. He was *Englische*.

He froze at the realization. A granddaughter? he thought. Why would my granddaughter sit on a ladder and sing? Why would she be in love with an *Englische* man?

Sweat broke out on his forehead. She was sitting at an Eck table with the *Englische* man. They were married.

Daniel shook his head. It didn't make sense. Amish and *Englische* cannot marry.

Daniel tried to remember the words of the song, but they failed him. Yet, he knew them. He could hear the words both his granddaughter and the *Englische* man were singing.

The dream troubled him; he'd had a similar dream years ago but the *Englische* man was not part of that dream.

CHAPTER ONE ~ It Begins

Monday, May 13, 2013 8 a.m.

Rachel hummed her various tunes as she worked. Even at this early hour, she was amazed at the number of dirty dishes from breakfast. Rachel rinsed and cleaned the dishes then placed them into the trays to be sent through the heavy-duty washer. She glanced at the opposite end of the washer. She nodded. *I can send at least another two or three trays through*, she thought.

"Say, Rachel," Katy Hack called as she chopped lettuce. "Instead of humming those songs, why don't you sing them for us."

"Yes," Viola Stuble agreed. "I'm older than both of you put together, so what I want, well, that's what goes. Sing, Rachel. Sing."

Rachel stopped humming and broke into *Where're You Walk,* one of her favorites, filling the kitchen with her voice.

Joshua Beiler, the general manager for the restaurant sat outside the kitchen's swinging doors, working on next week's menu and specials with Chef Harold Abbott.

"Did somebody turn the radio to a station with opera?" Joshua asked. He cocked an ear toward the swinging doors to listen closer.

Harold shook his head. "No, that is Rachel singing. She has a beautiful voice."

"Rachel... Rachel..." Joshua mumbled as he tried to place the name. "Oh, the 3D girl we just hired." He grinned. "I don't know who came up with the 3D name, but I do like it better than Dirty-Dish-Duty. He leaned back in his chair. "She can sing?"

Harold shrugged. "You're hearing her. That's her."

"We start a new production at the theater in six weeks." Joshua paused. "I want her to try out for Ladder Angel. Her voice is angelic and a perfect fit for the spot in the play."

"She won't do it," Harold said, shaking his head. "She's Amish."

"We'll see," Joshua replied and once more studied the sheets of paper in front of him. "We'll keep the potato carrot bisque and add this chicken lemon rice soup as a second option for the daily soups."

Harold nodded and continued to listen to Rachel sing. He enjoyed listening to her voice.

\# \# \#

Monday, May 13 2:30 p.m.

Joshua Beiler sat at his desk going over the accounts when the soft rap on the door caught his attention.

"Come in," he said and watched Rachel enter. "Have a seat, young lady." He motioned to a chair.

"Have I done something wrong?" Rachel asked, hesitantly sitting.

"No. No," Joshua said. "On the contrary. It is what you haven't done."

Rachel frowned. "What I haven't done? I do dishes. Is there more?"

"You sing, Miss Graber," Joshua said. "I've heard your voice."

Rachel shrugged. "I am sorry. I will stop singing."

Joshua shook his head. "Oh, no, no, no... That isn't the issue." He leaned back in his chair. "Why didn't you tell me you could sing?" He paused. "What is the name of the one that sounded like opera." Joshua inhaled. "The one about walking."

Rachel shrugged. "Everyone can sing, Mr. Beiler." She smiled. "Not everyone wants to sing. The song is called *Where're You Walk.*"

"So, you're an Amish philosopher who sings opera," Joshua said with a grin. "Interesting." He leaned forward over his desk. "What I want you to do is try out for the new play at the Blue Gate Theater." He paused. "Specifically, the ladder angel."

"I am Amish," Rachel said, remembering the *Rumschpringe* stories of her grandfather and his trip to New York City. "I am not an actor."

"There is no acting, Miss Graber," Joshua said. "You will sit on a ladder... okay, call it a staircase, and you will sing." He shrugged. "That's it."

"No, Mr. Beiler," Rachel said. "That is not it. I am Amish and we do not play act." She clasped her hands together in a firm grip. "I am sure there is a costume involved."

Joshua squirmed in his seat, trying to figure out the best answer.

"Amish do not wear costumes." She stood.

"Please." Joshua stood and once more motioned for her to take a seat. "Please sit, Miss Graber. Let's not be hasty." He watched her slowly sit back in the chair and he sat then rubbed his first two fingers over his lips as he thought. "No costume. I think we could accommodate that." His mind ran rampant in thought. "In other words, you would consider doing the song if you could wear your daily Amish clothes?" He paused. "Or, perhaps a piece of white cloth draped over the front of your Amish dress from shoulder to shoulder?"

Rachel froze. She had been caught in her own words.

"Tell you what, Miss Graber," Joshua said. "I want to come try out for the part, sing the song and see what you think. If you are still against the idea, so be it." He stretched his hands across the desk. "Please?" he begged.

Rachel nodded, realizing that he would continue to ask if she said no.

"Thank you," Joshua said. "Tomorrow, 9 a.m., at the Blue Gate Theater. Come inside and you'll find me up near the stage."

Rachel stood to leave.

"You will be there tomorrow?" He cocked an eye at her.

Rachel nodded and left.

# # #

Monday, May 13 5:30 p.m.

"Mama?" Rachel called as she entered the house.

"In the kitchen," Bethany replied. "What do you need?"

"I must call Grandpa Yoder in Centertown," Rachel said. "It is very important."

"What is so important you must call him?" Bethany asked.

Rachel sat on the bench at the kitchen table. "They want me to try out for a play at the Blue Gate Theater."

Bethany nodded. "Go call Aunt Mary and wait for Grandpa Yoder to call you back." She turned to peel another carrot. "I will hold the evening meal for your return."

Rachel scampered out of the house and hustled toward the Miller farm where the Amish phone booth stood at the end of the driveway.

"Aunt Mary?" she asked as the phone at the other end answered.

"Yes. What do you need?"

"This is Rachel Graber in Shipshewana. I need talk with Grandpa Yoder. Can you get him and have him call me back?"

"I will Rachel. How are things there?"

"We are all fine, Aunt Mary," Rachel said. "I need Grandpa Yoder because they want me to sing at the theater. He knows what to do."

"I will get him and have him call you back. Tell Bethany I said hello."

There was a click and the line went dead. Rachel hung up and waited.

She sat in the small building wondering how long before Grandpa Yoder would call her back.

The phone rang, startling her. She answered.

"What is the problem, my dear grandchild," Daniel Yoder asked.

"Grandpa." Rachel began to cry. "I have been asked to try out for a play at the Blue Gate Theater." She inhaled deeply, stifling the tears. "They want me to sing."

Daniel paused to think, remembering his *Rumschpringe* in New York City and the issues of costumes and songs. A tear welled as he remembered his close friend, Adam Brown from Australia who was killed.

"There is no problem in singing, Rachel," Daniel said. "Costumes? Exactly what costume do they expect you to wear?"

"I am not exactly sure, Grandpa," Rachel replied. "He said something about me wearing my Amish clothes with a cloth draped across me in front. I will sit on a ladder."

Daniel weakened. The dream came back, vivid. He saw the girl on the ladder singing. He knew it was his granddaughter. Now, he saw her face clearly. It was Rachel. Daniel tried not to let his voice waver too much,

"I think you should do it, Rachel." He hesitated, wondering if he should reveal more. "I see no shame in doing it." Again, he paused. "It is not the Amish way, but I do not think you will be shunned for the action. Check with the Bishop and get his approval, but first, find out exactly what they expect of you."

"Thank you, Grandpa," Rachel said. "I will do that. When are you and Grandma coming to visit?"

"Soon, Rachel. Very soon. I must go now." He hung up.

Rachel hung up the phone and ambled her way back home on the dusty road. She sighed. *Tomorrow, 9 a.m., I will sing for Mr. Beiler and find out what is expected. Then I will talk with Bishop Zwyer.*

CHAPTER TWO ~ The Try Out

Tuesday, May 14, 2013 9 a.m.

Rachel hesitantly opened the door to the theater. *Should I knock?* she thought, but decided to just go on in. The theater was dark with only lights highlighting the stage.

"Bring up a blue light over on the ladder to the right," an older gentleman yelled. "No, not the red. The blue. I said BLUE!!"

"Is Mr. Beiler here?" Rachel asked as she walked between the tables.

"Over here, Miss Graber," Joshua Beiler yelled, standing up from a corner table. "Jack! This is girl I was telling you about." He motioned to the older man stomping in front of the stage. "Come here."

Rachel joined him at the table as Jack fumed toward the same table.

"Jack Sonner, this is Rachel Graber. Rachel, this Jack Sonner. He's the director of the new play, *Romance in an Amish Dream*."

She stretched out to shake his hand. "Nice to meet you."

"So, you have the voice of an angel, as Joshua has told me repeatedly."

"I sing, Mr. Sonner," Rachel replied. "Voice of an angel?" She shrugged. "I truly doubt that."

"Allow me to be the judge of that," Jack said. "What I want you to do is go up to the stage. See that ladder to the right?"

Rachel nodded.

"I want you to sit on the third rung from the top and sing this." He pulled folded sheets of music from his hip pocket.

Rachel gazed at the music sheets and the words. She scrutinized the notes and questioned some of the words. She flipped to the second page, then thumbed through the next three pages.

"This is a lot of music," Rachel said. She glanced at Joshua. "I thought you said a song."

"It is one song, Miss Graber," Joshua said. "He gave you all the songs for the full play." He pointed at the first page and the song there. "Sing this one. Let him hear your voice."

Rachel once more studied the first page.

"You can read music. Yes?" Joshua asked.

Rachel cast a glance at the manager. "Yes, my grandfather made sure I knew how to read notes when he taught me how to sing."

Joshua frowned. "Your grandfather taught you to sing? Is he not Amish?"

Rachel smiled. "Yes, my grandfather is Amish. He is a teacher at the Amish school in Centertown, OH. He is the one who taught me to sing the song you heard me singing in the kitchen yesterday."

Joshua's eyebrows knitted into one long, hairy caterpillar across his face. "Your grandfather sings opera?"

"Yes," Rachel said. "He learned to sing light opera in school and then went to New York City on *Rumschpringe* and was to have the lead in an off-Broadway play, *Specters of Ghostly Raw*. The original lead was killed and my grandfather, Daniel Yoder, was to take his place.

"Daniel Yoder?" Jack questioned. "An Amish man?"

"Yes," Rachel replied. "He is my grandfather."

"I knew him," Jack said. "I was in that play; one of the backup ghosts." He shook his head. "What a mess that was. The lead, his name was... was..."

"Adam Brown," Rachel said. "He was from Australia."

"That's right," Jack said. "The old lady with the purse strings killed him for the rights to his play."

"*The Fair Dinkum Bogan* as Adam wrote it," Rachel said. "Or *Australian Dreams* as it was finally called by Preston Powers."

"You know your history," Jack said. "I was in both plays with Preston and Peter. When your grandfather walked out of *Specters*, they were beside themselves."

Rachel grinned. "My grandfather is Amish. Broadway was not for him."

"Do you want to be a star?" Jack asked.

"No," Rachel replied.

Jack shrugged. "Fine. Now, get on stage, on the ladder and I will start the music for you to sing."

Rachel walked up the side of the stage and stepped up to rungs to sit on the third rung from the top. The music started. Rachel held the page of music up and began to sing.

> *As the sun begins it journey*
> *Across the sky of blue*
> *The flowers lift their heads*
> *In adoration praise.*
> *I believe in the Lord*
> *For His word is true.*
> *I believe, I believe,*
> *For His word is true.*

Jack leaned toward Joshua. "You're right. The voice of an angel. She's perfect for the part." He paused and glanced at Joshua. "She's Amish. Will she do it?"

Joshua frowned. "I don't know. She already told me she doesn't play act and won't wear a costume." He nodded at Rachel. "What if we draped a shimmering piece of fabric over the front from shoulder to shoulder? Would it appear to be angelic?"

Jack nodded. "That could work." He analyzed the image of Rachel on the ladder. "Plus, we could attach wings to the ladder that appeared to be attached to her." He shrugged. "That could work, maybe."

Joshua nodded.

"Thank you, Miss Graber," Joshua yelled toward the stage. "Please, come join us."

Rachel stepped down from the ladder and hustled toward the waiting men.

"We want you for the part, Miss Graber," Joshua said.

"Yes," Jack added. "You're perfect."

"I do not act," Rachel said.

"You won't be acting," Jack said. "You will sit on the ladder and sing at the appropriate times during the production."

"Amish do not wear costumes," Rachel blurted.

"No costumes," Joshua said. "Remember, I asked about a cloth draped across you. You'd still be wearing your Amish clothes under it."

Rachel stood there, analyzing the proposition. *How do I get out of this?* she thought.

"Think about it, Miss Graber," Joshua said. "You can let me know tomorrow or the day after."

Rachel nodded and left the theater.

# # #

Tuesday, May 14 about 10:15 a.m.

"So, Rachel," Katy began. "How did the tryout go?"

"They want me to sing the part for the show," Rachel replied.

"Did you hear that, Viola? They want her."

"You realize if she does that, you will be back on 3D." Viola grinned.

"If it be, so be it," Katy said. "I'll be in the front row of tables to see that play." She grinned. "Maybe every night."

"You don't make that much money," Viola said. "But I will join you on opening night to see our girl singing her heart out."

"I am not sure I wish to be in the play," Rachel said. "I am Amish."

Katy wiped her hands on her apron and rushed over to Rachel.

"Miss Rachel Graber," Katy started. "You are talking nonsense. Do you want to spend the rest of your life doing dirty dishes in this kitchen? Or, do you want to be a star? Singing. Making people happy?"

"I am Amish, Katy," Rachel restated. "I do not wish to be a star."

Viola dried her hands on her apron and approached.

"Fine," she said. "You don't want to be a star. If I have to, I'll fire you and then you'll have to take that job." She placed a hand on her hip. "Do you want me to do that?"

Rachel hung her head. "No."

"Fine," Viola said. "You march up to Mr. Beiler's office and tell him you'll take the job as a singer at the theater." She placed her hands on Rachel's shoulder. "Trust me, dear. You'll enjoy it. I've listened to you sing. It is your passion." Viola turned Rachel toward the double swinging kitchen doors. "Now, scoot. Mr. Beiler and your future awaits."

# # #

Rachel knocked softly on the door to Joshua Beiler's office.
"Come in," he called.
Rachel opened the door and entered.
"Ah, Miss Graber." He stood. "Have a seat."
She moved across the room and sat at the chair in front of his desk.

"I came to tell you I will sing," she said.

"That's great," Joshua said. "I didn't tell you earlier, but you will be making more money."

"I will?" Rachel asked.

Joshua nodded. "I think about thirty or forty dollars more a week."

Rachel nodded. "That is nice."

"Rehearsals start in two more weeks. Until that time, I will have you continue to do your job as 3D. But, starting Monday,

June 3, you will be at the theater each day, Monday through Friday, learning your part in the show. Understood?"

Rachel nodded.

"Fine," Joshua aid. "Now, here are the pages of the songs you need to learn to sing." He smiled. "You won't be holding them during the live performances. So, start memorizing."

Again, Rachel nodded. "I understand."

He stood. "Thank you, Miss Graber. I know Jack will be thrilled to know you are on-board as the ladder angel." He grinned. "Jack really loved your voice."

Rachel lowered her head, hoping she wasn't blushing. "Thank you." She stood to leave.

"I am sure this will be a wonderful experience for you, and the play will be a major success."

Rachel approached the door. "Thank you."

"Will your grandfather be coming to the performance? I'm sure Jack would like to touch base with him." He shrugged. "I'm guessing it has been several years."

Rachel nodded. "I am sure Grandpa Yoder will be here." She opened the door and left.

CHAPTER THREE ~ Punishment

May 16, 2013 4:46 p.m.

Less than a year and I'm so out of here! Evan slammed the bedroom door, punched the power button on the stereo, and leaped through the air to flop onto his bed. He grabbed the full-ear-covering, external noise canceling headphones from the bedside table, and snapped them over his ears.

"Screw them all," he mumbled as the twangs of a country song blared in his ears. "He has no idea what I want." Evan didn't hear the insistent knocking on the door.

"Since you won't answer." Nathan opened the bedroom door and stepped inside. He reached over and powered down the stereo system.

Evan responded instantly, glaring at his father, climbing out of the bed, stomping to the stereo and shoving his father's hand away before pressing the power back on. "You have no right," he screamed. "That's mine. Leave it alone."

Nathan grabbed the headphones and snapped them off Evan's head. "In actuality, this whole system is mine. I bought it, you took it." He placed the headphones on the console. "Now, you're going to listen to what I have to say. I've put up with your crap, and listened to your rantings." He glared at Evan. "So, you sit and listen to me. I'm your father."

"Sure, Dad." Evan slurred the words at the older man in the expensive suit standing before him. "Tell me how much you love me. Tell me how lucky I am to have all this." The young man stretched out his arms and waved at the bedroom walls. "Yeah, like you always do. Tell me all about how good I have it." Evan looked down at the watch on his wrist. "Oh, wait a minute. Don't you have a date with somebody, somewhere, in about three minutes. Isn't this where you give me a hug, pass me fifty bucks and head out the door to party with a client?"

"You're only seventeen, Evan. You don't know everything about the world." Nathan edged closer to the door while glancing at the watch on his wrist. "Yes, I do have an engagement. And yes, it is a meeting with a very important client. You see those skis, that surfboard, your clothes, and this stereo?" He pointed, jabbing his index finger at the different items spread throughout the room. His eyes finally came to rest on Evan's feet. "When I was a kid, I didn't get two-hundred-dollar sneakers or three-hundred-dollar watches."

"Yeah, well, Dad..." Evan didn't hold back on the snide. "You love me, remember? This is how you show me how much you love me."

Nathan raised his hand but let it fall back to his side. "Without my clients, you wouldn't have any of this. To be successful and have all this, I need to work. I'm sorry you're alone. Your mother died six years ago, but there was nothing I could do about that. It was an accident."

Evan glared at his dad. "You're the one who took her off life support. That wasn't an accident. It was you who finally killed her in the end. Sure, the thug did some damage, but you, YOU alone took her off the machine that was keeping her alive." A tear welled up. "While she was on the machine, at least there was hope."

"We'll talk about this when I get back home tonight." Nathan grabbed the bedroom door handle. "I'll be back." He reached into his pocket, pulled out the money clip, snapped a couple of bills free of the clip and placed them on the book shelf by the door. "Call for pizza, Chinese, whatever," he mumbled. "I should be home before ten. Get your homework done. We'll talk then."

Evan watched the door close and listened to it click shut. "We'll talk then," he whispered in mockery of his father's words. In one swift, quick movement, Evan lifted his right arm up, catching the bend with his left hand to stop it at mid-chest, allowing his hand to snap up and the sole finger flip defiantly into the air: the bird. "Up yours, Dad!" He reached over and snatched the bills and wadded them into his jeans pocket. "Sure, I'll get Chinese. Happy Dragon is only three blocks away and I can get me a beer without anyone asking my age."

He snapped the power on the stereo system while pulling the headphone plug out. Music blasted through the room. Evan joined the song, singing as his voice blended with the country singer. He picked up the guitar and strummed with the song.

Yeah, less than a year, he thought. I am so outta here and will be touring with some band, any band.

# # #

Nathan hated the way Evan blamed him for Barb's death. Yet, there were secrets Evan didn't know. He silently leaned against the hallway wall and listened to Evan vibrate the walls with the loud music behind the closed door. Nathan's mind blurred with the images and memories of his wife in the hospital. The police thought it started as a simple hold-up which escalated to her being beaten, hit in the head with a brick and finally, brutally and sexually molested. He saw Barb's pained face in the recovery room after the operations. There was no way she would live. Even if she did respond and came out of the coma, she would be more vegetable than human. The doctors gave her less than a ten per cent chance of survival. For five days he was by her side, ignoring everything, and everyone, before he finally pulled the plug on the respirator. Evan didn't know about the rape. Nathan took a deep breath and softly let it out before walking the long hallway to the front door of the apartment: the big apartment filled with too many memories.

#

Evan strolled the street. He had his hood pulled up over his ball cap and his hands shoved down into his jeans. He wasn't looking for trouble, but he carried an air of trouble about him. People avoided looking at him, or even getting close.

He gazed up at the stupid neon light of a red dragon changing from smiling to non-smiling and then back to smiling, again. Happy Dragon glowed in golden neon. Evan yanked open the door and entered the restaurant.

"Ah, Evan, you come eat here tonight?" Lin Ho smiled and welcomed the young man to the restaurant. "You lucky tonight. My brother has new shipment. You work, yes?"

Evan watched the small Chinese man. "I eat." He hesitated. "How much work?"

"Big shipment. Very big. Need much help. You make plenty money."

"Sure, I'll help after I finish eating." He smiled at Lin. "Make it Gong Bao Chicken and a bottle of Tsingtao."

Lin Ho bowed. "Follow me to seat." Lin scurried toward the back, near the kitchen doors. "You eat then I take you to my brother." He bowed again and chattered Chinese to a waitress who quickly disappeared and returned with the bottle of Tsingtao beer.

Evan consumed his meal, paid, leaving a nice tip before following Lin Ho. This time Lin rushed him through the kitchen and out the back door to a waiting car.

"He take you to my brother, and he wait for you. My brother pay you good."

Evan was always leery of being shanghaied, but felt pretty comfortable with Lin Ho. The driver zipped through the streets and alleys, finally stopping at the wharf. "We here," the mysterious and up-to-this-moment, silent driver said.

Evan got out and quickly spotted the activity. Another short Chinese man approached.

"You name Evan?"

Evan nodded.

"You work hard, I pay good. Follow me." The man headed back toward the activity. "Carry this inside. Follow man ahead of you. Repeat until all moved."

Evan watched for a few seconds as the collection of about six men marched from the warehouse to the ship, where they grabbed a bag, heaved it onto their shoulder and marched back to the building. He shrugged. *Definitely a no-brainer*, he thought. Evan stepped into the line and grabbed a bag, hoisted it onto his shoulder noticing it wasn't as heavy as he thought it would be, and followed the silent man ahead of him.

Three hours later Evan got back in the car and counted his money as the silent driver wove a path back to the restaurant. Evan got out and made sure the one hundred plus dollars he'd earned was safely stuck in his pocket. He headed home.

# # #

Thursday, May 16 10:20 p.m.

Nathan glanced up when the door opened.

"Where have you been?" he yelled as Evan entered the apartment. "You look like... like... What have you been doing? Fighting?"

"No," Evan replied. "I went to get me something to eat." Evan headed down the hallway toward his room. "Chinese, if you need to know."

"Get back here, Evan. We aren't finished. I want answers."

Evan twirled on his heel and glared at his father. "Me, too. I want answers. Where were you? Who did you see? What were you doing?" He narrowed his stare at his father. "See? I can play your game."

Nathan's eyes widened in surprise at his son's latest belligerent actions.

"If you must know, Dad." Nathan heard the slurred last word from Evan as the boy flung his hoodie through the open bedroom door. "I got me a Chinese meal of Gong Bao Chicken and then I worked out with some new friends. Finally, I came home. Now, does that make you happy?" The boy spun around and headed into his room, and as tradition had been established, slammed the door behind him.

Nathan knocked on the door before opening it and walked to Evan's bedside. He held an envelope in his hand. "Since you seem to be answering questions, answer this one. Why is Mrs. Anderson sending me a letter about your refusal to turn in homework? You don't feel it is necessary to hand in English term papers?"

Evan rolled over on his bed to face his father. "You tell me, Dad. You obviously did term papers on book reports when you were in school. Be honest. Did it help you with your work tonight? Exactly how many of those book reports have been critical in locking down a deal?"

"Fine," Nathan said and walked to the large window. "I'm not going to fight you about book reports. If they fail you, so be it. You fail." He looked out on the night scape of the big city, watching the lights flicker far below. "You don't seem to have any focus. It's obvious you have no respect for me." He stared at his son's athletic build. "You're willing to spend time working out, but not get a job. I've been thinking. For summer break, which will be in three short weeks, you'll spend the time with your grandmother in Indiana."

"What?" Evan rolled off the bed and stood. "With who? Where?"

"Grandma Kurtz in Shipshewana, Indiana. I'll call her tomorrow to set it all up. Maybe during the summer, she can knock some sense into your stubborn mind."

"Who is Grandma Kurtz?"

"My mother. I'll be honest, I left on bad terms and haven't visited her since my father passed away." He turned from the window and looked at Evan. "You were very young."

"If you don't like her, why are you sending me there?"

"I didn't say I don't like her. She and I don't see eye to eye on everything, but she raised me and I don't think I turned out all that bad. Maybe she can kick your ass and get you down the straight and narrow path before it is too late." Nathan snapped the envelope in his hand. "You have one year left until graduation with a couple of weeks left this school year, and they're already talking about kicking you out of this school. Do I need to recount all the schools you've been to in the last five years?" He slumped into the chair by the window. "Evan, I really don't know what to do anymore. I've tried to give you everything you want. Maybe my mother can give you what I've been overlooking." He sighed. "She's a very smart woman."

"I didn't even know I had a living grandparent," Evan said. "Where is this Ship-whatever place?"

"In northeast Indiana. The town is about six hundred people, mostly Amish. It's a busy place, but nothing like here."

"Amish?"

"Let's put it this way, Evan. In Shipshewana, you're going to find life very different. The Amish are a very simple folk who are. —" Nathan smiled. "Tell you what. You'll find out when you get there." He stood up and walked to the door. "As I said, I'll get a hold of my mother and see if you can live with her for the summer."

"You can't make me do that." Evan folded his arms defiantly in front of him.

"You're only seventeen, Evan. Until you are eighteen, you're a minor and as much as you hate it, you have to do what I tell you. This August, when you turn eighteen, you can move out. If you decide to do that, we'll call it an early Christmas present." Nathan opened the door and stepped out. "Good night, son." He closed the door.

Evan dropped onto the bed and slammed his hands onto the mattress in frustration. "When I turn eighteen, you wait and see. I'll move out, that's for sure." He grabbed the headphones and slipped them over his head, and pushed the remote power button. "Just you wait and see." Johnny Cash sang *Will the Circle be Unbroken?* but it didn't soothe as memories of his mother's accident and funeral surged forward.

CHAPTER FOUR ~ The Play

Monday, June 3, 2013   8:45 a.m.

Rachel was hesitant, but opened the door of the theater and walked between the many tables toward the stage. Jack Sonner sauntered back and forth in front of the stage.

"What do I do, Mr. Sonner," Rachel asked.

"Well, little lady," Jack started. "You get up there on stage and sit on that ladder. When the music starts, you sing the new first song. Understood?"

Rachel nodded and headed to where she had been directed. She sat on the ladder and waited. The music started and she sang.

This is my story; this is my song.
Praising my savior all the day long.
Angels, descending, bring from above,
Echoes of mercy, whispers of love.
I believe. I believe in my God.

Rachel sang the next two verses. Nothing was happening. She frowned.

"That's perfect," Jack yelled. "Now, angels on stage right. Where are you? You're supposed to be coming down the stairs after she finishes the first verse. Move it. Move it."

"We were waiting for Helen; she's the lead angel." A young female voice called from above the stage. "She's here now."

"Fine," Jack yelled. "From the top. Ladder angel, sing your part from the beginning."

Rachel frowned. *Ladder angel?* she thought. *I am ladder angel?*

Once more the music started from the beginning and Rachel sang her part. As she began the second verse, angels appeared on the staircase on the opposite side of the stage. Rachel watched, fascinated, but continued to sing.

At least most of the music seems Christian, she thought. *Now, I will see what the play looks like. I can still back out if I do not like it.*

"Let's sing the second song, *Believe In The Faith*" Jack bellowed. "I want my field workers on stage, now. Ready?" He gazed at Rachel.

She nodded.

Hallelujah! Hallelujah!
The most high Lord God, Jehovah!

In the quiet of the morn,
As the sun gently warms,
Amidst the fields and farmsteads, we stand.
With a heart full of trust,
In the Lord we adjust,
Living by His loving, divine hand.

CHORUS: Oh, believe in the faith we hold,
In the stories from days of old,
In the hymns that lift our soul,
In our God, who makes us whole.

In the rustle of the sheaves,
As the wind gently weaves,
We find solace in His gentle breeze.
In the quilted starry night,
His presence shining bright,

Guiding us with everlasting ease.

Oh, believe in the faith we hold,
In the stories from days of old,
In the hymns that lift our soul,
In our God, who makes us whole.

Through the trials we face,
By His love and grace,
We find strength to endure the test.
In the humble way we live,
We find peace He'll give,
With each step, we are truly blessed.

Oh, believe in the faith we hold,
In the stories from days of old,
In the hymns that lift our soul,
In our God, who makes us whole.

In the warmth of kinship's bond,
We find our hearts respond,
To the love that binds us as one.
In our simple, faithful song, we'll carry on,
In His light, till our days are done.

Oh, believe in the faith we hold,
In the stories from days of old,
In the hymns that lift our soul,
In our God, who makes us whole.

In this simple life we live,
We find comfort and reprieve,
Trusting God's plan with all we are.
Believe in His love,
Shining from above,
In His embrace, we'll never be far.

"Absolute perfection," Jack gushed, watching the actors work in the imaginary field with imaginary tools. Rachel began the song, but all the cast joined in at the chorus after the first verse.

# # #

Monday, June 3   7-ish p.m.

The knock on the door startled Bethany who was reading the Bible. Jeremiah strolled to the door to answer.

Amos Hockstetler stood there gazing at the countryside.

"Yes?" Jeremiah asked.

"Rachel has a phone call," Amos said and pointed to the buggy. "I brought the buggy so she can ride back with me. It was Daniel Yoder."

Rachel jumped up from the kitchen table. "I will be back."

Jeremiah watched the buggy pull out from the driveway, stepped back into the house, and closed the door.

"I wonder why your father called Rachel?" he asked as he sat in his favorite chair.

Bethany shrugged. "I think they are discussing her participation in the new play at The Blue Gate Theater." She smiled at him as she found her place in the Bible. "Today was the first day of rehearsals."

Jeremiah nodded.

# # #

"Grandfather?" Rachel asked as the phone was answered.

"Rachel!" Daniel said. "How did the first day of rehearsals go? Is the play one you are comfortable with?"

"Yes, Grandfather," Rachel replied. "I have memorized all the songs and I sang them without any problems." She paused. "I saw the whole play, I think. It is about a young couple, one who is a believer and the other is not. Maybe I did not see all the play because it really did not seem to end and I still had four more songs to sing."

"Take it one day at a time, Rachel," Daniel said. "You will see all of the play."

"Oh, Grandfather," Rachel said. "The director of the play is a person who knows you. Do you remember a Jack Sonner?"

"The name seems familiar," Daniel said.

"He was in the play, *Specters*, as a backup ghost. He knew Adam Brown and worked in several plays. He remembers you leaving the play to come back home."

"Yes, Jack Sonner," Daniel said. "I do remember him. I must visit and see him." Daniel snickered. "Of course, it has been a few years since I last saw him. I may not recognize him."

"Do not worry," Rachel replied. "I will make sure to introduce the two of you." She smiled, knowing Daniel couldn't see her. "I know both of you."

"Can you tell me more about the play?" Daniel asked.

"The couple are in love. They have other friends. There is singing and dancing. The angels, not me, also sing and walk among them on the stage. I just sit on the ladder and sing my songs when I need to."

"Interesting," Daniel replied. "Do you wear a costume?"

"Not really," Rachel said. "I will have a cloth draped over the front of me. I get to wear my Amish clothes underneath."

Daniel smiled, remembering his time on stage and the costumes he was supposed to wear. He blushed, remembering the costume for Mephistopheles. He shook his head. *That is why I came home*, he thought.

"Continue to pursue this play, Rachel," Daniel said. "If, at any time you are not comfortable..." Daniel took a deep breath. "Walk away. I did. I am Amish. You are Amish."

"Yes, Grandfather," Rachel murmured. "I will."

"Good bye, Rachel," Daniel said. "Is all well with the family?"

"Yes," Rache replied. "Good bye."

"Good bye."

CHAPTER FIVE ~ The Countryside

Saturday, June 8, 2013 9 a.m.

Evan slumped in the car seat watching the repetitious scenery pass. His father attempted conversation, but Evan kept silent. The ride continued in mutual silence.

Suddenly, the road caught Evan's attention. It had widened but only on the berm. He found it interesting, especially the occasional droppings. Then he saw it. The buggy came into sight and he couldn't believe his eyes.

"What the..."

"They're called Amish," Nathan said. "I told you things were different in this area. We're in an area where the Amish live. They have no use for the intricacies of modern life." The car pulled beside it and Evan stared the horse pulled buggy. "The Amish don't even have electricity in their homes."

"How do they watch television?"

Nathan laughed. "They don't."

Evan hesitated, frozen in fear. His mind raced at the possibility he didn't want to admit. "Grandma Kurtz isn't Amish, is she?"

"No, Evan. She's not Amish. She has electricity, even a television."

Another buggy came into sight and Evan watched the wheels spin and the horse trot down the berm. Nathan slowed the vehicle and Evan saw the people inside. They were all dressed in dark clothes. Evan shook his head.

"How long before we get there?"

"We're nearing Middlebury. Shipshewana is just down the road and your grandmother's place is just beyond there. She lives in the country."

Evan stared out the window. This was all country, nothing like New York City. In fact, Elkhart seemed like the only large city near them and it was quite a distance behind them. It had been a long, silent flight from New York to Chicago and then catching the puddle hopper to Elkhart. His mind raced with possibilities. *If grandma has a car, I can borrow it, and at least party in Elkhart. What she doesn't know, won't hurt her*. He nodded approvingly at his decision.

"I guess now would be a good time to inform you of some of my mother's wishes." Nathan tried to smile.

"Rules?" Evan recognized the subtle word 'wishes' as just another word for rules. He looked out the window. The smiling face of the little girl in the Amish buggy they were passing forced him to smile. She waved.

"Call them courtesies. Your grandmother only expects a few conditions of your staying with her during the summer."

Evan rolled his eyes, folded his arms across his chest, and continued to watch the passing scenery of houses, barns, fields, and small cluster of woods.

Nathan continued. "One, you will remove your shoes upon entry into the house. Two, you will sit and join her at the dining room table to eat your meals. In other words, you will not be eating in front of the television." Nathan glanced at Evan and could tell he was listening while appearing indifferent. "Three, you will get a job. Four, you will be home no later than nine-thirty at night. Five, you will show her respect, and not use foul language in her presence."

Evan sighed and glared at his father. "Nine-thirty? She does know I'm seventeen, almost eighteen? I'm not some little kid."

"Trust me, Evan. I was raised in Shipshewana. Nine-thirty is plenty late enough." He slowed the vehicle. "In fact, this is Ship-she now." Nathan turned the car onto Route 5 where a small caravan of three buggies on the opposite side of the road quickly moved toward the intersection.

Evan sat up in his seat and scrutinized the landscape of small buildings, a myriad of black buggies and cars. He saw a mixture of people walking around dressed in dark colors, while others wore more conventional clothing.

"Are you kidding? This is where I'm going to spend my summer?"

His father continued on South Van Buren Street toward the middle of town where the red light blinked continuously day and night to indicate town center proper.

Nathan pointed. "This is downtown Shipshewana, Evan. As you can plainly see, no Chinese restaurant, and very little entertainment. Life here is very low tech."

"You can't leave me here," Evan protested, his eyes wide. "Take me back home, and I promise you, I'll get better grades, and be the perfect son."

"Sorry, Evan, but your grandmother is very excited at the prospect of your being here to help her around the house. You will survive." Nathan grinned. "Hell, you might even enjoy it."

Hell, Evan thought. A *very appropriate term for my imprisonment here.*

Nathan stopped, turned right at the light, headed east before finally turning into the driveway of a farmhouse.

Evan stared at the long lane leading back off the road. It was lined with tall maples on each side which created a shaded tunnel over the gravel driveway. He glanced at the large yard stretching out in front of the brick and white wood-sided two-story house.

"Who mows the yard?" he asked.

"Knowing your grandmother, probably she does." Nathan smiled. "But, more than likely, it will be you doing it during the summer this year."

Evan slumped back into the seat and rolled his eyes. "Never mowed a yard in my life." He glared at his father. "Not about to start now."

Nathan shook his head. "Son, you're going to have very long earlobes by summer's end if you go in with that attitude. My mother has no qualms about tugging you about by pulling on your ear." He snickered and rubbed his right ear. "You have no idea how many times she marched me out to the barn to milk cows. She'd clamp her thumb and index finger on my earlobe and lead me out there." Nathan shook his head. "You can't get out of her grip."

"I don't plan to milk cows, either," Evan said.

Nathan pulled up near the house by the two-car garage. "She no longer has a dairy farm." He turned off the car and faced his son. "Don't plan on a summer of sitting around watching cartoons on the television." He gave a feeble smile to Evan. "You're going to get up early in the morning, eat healthy meals, do chores and be very glad to hit the bed early in the night."

"I ain't her slave," Evan snapped.

"No, Evan, you aren't her slave. You're her grandson and you are here this summer to get to know her and help out as much as you can."

Evan opened the car door and crawled out, stretching to ease the muscles which had started to cramp from being in the car so long.

A lone woman stood on the back porch steps. Evan could see her analyzing and watching him. She moved.

"Nathan!"

Evan watched as the thin, older woman scampered down the steps from the back of the house and race toward them. Her arms were open, ready to hug her son.

"Hi, Mom," Nathan mumbled and embraced his mother. He pushed her away and held her hand as he moved to the front of the car where Evan now stood. "This is Evan, my son." He reached out and pulled Evan closer. "This is Adeline Kurtz, my mother, your grandmother."

Tears welled in her eyes and she grabbed the young man's face in both her hands and pulled him closer for a kiss. She stood only five foot four inches against Evan's tall six-foot stature. He bashfully bent down to her.

"You have grown, Evan. You weren't even walking the last time I saw you." She stared into his eyes, searching, then turned to Nathan. "It is so good to see you. How long are you staying?"

"Not long." Nathan glanced at the late afternoon sun. "I have to get back to Elkhart to catch my flight to Chicago and then back to New York." Nathan looked at his watch. "I probably should head out in the next ten to fifteen minutes."

Evan jerked his head toward his father. "I thought your flight was tomorrow?"

"Something has come up and I need to be back at the office tomorrow." He gazed about the farm. "The place looks good."

"Nathan," his mother whined. "I thought you'd at least stay longer. Maybe supper?" She placed her hands on hips. "Are you still angry?"

Evan shrugged. "Don't sweat this. He does it all the time." Evan glared at his father. "I call him 'Mr. I-Can't-Be-Around-Dad' since he never is." He walked to the backseat of the car and pulled his two suitcases out. "I got my stuff out, you can leave now." Evan headed for the back door of the house.

"I guess if you have to leave..." Adeline stretched up to kiss him. "Have a safe trip home, Nathan. I love you." She turned and followed Evan toward the house, the bounce no longer in her step.

"I'll call you," Nathan yelled.

"Sure. Whatever." Evan continued toward the house, ignoring his dad.

\# \# \#

Saturday, June 8 3 p.m.

Nathan crawled into the car and started the engine. He put it into gear and backed up so he could head down the long lane. He honked the horn but nobody waved. Nathan took a deep breath. *My mother will get Evan straightened out unless... unless I'm the problem.* He paused in thought. *Could I be the problem?* Nathan turned onto the country road, passed an Amish buggy and headed to Shipshewana and home in New York City via Elkhart, Indiana, and Chicago, Illinois.

# # #

Evan stood uneasily at the back screen door. He watched his grandmother slowly trudge up the steps. At the last minute, he grabbed the door and held it open for her.

"Come in, Evan," she said. "I'll show you to your room."

"Would you like me to call you 'grandma' or something else?" He slipped off his shoes and placed them on the small rug by the door.

Adeline turned around, catching his movements, and smiled at the young man. "Grandma is fine or, if you like, you could call me Grandma Addie." She grabbed his hand and held it to her cheek. "I hope we have a nice summer." She kissed the back of his hand then let go and moved slowly toward the wooden banister of the staircase. "Your room can be the one at the top of the stairs. The bathroom is next to it." She hesitated and took a deep breath.

Evan frowned. This was not the same woman who had charged out of the back door just a few minutes earlier.

"If you don't like that room, feel free to pick any of the other three up there."

"Which room is yours?"

"I sleep down here." She took a deep breath before grabbing the banister again. "I and the steps just don't get along these days." She smiled feebly at Evan. "Getting old, you know."

Evan frowned. "But I saw you come charging out of the house earlier."

"It was for Nathan. He mustn't know."

"Know?" Evan's curiosity was piqued. "Know about what?"

She patted Evan's arm. "All in due time, Evan. Now go unpack. The evening meal will be ready in about another twenty minutes. I hope you're hungry."

"Something smells... well, sort of good."

"It is one of your father's favorites when he was younger. Tonight we will be having spareribs in sauerkraut with peppers."

"Sauerkraut?"

Adeline once more patted Evan's arm. "Go unpack. We can get to know each other during the evening meal."

Evan grabbed his two suitcases and slowly trudged up the polished, dark, wooden staircase to his new bedroom.

"Don't get lost up there. Oh, remember, there are two staircases, so don't confuse them. This one comes down near the back door and kitchen. The other one comes down by the front door by the living room."

"Thanks, Grandma Addie."

Adeline smiled and watched the young man disappear up the stairs. She grabbed her chest as the pain swelled.

"Dear Lord, allow me the summer." She gazed up the stairs and nodded. "He's a good boy. Perhaps the circle will finally be completed." Addie took a deep breath as the discomfort eased. "Only time will tell if it be Your will, Lord. Amen."

CHAPTER SIX ~ Grandma's

Saturday, June 8 4 p.m.

Evan pushed the old, polished door to the room. It creaked as it opened.

Got to get that oiled, he thought. *Don't need her hearing me every time I open it.* He immediately thought of his grandmother. *I don't know why, but I like the old woman.*

White sheers fluttered in front of the open windows. The plaster walls were painted off-white, and a heavy braided oval rug welcomed him to the side of the bed. He glanced at the polished brass railing which encased the ornate brass scrolls and bars of the headboard. A quilt comprised of blue and white diamonds covered the bed.

Evan placed his suitcases on the bed and snapped them open. He frowned. There was no closet. The only door was the one he came through. He noted the heavy oaken dresser and its many drawers. Beside the door was a large oaken cabinet with two doors. He opened one and realized it was a closet, an armoire, for his clothes. A light cedar scent filled the room. Evan enjoyed the aroma. He was reminded of his mother, it confused him. He hung his shirts and pants in the armoire. He shrugged and began to place his socks and underwear in the drawers of the dresser.

Evan discovered a scrapbook in the bottom drawer. It had the title *Pogo* and was filled with old cartoon strips from the newspaper. He gazed and read a few, realizing this could good material to read at night if he had to go to bed early.

He gazed at the suitcases. They were empty. *Just like my life. Not much in it, and now empty.* Evan closed the suitcases, listening the hollow click of the snaps as he latched them. He placed them under the bed. A wind blew and the curtains billowed in the breeze. Evan moved to the window and pulled back a sheer with his index finger. He stared at the driveway below, the line of trees and the great expanse of fields to the west. In the distance was Shipshewana.

Evan glanced at his watch. 4:22 p.m. He bent down and sat on the floor by the windowsill. He watched the activity outside. A squirrel bounded between two maple trees and then scampered up one. A robin flitted from tree to tree. Further back, closer to the barn, Evan spotted a tall pole with three beams. At the end of each beam was a large birdhouse with several openings. Darker colored birds he didn't recognize swooped and flew around the area, dodging in and out of the openings.

"What time do you normally eat your evening meal?"

Evan shook his head to clear the melancholy cobwebs, stood, and walked to the bedroom door. He headed toward the stairs he'd come up.

"It doesn't matter to me, Grandma. What time do you eat?" He could see her at the bottom of the steps. "I got everything unpacked," he said as he hustled down the stairs.

"I usually eat supper about five in the evening but if you'd like it later, I can change things."

Evan snickered. "No, Grandma, that will be fine."

"I get up early," Adeline said. "Breakfast about six in the morning and somewhere near noon I will eat a lunch." She curled an index finger at Evan. "Let's go to living room." She headed toward the front of the house. "We can get to know each other there."

Evan followed, watching the older woman as she appeared to strain at each step, cautiously touching the wall for support. "Something smells good."

Adeline stopped at the dining room entrance. "Oh, my! I totally forgot about supper." She stared at Evan in bewilderment.

Evan took in her appearance: slightly paler, a little confused, and unfocused.

"Is everything okay?"

"You go sit at the table there." She pointed into the dining room. "Pick any chair. I'll bring in supper."

"Let me help you," Evan countered. "Show me some pot holders and I will get whatever is in the oven for you."

Adeline opened a drawer and handed Evan two oven mitts. "Just put it on top of the stove. I'll put it on a platter."

He lifted the heavy cast-iron oval pan from the oven onto the stove and pulled the lid off. "What is this, again?"

Adeline stabbed a fork into the pan and lifted a rack of ribs which she placed on a platter. She scooped out potatoes, sauerkraut, onions and green peppers which she put around the ribs. "Your father would have enjoyed this," she mumbled. "Pity."

"I don't think I've ever had it, but I'll give it a try." Evan grabbed the platter. "I'll take this to the table." He headed into the dining room and hurried back.

"I drink water with my meal," Addie said.

"I usually have beer with my Chinese meals," Evan said, noticing her frown.

"We don't drink alcohol." Addie raised an eyebrow.

"Water works for me, Grandma." He grabbed two glasses and filled them from the faucet. "Ready to eat?"

Adeline smiled at Evan and then headed for the dining room. "It will be nice to have someone to talk to during the meal."

Evan sat across from his grandmother and watched the woman bow her head, yet cock an eye in his direction.

"We give thanks, Evan. Bow your head and I will say Grace.

Heavenly Father, thank you for the bounty we are about to partake. Let it nourish both our body and soul. And thank you for bringing Evan into my life. In Jesus name, Amen."

"That was nice, Grandma. Thanks."

"Well, I'm not sure exactly what your father wants me to do, but we will figure it out as time passes." She looked up from her plate to give Evan a knowing smile. "Leopards don't change their spots."

"My father thinks I am lazy and have no ambition, no goals." Evan took a stab at the sparerib with his fork.

"Pick it up with your hands and enjoy the food. No reason to try and be neat. Spareribs are like any other ribs, you just enjoy them, getting as messy as you need. The you get cleaned up when done."

Evan grabbed the ribs and gnawed on the bone, sucking the soft meat into his mouth. "This is good. Dad probably told you I've been kicked out of almost every school I've been in for truancy, disrespect, disorderly conduct and... Well, you name it, I probably got blamed for it."

Adeline stuck a rib bone in her mouth and then pulled it out while sucking on it. "So, what you are saying is that you're a smartass, snot-nosed, know-it-all brat who feels the world owes you something." She held up her hand to silence Evan. "But you said something I caught. You get blamed. Why did you say that?"

Evan shoved a forkful of potatoes into his mouth and glanced about the room at the photos on the wall as he chewed before answering. "Everyone figures I did it. If dad can't find something, I took it. The local gang punches me in the eye, I started it. A mirror in the lobby gets broken, it had to be me. Stuff like that." Evan took a mouthful of sauerkraut, and then shivered from the taste. "Not sure if I like this stuff. Kind of bitter."

"Sprinkle some sugar on it, if you'd like. It might taste better." Adeline smiled.

Evan grabbed the sugar bowl and dusted his sauerkraut. He took a bite. "That tastes a lot better. So, my dad likes this stuff."

"At one time," Adeline replied softly. "At one time. So, tell me, Evan. Did you break the mirror? Did you start the fight?"

"No. The Red Chiefs — that's a punk street gang — followed me into the apartment lobby and started a scuffle. Three of them against me. One swung at me and I ducked. He broke the mirror. When I came back up, another one caught the side of my face, nailing me in the eye." Evan absently rubbed the area in memory. "They ran just as security came around the corner. I got blamed for it. Dad had to pay for the new mirror."

"You have no ambition?" Adeline scooped some green pepper, onion and sauerkraut together on a fork to eat.

"My dad is never around. He doesn't know. Like the other night he went out with some clients and I had Chinese food at a local restaurant. Mr. Ho's brother needed some help, so I went to the docks and helped. I earned over one hundred dollars unloading a shipment. Mr. Ho has me do work around his restaurant, too. I'm willing to work. All I ask, respect me."

"And your dad doesn't?"

"Dad doesn't even know I exist, for the most part. Ever since mom died, he spends all his time at work or with clients. I'm like a pet cat. He comes back to the apartment to sleep and make sure I've got food and water."

"That's rather harsh, Evan."

"Did you see how fast he wanted to get away today, Grandma? That was harsh. He couldn't stay to make sure I was situated, or even to visit with his own mother."

"Not everything has been easy for Nathan."

"Yeah." Evan pointed at the pictures behind her. "Who is that woman? I'm guessing that one is my dad's graduation picture. But that one, that isn't my mother." He pointed to the other wall. "That's her there." He squinted. "I think she's holding a baby. Me?"

"Yes, that is you and your mother. Behind me are the pictures of my children: Nathan and Alyssa."

"Alyssa? I've never heard my dad talk about a sister." Evan shrugged. "Of course, he never really talked about me having a grandmother, either."

"It was many years ago. Alyssa was killed in an accident the summer she graduated from high school." Adeline glanced over at Evan's empty plate. "Would you like some more?"

"No, I'm full." Evan hung his head. "I'm sorry. I didn't know. How did it happen?"

"I'll clean up the dishes. Why don't you go out on the front porch and relax in a chair?" Adeline stood and gathered her plate and silverware.

"I can help."

"No, Evan. I'd prefer to be alone right now, if you don't mind. I have some things to think about." She gazed at him and smiled. "Give an old lady some privacy."

"Sure, grandma." Evan ambled out of the dining room and across the living room to the front door which was open. He pushed on the screen door and stood for a few moments on the porch before locating a rocking chair that took his fancy. The country quietness engulfed him. In the distance, across the huge expanse of front lawn, on the road, Evan could see a black buggy on its way to the east. He smiled.

# # #

Saturday, June 8 5:45 p.m.

Adeline let the screen door close behind her. "A penny for your thoughts," she said. "Enjoying the peace?"

Evan nodded and continued to rock.

"I hope you have something respectable to wear to church tomorrow morning." Adeline watched Evan for a reaction as she sat in the rocker next to him.

"I don't do church or that religious thing, Grandma."

"We attend church in this household, Evan." She leaned forward in her rocker and stared at him. Adeline reached over and put a hand on his. "It isn't an option. If Satan decided to stay overnight on Saturday, he'd be expected to go to church with me the next morning. The Shipshewana United Methodist Church accepts everyone." She smiled. "I'm sure you have a nice button-down shirt, good slacks and shoes you can wear."

Evan held the rocker still. His mind raced with possible excuses. "I just got here. Can I wait until next week to go?"

"I thought you'd come up with a better excuse than that, Evan." She snickered. "You might as well go this week and start your first full day in Shipshewana giving thanks to the Lord. Besides, I've already told most of the members my grandson was coming to visit. Wouldn't I look foolish walking into church tomorrow all alone?" She winked.

Evan squirmed in the rocker. "Can I at least think about it?"

"Of course, Evan. Tomorrow morning I will make breakfast, and then we'll get ready to go to church and enjoy the service. I'll even put a chicken in the oven so it will be ready to eat when we get home. After our Sunday dinner, we can sit out here and discuss what you decided."

"Grandma, I think you just scammed me."

Adeline reached over and grabbed his right earlobe between her thumb and index finger. "I'm a sweet old lady who always gets her way." She tugged on his ear, let go, then laughed heartily.

Evan massaged his ear and frowned at the older woman. "Dad warned me about the ear pulling. I thought he was kidding."

Adeline cackled with laughter. "I dragged your father by his ear around this farm so many times, I thought he was going to embarrass those natives in *National Geographic* because he had longer earlobes." She set her rocker to moving. "I nearly tore his ear apart when he started wearing that diamond stud piercing."

Evan had matched Adeline's speed but stopped dead at her words to stare. "Wait a minute! My dad wore an earring?"

"There's a lot you don't know about Nathan... I mean, your father. You're here for the summer. We'll talk. I'll show you pictures."

"Can I ask about Alyssa?"

Adeline slowed. "She's family. You're family. You have the right." Adeline folded her hands together and stared at the field to the east. "You saw her picture, she was a beautiful girl. Alyssa was bright. Real smart, smarter than her older brother." The old woman paused and breathed deeply. "She had a scholarship for college and was getting things around to attend that fall." Adeline sniffled. "Then she was killed in that accident and all the dreams ended."

"You mean her dreams ended." Evan saw the tears on his grandmother's face. "If you want to stop."

"No, it's okay, Evan." Adeline pulled a hankie out of a pocket and dabbed away the tears. "All the dreams, Evan. Yes, her dreams ended but my dream of helping my daughter pick a wedding dress also ended. My dreams of sharing that moment with my daughter when she became a mother, shattered. Your grandfather's dream of walking his little princess down the aisle withered like snow on a hot surface. My dreams of a family died when your grandfather and father argued over..." She gazed at Evan. "Has your father ever told you why he doesn't visit here?"

"No."

"I think he should be the one to tell you his side of the story, before you hear anything from me."

"What kind of accident killed Alyssa?"

"She was out with some friends and they decided to go to Yoder's for the youth sing-fest at their barn. Normally it is a closed function for the Amish only, but this was part of Jeremiah Yoder's *Rumschpringe*."

Evan frowned.

"*Rumschpringe*. It is a period when a young Amish person experiments with the outside world before deciding to join the church and settle down into the Amish lifestyle. Call it their wild period where they smoke, drink, dance and do that which they're not allowed to participate as an Amish member."

"Alyssa wasn't Amish, was she?"

"No, but she had many friends, both Amish and non-Amish. There were five of them in the buggy, two Amish and three *Englische*." She glanced at Evan and saw the puzzled look. "In the Amish world, you are either Amish or you're *Englische*. If you're not Amish, you're *Englische*."

Evan nodded.

"They were in the buggy headed to Yoder's barn and were out on US-20... that is the highway you came in on from Middlebury. A semi came around the curve too fast, went left of center, over compensated and hit the buggy. They were all killed instantly. According to police reports, Jeremiah didn't have a reflector on his buggy nor a blinking battery-operated light." Once more Adeline paused and stared out at the field. "I personally know the Yoders. They were one of the first Amish families to embrace the new reflectors and had them on all their buggies. In fact, Jeremiah was proud of his new battery-operated blinking light for his buggy." She held her head high. "Amish aren't supposed to stand out but Jeremiah was a strutting rooster, if ever there was one. He really fancied Alyssa." Her face beamed and she grinned momentarily at the memory and then once more was solemn. "It was a tragedy both for the Amish community and the town of Shipshewana." Suddenly, she started to cry.

"I'm sorry, Grandma. I guess I shouldn't have asked." Evan was out of his rocker and at her side trying to comfort. "Guess we should go in and I should start checking my clothes for tomorrow morning's church."

He helped her out of the rocker and into the house.

# # #

Sunday, June 9, 2013 12:10 p.m.

"How's the chicken, Evan?"

"It's delicious, Grandma. I've never had it prepared like this before."

"Well, enjoy. There's plenty." She took a bite of mashed potatoes. "Did you enjoy church this morning, Evan?"

"It was okay. Joe Holgate seemed like a pretty good guy." He watched her for any reaction. "He said he'd show me the town's hot spots next Friday or Saturday night."

"Joe is a nice kid, but be wary. There is something about him that just doesn't click for me, so I tend not to trust him."

"I was worried there wouldn't be anything to do here." Evan twirled the chicken leg in his hand. "Dad said there wasn't even a Chinese restaurant here."

"Just what do you plan to do this summer? Do you want a job? Loaf? Read? Watch TV?"

Evan sheepishly glanced at Adeline. "Dad said I was supposed to help you."

"Oh, honey, that is sweet, but I've been handling this farm all by myself since your grandpa passed away." She cut a slice of breast meat, swished it in gravy then flicked into her waiting mouth. "May I suggest you get a job?"

"Doing what?"

"We have a couple of grocery stores, some hardware locations, even a few restaurants where you could be a busboy. Plus, I'm sure the auction and flea market area could use help."

Evan gazed around trying to figure out how to approach the next subject. "I guess I could do that. Uh, are you going to drive me into town or do I get to borrow the car?" His mind drifted to the bright red 1967 Chevrolet Nova that his grandmother had driven them to church that morning.

"Since I don't have you on the insurance, it's either I drive you or you use your dad's old bicycle to get into town." She peeked at him from the corner of her eye. "The Amish go buzzing by here on bikes constantly so I know it won't kill you. Town is only about two miles to the west, about fifteen minutes away."

Evan stabbed a couple of green beans onto his fork. "It would be nice if you drove, Grandma, since you know where all these places are."

"I have to go to town for groceries and a few errands, so that will be just fine. We'll leave about 8 a.m."

# # #

Monday, June 10, 2013 8:15 a.m.

Adeline pointed. "That is a bulk store." She grinned. "I already spoke to Ezra Wyse and he said he'd take your application and give you chance."

Evan gave the building a cursory glance. He remembered it from the day they'd come in. US-20 was less than a quarter mile away. On the north side of the building, he could see about six buggies lined up. The horses stood quietly waiting for their owners to return.

Evan opened the car door. "Guess I can go and check it out."

"I will pick you up this afternoon, a little after five."

Evan frowned. "What if I don't get hired?"

"If Ezra don't hire you, I'd suggest you stop at the next business going north. When you get to the blinking light, turn right, trying the different places. When you get to the edge of town, about a block, cross the street and head back to the light. If you still haven't found a job, head north to the end of town, cross the street... I believe you've got the idea. Just continue trying to get a job."

He closed the door and leaned in the open window. "If I don't get a job?"

Adeline smiled. "Then just keep walking until you get back to the farm."

Evan grimaced and stared at her. "You believe I'm going to get a job, don't you?"

Adeline reached over and patted his hand. "Honey, I believe in you. These people will, too, if you give them a chance. In the city, well, nobody trusts anybody. Out here, in the country, people trust one another until the person proves otherwise. Right now, I need to take care of some other business, and then I'll be back to shop."

Evan shook his head before finally shoving himself away from the car. "See you tonight, Grandma." He paused. "Thanks."

She drove the car away and Evan watched for a few seconds before heading into the store.

"Is Mr. Wyse available?" Evan asked the young girl working one of the checkout counters.

"Which Mr. Wyse do you wish to see? Mr. Abe Wyse? Mr. Ezra Wyse? Mr. Noah Wyse? Or Mr. Samuel Wyse?"

"That would be Mr. Ezra Wyse. Is he available?"

She glanced about the building. "That's him by the greeting cards."

Evan nodded to the young girl. "Thanks." He quickly walked over to the older, tall man. "Mr. Wyse?"

"May I help you?"

Evan offered his hand to shake. "My name is Evan Kurtz. I wondered if you were hiring any help right now?"

Ezra stepped back and momentarily scrutinized the young man before him. "So, you're Addie Kurtz's grandson. Have you done any stocking or grocery work before?"

Evan shrugged. "I haven't worked in a grocery store but back in New York City I worked for Mr. Ho at the docks from time to time, loading and unloading shipments."

Ezra shook his head. "I didn't mean using a tow-motor."

"I didn't use a tow-motor, sir. I carried the bags, sacks and crates on my shoulders. Some of them were well over a hundred pounds each."

"I'm sorry. We do everything here with pure manual labor. I take it a fifty-pound bag of potatoes wouldn't be an issue?"

Evan smiled. "No, sir. No problem at all."

"When can you start?"

"Any time you'd like, Mr. Wyse." Evan gazed about the store. "I can start now, if you'd like." He grinned. "Otherwise, I have a long walk home since my grandmother won't be back until about five."

Ezra slapped Evan on the back. "Your grandmother knew I'd hire you." He turned. "Follow me to the office. We'll get the paperwork done and then you can start."

CHAPTER SEVEN ~ Learning The Amish

Monday, June 10 8:45 a.m.

"Sign your name and we're finished." Ezra slid the paper toward Evan. "It's for taxes and to get you on the payroll."

Evan signed the document and handed it back.

Ezra pulled up a clipboard and ran his finger down the sheet. "Zak has Wednesday off, so if I let you have Thursdays off..." He nodded and looked at Evan. "That will work. Everyone has Sunday off around here plus one other day. We also have two shifts, early and late. The early crew comes in at seven while the late crew comes in at nine-thirty. You work eight hours with a half hour for lunch. The doors open at seven-thirty and close at five-thirty with the late shift ending at six." He grinned at Evan. "That allows for cleanup and final stocking. It also gives the checkouts time to balance their drawers."

Evan nodded.

"So which shift would you prefer? Does Addie like to sleep in? You want to work the late shift?"

"Grandma gets up early, sir. Breakfast is at six in the morning. I see no problem with the early shift."

"Fine, Evan. Let me try you out on the early shift since that's the same shift Zak works. The Amish are early risers, too."

Evan hesitated.

"Something bothering you?"

"How many Amish do you employ?" He glanced nervously about. "I mean, I've never met an Amish person before. Until a few weeks ago, I didn't even know they existed."

"Most of my employees are Amish, Evan. Is there a problem?"

"Oh, no sir," Evan said.

A young man dressed in dark pants, blue shirt, and wearing suspenders stuck his head into the booth. "You wanted to know when..." He stopped and stared at Evan. "I am sorry, I did not know you had a visitor."

"That's fine. Come in, Zak." Ezra stood up and pointed to Evan. "Isaac Graber, this is Evan Kurtz. I just hired him." Ezra turned to Evan. "So, Zak, I want you to show Evan the ropes over the next couple of days. You know, the ins-and-outs of stocking, warehouse, produce, the whole she-bang."

Zak stepped into the office and leaned against the door jam. "You mean today and tomorrow?"

Ezra slapped Evan on the back. "I figure Evan's a quick learner." He winked at Zak. "We'll find out soon enough."

Zak leaned in to shake hands with Evan. "Welcome. Nothing like the present to jump in. We have to bring in new stock from the Holcombe delivery truck." He turned to Ezra. "You wanted to know when they came."

"Thanks, Zak. Tell them I'll be out shortly and take care of it." He turned back to his desk. "You can show Evan how we do things around here." He rummaged through the papers cluttering the desk.

"Follow me," Zak said and backed out the door to disappear.

Evan stepped down the four stairs from the office booth to follow Zak. He glanced at the entrance to see his grandmother coming in the door. She smiled, nodded, and began her shopping.

"We are a small group of workers here," Zak said, catching Evan's attention. "That is Mary Schmucker at the checkouts right now. Over there," he pointed, "is Mary Troyer working on the produce."

Evan nodded as they rushed around a corner and headed down the aisle between spices and frozen goods.

"In the back, Mark Zook is unloading the Holcombe truck on the dock. It is just the four, uh, five of us until the rest come in later. Full shifts are on Monday, Friday and Saturday."

"Those are busy days?" Evan strode beside the Amish boy who nodded in agreement.

Zak pushed the double swinging door open and Evan realized they were in the back of the store. Cartons and crates of foodstuffs balanced precariously against each other. Quickly maneuvering around the stacks, Zak made his way to the large open doorway.

"We will go help Mark on the dock." He slipped through the interweaving strips of heavy plastic to the outside.

Evan felt the sudden temperature change. He now realized how cool the back of the store was. The summer heat was climbing.

Mark gazed up from his work where he wrangled huge bags from a wooden flat.

"This is Evan," Zak said, pointing at Evan before grabbing a bag. "He is a new hire, Mark."

Mark stuck out a hand to shake and then nodded to the stack of bags. "Help yourself and follow Zak. I will be right behind you in case you get lost." He laughed.

Evan lifted a bag onto his shoulder and followed Zak. He turned to see Mark following. He felt a little self-conscious for wearing blue jeans and a plaid shirt. Both of his fellow workers were wearing dark pants, blue shirts and sporting suspenders.

# # #

Zak strolled up an aisle toward Evan, greeting customers as he passed them.

"It is now nine-fifteen. It is time for us to take a break, Evan. I'll show you where the lunchroom is located." He leaned down and grabbed the last two #10 cans of beans from the case and put them on the shelf. "Mark will handle things for the next fifteen minutes while we enjoy getting away from here." He smiled at Evan. "Besides, the late shift will start coming in shortly."

"Mr. Wyse didn't mention anything about a break," Evan said following Zak through the store.

Zak turned and stared at Evan. "Have you never worked before?"

Evan shrugged. "I've done odd jobs as needed." He grimaced. "Really never needed to work."

"You *Englische* are a strange lot. Some feel they must work all the time, and yet, others feel they need not work."

"*Englische?*" Evan glared at Zak. "My mother is Irish, born and raised in Dublin, Ireland. I'm definitely not English."

Zak smiled. "You are *Englische*. I am Amish. That is how we Amish differentiate our lifestyles. Amish live a simple life as compared to those of you, the *Englische*."

"Uh-huh," Evan mumbled, unsure of how to continue the conversation, all the while remembering Grandma Addie's talk about it.

Zak put an arm over Evan's shoulder and urged him on. "Come. We will enjoy a cooling glass of water and relax before we are busy once more." He pointed to the right. "There is the lunchroom. We can rest in there, or at least get a water. I think I will relax on the back dock and enjoy the fresh air."

Evan stumbled along, unsure of what to do. Working before had always been simple, manual labor, with no need to think beyond the fact of getting the work done. A simple job, a payment, and he was done. This was full time employment. He smiled as the realization came to him... this is a real job. Evan followed Zak into the lunchroom, grabbed a glass of water and sat at the table as Zak continued to the back dock.

Evan sat at the table, enjoying the leisure, listening to the music when Zak walked back in.

"Ready to get back to work?" Evan asked.

Zak frowned at him. "No. I will start when it is time. Are you a delivery man?" He turned and walked away from Evan, not waiting for an answer.

Evan watched Zak disappear beyond the door. He was confused. The young Amish man had been pleasant all morning and now he acted like Evan was a stranger, even asking if he was a delivery person.

Zak came back into the room.

"What are you delivering?" he asked.

Evan frowned, finally noticing Zak now had on a white shirt. *Had he changed shirts while on the outside dock? Zak and Mark had on blue shirts.*

"Why are you acting so strange, Zak?"

"My name is Zeke."

"Huh?" Evan reared back in his chair to scrutinize the man before him.

"Oh, Zeke," an identical looking man said coming in from the dock. "This is Evan Kurtz. He is a new hire today."

Evan stared at the two men standing before him. One wore a blue shirt, the other wore a white shirt.

"Evan, this is my twin brother, Ezekiel. We call him Zeke."

Zeke stood aloof, staring at Evan. "Evan Kurtz," he said. "The name is familiar."

"My grandmother, Adeline Kurtz lives to the east of town," Evan offered, standing and extending a hand to shake.

Zeke stared at the hand, but made no offer to shake. Evan dropped his hand.

# # #

"Adeline Kurtz... Kurtz... ah, yes, Adeline Kurtz." He turned to Zak. "Her husband was John Kurtz, son of James Kurtz." He cocked his head to the side. "James was cousin to Paul Hershberger. James was your great-great grandmother's brother. Do you remember?" He paused. "Kurtz? Kertz?" He paused again. "U? E?"

Zak's eyes danced as he put all the names together. Suddenly, they widened.

"Meidung!" Zak blurted. "No! Ex-communication."

"Yah," Zeke said and walked away.

"I am sorry," Zak mumbled and followed his brother.

Evan jumped from his chair to chase Zak. Grabbing him by the shoulder, he turned Zak to face him.

"What?" Evan asked.

Zak pulled away and continued to walk. Mark walked into the room, as he noticed Evan, he turned his head and ignored him. Evan was confused. *What happened?* he thought. *Let me go ask Mr. Wyse.*

Evan hastened to the front office, passing several of the employees. None of them would look at him or acknowledge his presence. He took the stairs two at a time. Short of breath, he knocked on the open door frame.

Ezra Wyse looked up from his desk. "What is it, Evan?"

"I don't know. Zak and I went on break. I didn't know he had a twin brother who came in—"

Ezra laughed. "Oh, I forgot to mention that itty-bitty detail. Yeah, Zak and Zeke are twins. So, to keep things easier for me to tell them apart, I make Zak wear a blue shirt and Zeke has to wear a white shirt."

"That's not the issue," Evan replied and took a deep breath. "Zeke heard my grandmother's name and he said something about a cousin and they won't talk to me."

Ezra frowned. "Is anyone else talking to you?"

Evan shook his head. "Nope. None of them. In fact, they turn their backs to me when I approach."

Ezra placed a hand over his lower face, pulling it down over his chin. "Did somebody say '*Meidung*' by any chance?"

"That might have been the word, plus something like ex-communication." Evan stood there frowning and nodding his head. "What is that?"

"You, lad, had been shunned, and I mean big-time. Did you say ex-communication? I didn't think I'd have to address the issue here at the store, but I see there is a problem. Sit." He motioned to a chair. "I'd best explain this to you."

"Shunned?" Evan sat. "What did I do?"

"You? Nothing." Ezra sat and placed his clasped hands on the desk. "The Amish... okay, Evan, let's go it from another direction. What do you know about the Amish?"

Evan shrugged. "They like to wear black, don't have electricity and ride around in buggies."

Ezra shook his head. "This is going to take a lot of explaining." He eased back in his chair. "Right now, as I see it, I have two choices. I let you go home until I get this figured out, or I send home all the Amish working here." Ezra cocked an eye in Evan's direction. "I hate to do this to you, but I think you'd best be headed home today and wait for me to call you back to work."

"I'm fired?"

"No, Evan, I'm not firing you. In fact, from what I've seen of your work today, I'm impressed. You're a hard worker and I really don't want to lose you, but, at the same time, I can't let the majority of my staff go home. Put simply. They won't work with, talk to, or acknowledge your presence. That's going to make it difficult for you to your job. Do you see the predicament?"

"I can work in silence, Mr. Wyse."

"That's not the issue. Zak is… was training you. Without him to guide you, what will you do? Will you know what to do next? Will you know when the shipments arrive? Will you know when you're needed up front to help pack? I would have to be on the floor the whole time to let you know what to do and when to do what. Do you see the complications. You have been shunned. To them, you don't exist. They won't talk to you."

Evan frowned. "But…"

"Shunning is complicated, and ex-communication is worse. You and I could be standing side by side and Zak could up to me and tell me to tell you hello, but he'd tell me that and I'd have to repeat it to you. Your response to him would again have to be spoken by me. I would be an interpreter, repeating exactly what I heard. Plus…" He frowned. "I wasn't aware shunning to be carried for generations, Evan. If one leaves the Amish after they are baptized, until they return, and seek counsel and acceptance back into the community, they are ignored." He leaned closer. "I mean it. The Amish will shun and disown their own family members. It's a very complicated ruling. Ex-communication has even stronger rules. I will need to find out more." He paused. "Do you want me to call your grandmother?"

"No," Evan replied. "I will walk home." He stood and offered his hand to Ezra. "Let me know when I can come back to work."

"Talk to your grandmother. Have her explain it." Ezra shook Evan's hand. "I will attempt to fix this in the next day or two." He offered a sly grin. "Don't attempt to get a job elsewhere. You've been shunned and by this evening, the whole Amish community will know it and you won't have a snowball's chance... you won't get hired and if you do, you'll be let go very quickly. Stay calm until we get this straightened out."

# # #

Monday, June 10 11:20 a.m.

"Grandma?" Evan slipped his shoes off near the back door and placed them on the carpet piece.

"Evan?" Addie stood by the kitchen sink washing dishes. "You're home early. What happened?" She wiped her hands on a towel and placed it by the sink.

"Mr. Wyse sent me home. There was a problem at the store."

"A problem? Come. Sit in the living room." Addie moved to the front room. "What sort of problem was there?"

"Have you heard the word '*Meidung*' before?"

Addie eased into the stuffed chair. "Yes, Evan. I've heard that word before. It is Amish. Why?"

"Seems I've been shunned for some reason. Can you explain it?"

Addie straightened her dress and then folded her hands together on her lap. She smiled at Evan.

"Well, dear, this is going to take a little while."

"Seems I have the time, Grandma. I don't get back to work until this is straightened out. Mr. Wyse wasn't sure how long it would take, but until that time... Well, I don't have job."

"Back in the forties, your great-grandfather, James Kurtz... well, he left the Amish."

"Huh?" Evan sat up in the chair. "We're Amish?"

"No, Evan. Your great-grandfather was Amish. He met your great-grandmother on *Rumschpringe* and they dated. They broke up and he went back to Amish and got baptized. Do you know what that means?"

"Yeah. I've been baptized."

"No, Evan. In the Amish community, to be baptized is to become one with the community. That means you will live by the rules of the community. They call that an *Ordnung*. It is a set of rules that guide their everyday life. It decides everything for them — even the size of the brim of a man's hat, what color dress a woman may wear, to whether the buggy can be enclosed or not. Once you're baptized, you agree to these terms." Addie waved her hand in the air. "Never mind. Anyway, James was in town and saw Eliza Waldvogel. Well, they struck up a conversation and they decided to get married. She wouldn't become Amish." Addie smiled. "From what I've heard, she was very much like your mother, except she was German. So, James left the Amish. Being baptized, and a member of the community, that is a bad thing. He was shunned by his family for dating her, and ex-communicated when he married her."

"So, because my great-grandfather left the Amish, I'm in trouble?"

Addie's brows knitted together in a frown. "Only part of the problem, Evan. When they ex-communicated James, he changed the spelling of his name from Kertz to Kurtz." She shrugged. "Since his Amish family disowned him, he disowned them. What surprises me. I mean, Nathan and Alyssa had many Amish friends. They were never shunned." Addie tapped her lower lip with an index finger. "So, who shunned you?"

"Zeke Graber. I was working with Zak Graber when his twin brother came in. He's not very nice. Anyway, I was introduced to Zeke and the next thing I knew, they were walking away from me. Oh, and they mentioned a cousin. Paul somebody."

Addie smiled. "Paul Hershberger." She nodded. "It all makes sense now."

"It does?" Evan asked.

"Now it gets even more complicated. James' cousin was Paul Hershberger. His sister, Emma, married an *Englische* man named..." She thought for a moment. "Yes, Dan Noble. Their daughter, Martha, married an Amish lad named Daniel Yoder." Addie gazed at Evan. "Are you following this?"

Evan sighed. "Trying to."

"So, Daniel Yoder's daughter, Bethany, married Jeremiah Graber who is the father of the twins." Addie patted her bosom. "That was very strenuous trying to remember all the lineage." She giggled. "The Amish do it without even a blink of an eye."

"I know," Evan said. "Zeke rattled it off and then bam! I was shunned."

Addie stood. "Don't worry, Evan. I'll go talk to Bishop Zwyer." She walked over to Evan and patted his shoulder on her way to the kitchen. "I think this can be cleared up very quickly. Are you ready to eat lunch?"

"Having just walked home, yes, Grandma, I'm hungry." Evan laughed. "Are you going to see this guy today?"

"I will see Bishop Zwyer this afternoon." She placed a hand on the kitchen doorway for support. "If you wish, you can go out to the barn and check for eggs before lunch and then, well, just enjoy the afternoon."

Evan stared at his grandmother. "Can't I join you?"

"I think this is best addressed by one who knows the Amish. If things get too..." Addie hesitated. "Let's call it awkward, maybe then I'll bring you into the fray." She giggled. "Okay?"

Evan nodded and headed out the back door to the barn.

# # #

Adeline Kurtz took her time going up the steps to the Zwyer home and then knocked on the door.

Mary Zwyer answered the door. She nodded at Addie. "How can I help you?"

"I'm here to see Bishop Zwyer," Addie said.

"Come in," Mary said. "He is in the main room, resting."

Addie followed Mary through the house to the main room where Bishop Zwyer sat in his chair, eyes closed.

"You have a visitor," Mary said. "It is Mrs. Kurtz." Mary's voice was cool and distant.

Bishop Zwyer opened his eyes and stretched in his chair. "Sit, Mrs. Kurtz." He motioned to a nearby chair.

Addie strolled to the chair and sat.

"To what do I owe this visit?" Bishop Zwyer asked.

"You know full-well why I am here," Addie said. "My grandson has been shunned by the Graber family and the Amish community." She took a deep breath. "This silly family feud must end." She eased back into the chair. "My grandson, Evan, has done nothing."

Bishop Zwyer tugged on his beard as he thought.

"You didn't shun my children." Addie glared at the bishop. "My daughter, Alyssa, was friends with so many of your youth before she was killed."

Bishop Zwyer nodded. "Aye. I allowed that luxury. I thought perhaps we should have enforced the ex-communication, but, as you said, it was your father-in-law, not Alyssa's fault."

"So, what changed your mind, Bishop Zwyer?" Addie snapped.

"The accident. It was a sign that we should have enforced the shunning."

"A sign? That is a lot of bull pucks, Bishop. My daughter had nothing to do with the accident, other than she was killed, just as the other Amish kids."

Bishop Zwyer wavered. "Maybe yes. Maybe no. She should have been shunned."

"Okay, Bishop," Addie started. "I understand your shunning rules, but why push it beyond the one who broke your law? My father-in-law has been dead for over twenty years. What good is it to punish his offspring?" The edges of her lips curled in an evil grin. "How long do you beat a dead horse before you realize it isn't going to work anymore? My grandson has no idea what his great-grandfather did, nor does he care." She paused, her eyes dancing in thought. "Yes, Ezekiel 18:20 says something about the father is not responsible for the sins of the son and the son is not responsible for the sins of the father; to each their own."

"We care, Mrs. Kurtz," Bishop Zwyer replied. "You bring up a good point."

"So, the Amish community, probably over fifty per cent of Shipshewana, is going to shun my grandson the whole summer while he is here?" She glared at Bishop Zwyer and spread her arms and hands out in front of her. "What do we do?"

Bishop Zwyer tugged on his beard as he thought. He stared out the window, moving his head, nodding ever so slightly as he considered each point.

"I will talk with Paul Hershberger and Jeremiah Graber. I will remove this shunning of your grandson." He inhaled deeply. "Is that your wish?"

"No, Bishop Zwyer,' Addie snapped. "I want it to be your wish."

"Let it be so," Bishop Zwyer with a sigh of relief.

"I will tell Evan," Addie said, stood and walked toward the door. "Have a lovely day, Mrs. Zwyer. It was nice to see you," Addie said as she opened the door and left.

CHAPTER EIGHT ~ Back To Work

Saturday, June 15, 2013 9:30 a.m.

Evan heard the phone ringing. It was Saturday and he wanted to sleep in.

"Evan! It's for you. Ezra Wyse is on the phone."

"Be right there," Evan yelled and rushed to put on his jeans, and slip a t-shirt over his head as he raced down the stairs.

He took the phone from Addie.

"Good morning, Mr. Wyse." Evan took a deep breath and leaned against the kitchen counter, stretching the wall phone's cord.

"Good morning, Evan. I thought I'd call and let you know how things are going. Seems your grandmother got the bishop stirred up and was able to straighten out this shunning business in a hurry. Bishop Zwyer informed the Graber family that James had been shunned and ex-communicated. Yes, it does involve his children and heirs, but they were lax about it for several years. That's when Alyssa Kurtz and the Amish were involved with the accident. A relative of Paul Hershberger's was also killed. He's been adamant about the shunning, but Bishop Zwyer was able to convince him to let the past remain in the past. Zak let me know last night that they were wrong and wanted to apologize for my firing you. I told them you'd be back to work on Monday." There was a pause. "You *will* be coming back to work on Monday?"

"I'll be there, Mr. Wyse. Am I still on the early shift?"

Evan heard Ezra snicker. "Yes, Evan. I'll see you bright and early Monday morning. Good bye."

"Good bye." Evan hung the receiver back on the wall phone.

"Thank you, Grandma Addie. I got my job back. I start Monday morning."

She nodded her head. "And we will thank the Lord tomorrow for this wonderful news." She put a plate of eggs and bacon on the table. "You are hungry, right?"

"Looks good, grandma," Evan said and sat at the table.

"First, young man, give thanks to the Lord and then enjoy your meal."

Evan lowered his head and said a small prayer. He wasn't too sure what to say but offered a grace.

Thank you for this food I am about to eat. Amen.

Addie raised an eyebrow, but decided not to say anything. She was slowly getting Evan where she wanted him.

"What do you plan to do today, Evan?"

He leaned back in the chair, a slice of bacon in hand. He waved the crisp slice in the air. "I was thinking of collecting eggs and checking out the barn some more." He munched on the slice of bacon. "You have a big barn, why don't you have more cows?"

Addie sighed and pulled the chair opposite him to sit on. "We did, at one time. I even had a couple of farm hands who helped to keep them milked after your grandfather passed." She smiled at Evan. "But life has a way of giving a person new perspective. I've leased most of the pastures out to other farmers." She gazed off into the distance, not focusing on anything in particular, remembering. "I can't do it, Evan. I'm getting old."

"But, Grandma Addie, this could be a real money maker."

"Money isn't everything, dear." She shook her head. "No, money isn't everything," she mumbled in a whisper.

Evan watched her. "You mean to tell me, every day, you go out there and milk that one cow?"

Addie laughed. "No, Evan, Gertrude gets milked twice a day. Once, in the early morning, and again, in the evening. I couldn't get rid of Gertrude when I sold off the other cattle. I kept her and I milked her, but, well, lately, I just don't have the energy to do it anymore. So, Leroy Volhaus, or one of his sons, come down and do it."

Evan frowned. "I never heard a car or truck come in."

Addie giggled. "They have the farm down to the east and across the road. They usually walk or bicycle over.

Evan gave her a look. "Amish?"

"No, Evan, they're not Amish. They're Mennonite." Addie thought for a minute. "Finish your breakfast, Evan. I want to take you to Menno-Hof." She stood.

Evan immediately reared back and frowned.

"It is the Amish-Mennonite Visitor's Center in town." Addie placed a hand on his shoulder. "Don't fret. I think a couple of hours wandering around in there and learning about our neighbors might help you understand the community better. We're a blend of Amish, Mennonite, and *Englische*."

Evan grabbed the last strip of bacon from the plate and started munching. He reached for the plate, but Addie slipped in and had it lifted from the table before he could get it.

"Grandma!" He gave her a scowl. "I could have put the plate in the sink."

"Yes, you could have, Evan. But..." She giggled. "I wanted to clean it." She motioned him up the stairs. "Go get ready. We're going into town." She cleaned the dish and rinsed it. "I need a couple of things from the yarn store. I'll drop you off at the center and do my shopping." She dried her hands on a towel. "Then I'll pick you up and we'll have a late lunch at the 5/20 Country Kitchen."

"Sounds good." Evan turned and hustled up the staircase to get ready.

The phone rang.

"Evan! It's for you," Addie yelled up the stairs.

Evan rushed down to answer the phone. *Maybe it is my dad,* he thought. *Please don't be Mr. Wyse telling me I'm fired.*

"Hello?" Evan said, grabbing the kitchen wall phone's handset and stretching the coiled cord across the room to the small table.

"Hey, dude. This is Joe Holgate," Joe said. "Remember me?"

"Yeah, sure," Evan replied. "From church."

"You free tonight? Want to have some fun?"

"You bet," Evan said. "What time?"

"I'll pick you up about eight. That okay?"

Evan frowned and decided that they should be back home by that time. He nodded. "Sounds good. See you then, Joe."

When Evan hung up the phone, straightening the coil as he replaced the handset back on the wall phone, he noticed his grandmother watching him.

"I'm going out with Joe tonight," Evan mumbled. "Is that okay?"

Addie grimaced. "What time do you expect to be home?"

Evan's eyes widened. "I don't know. Do I have a curfew?"

"No, Evan," Addie replied. "Just remember, we will attend church tomorrow morning." She hesitated. "Don't drink too much tonight."

"Grandma!" Evan exclaimed.

"You've already told me you drink Chinese beer or whatever, so I figure with Joe..." She shrugged. "I'm sure he has access to alcohol." She hesitated. "Be careful. This isn't New York City and the police don't have a lot to do, so under-age drinking is one of their favorite charges."

Evan nodded. "Thank you," he mumbled.

# # #

Saturday, June 15 9 p.m.

"So, where are we going?" Evan asked.

"First stop, Hanson's Garage," Joe replied. "Every Saturday night the guys get together for a small jam session."

Evan frowned. "Jam session?"

"I play bass guitar, Harold Miller plays drums, Arnold Hanson plays lead guitar, and Peter Hanson is lead singer." He paused. "Oh, yeah, and Tobias Snyder who is our sound person."

Evan nodded. "Uh-huh."

Joe pulled into the driveway of Hanson's Garage where two other cars were already parked.

Joe hopped out of the car, opened the back passenger door and grabbed his guitar case. "C'mon, Evan. The guys are waiting." He opened the garage door and disappeared inside. Evan followed.

"Hi, guys," Joe said. "This is Evan Kurtz from New York City. He's here this summer to visit his grandmother." He pointed at each of the three young men. "That's Arnold, Peter, and Harold."

Joe placed the guitar case on a table and pulled his bass guitar out.

"Let's get started," Joe said. "The quicker we get done here, the quicker we get to the campsite." He grinned. "And, you all know what that means."

Again, Evan frowned, unsure of where the conversation was going.

"Yeah," Harold said. "Girls and beer; two of my favorite combinations."

Peter Hanson moved the microphone to what was obviously center stage for them and tested the speakers. He motioned to Tobias and shoved a thumbs-up in his direction.

"We'll start with an old song," Peter said. He glanced at Evan. "We'll do *Slow Ride* by Foghat."

Evan grinned; this was one he knew.

The group started playing and Evan kept tempo with them. Under his breath, mouthing the lyrics, he sang the words.

"If you know the words, Evan," Peter said. "Get up here and sing with me." He shrugged. "We're cool."

Evan stood and joined Peter in front of the microphone, and belted out the song like used to do in his room when he was all alone.

Peter stood back, shocked. Joe quit playing to gaze at Evan. Arnold soon joined Joe and Harold finally hit the drums for the last time.

"Where did you learn to sing like that?" Peter asked.

"You were awesome, dude," Joe said. "You didn't tell me you sang." He chuckled. "You didn't sing like that in church last Sunday."

Evan shrugged. "I didn't know those songs. This one, I sing it all the time back in New York. I listen to music from the 60s, 70s, 80s, and I really enjoy country."

"What other songs do you know?" Peter asked. "Never mind. Here's the list of songs we sing. Do you know any of them?"

Evan scanned the list. "I know most of them except maybe four."

Peter looked at his partners. "Looks like we got us a new lead singer."

Evan shook his head. "No, you got the wrong guy. Nope. Not me."

Joe nodded his head. "Yes, we have the right guy. Let's take *Slow Ride* from the top, follow it with..." He took the list and pointed at the next five songs. "We'll practice these tonight."

Evan shrugged and took the list and looked at the other four men. Peter pulled a dusty piano from the corner. "I'll play piano."

An hour later, the group were back in the cars, headed for a campground north of town.

"Janice is going to like you," Joe said. "She broke up with her boyfriend two weeks ago and has followed Alison, my girlfriend, around constantly, hoping to find a new boyfriend."

Evan nodded in the dark. *Girls and beer*, he thought. *I'm pretty sure Grandma Addie isn't going to like this*. He shrugged. *Oh, well, it's my night.*

# # #

Sunday, June 16 7:30 a.m.

"Evan? Are you awake?" Adeline called up the staircase. "Breakfast is almost ready."

Evan rolled over and groaned. His head hurt.

I can drink one, two bottles of Tsingtao at Lin Ho's restaurant... He shook his head as he tried to put coherent thoughts together. *Never felt like this the next morning. I had five... no, I had eight? Nine?* Again, he shook his head to clear it. *Too many,* he thought.

"*Are you coming down?*" Adeline called.

"I'll be right there, Grandma," he replied and grabbed a pair of slacks and shirt from the armoire.

No, I should shower first before putting on clean clothes, he thought. He grabbed the clothes from the night before. There was a campfire scent to them. He shrugged. *I'll shower after breakfast.*

Once more he placed a hand to his head in an attempt to still the circling sensation.

Grandma is going to know when she sees me, Evan thought. *What do I tell her?*

He staggered to the door and used the hallway wall to stabilize his walk to the staircase. Holding tight to the handrail, he took each step of the staircase with deliberate caution. He stepped into the kitchen.

"You got home rather late," Adeline said. "Did you have a good time?" She gazed at Evan. "Yes, I think you must have had a good time." She smiled. "I remember your father coming home like that." She inhaled deeply. "You remind me so much of your father when he was your age."

Evan sat at the table and glared at the eggs. His stomach turned.

"I'm not that hungry," Evan said. "Maybe just some bacon."

"Not that it is any of my business," Adeline said. "How much did you drink last night?"

Evan inhaled deeply. *Do I tell her the truth?* he thought. "More than I should have," he replied.

Adeline nodded. "Perhaps a moment with Jesus at church will help to clear the head. Are you about ready to leave?"

Evan gazed at the clock; a few minutes before eight.

"Why so early?" he asked.

"We'll leave about eight-thirty," Adeline said. "I made some cinnamon rolls last night for this morning's coffee corner at church. I want to make sure I get them to the church early enough." She picked up the plates from the table. "Now, finish getting yourself about. A little cold shower might help." She glanced at Evan. "And a little after shave lotion to help cover that lingering smell." She wrinkled her nose. "By the time you get back down, I'll be ready to go."

Evan slowly walked up the staircase. *I wonder if Joe will be at church this morning,* he thought as the image of Joe and Alison nearly asleep by the tree on the other side of the campfire.

Reaching the top of the stairs, he bowed his head. *Thank you, Tobias Snyder for bringing me home.* He paused. *And Jesus for keeping me safe.*

CHAPTER NINE ~ Meeting Rachel

Monday, June 24, 2013 8:30 a.m.

Evan followed Zak around, learning the procedure for the day.

"Let us check the dock," Zak said, and headed to the back of the store.

Evan shrugged. "Sure." He followed.

Joe Holgate stood just inside the plastic barrier of the backroom storage area.

"Hey! Evan!" Joe yelled. "Thought I'd come see how you're doing today." He reached out and put his arm across Evan's shoulder. "I mean, you are my best new friend."

Evan frowned but it quickly changed to a smile. It was good to see Joe.

Zak frowned but stepped to the side and allowed Evan and Joe to pass.

A young lady strolled through the plastic barrier.

"Zak!" she called, noticing Joe.

"Rachel," Zak replied. "Why are you here?"

"I came with Zeke..." She paused and gazed at Joe. "I will be going to the Blue Gate Theater to do rehearsals. I thought I would stop to see you and possibly talk to Mary Troyer if she was not working too hard this morning."

Zak shrugged. "Not many customers today. Mary is stocking the candy shelves."

Rachel nodded and headed on into the store.

"Who was that?" Evan asked. "She is hot. Your girlfriend?"

Zeke strolled up behind Evan. "No, she is not Zak's girlfriend. Keep a civil tongue when you talk about our sister."

Joe, with arm still over Evan's shoulder, leaned in and whispered. "You're in trouble now, *Englische* boy."

Evan stepped back, letting Joe's arm fall to the side. He stared at Zeke. "Your sister?"

"Yeah, his younger sister," Joe said with a sneer. "The Amish have large families..." He glared at Zeke. "Right? What do you have? About twenty siblings?"

Zeke took a deep breath. "You know I have nine siblings, Joe. Just because Rachel will not date you..."

Evan gazed at Joe. "Date?"

"Aye," Zeke said, walking past Evan, striking Evan's shoulder with his. He glared at Evan. "I thought you would move seeing me coming."

Evan held his breath and slowly counted. *Keep your temper*, Evan thought. *Grandma Addie got you this job and nobody here knows you.*

"My mistake," Evan mumbled. "Sorry."

Zeke continued to the dock outside.

"Well, my work is done here," Joe said. "Guess I'll go see who's up front." He grinned and walked into the store. "Maybe I can get Mary to go out..." His voice trailed.

Zak put a hand on Evan's shoulder. "Give Zeke time, Evan. He will come around." Zak shrugged. "He is leery of the *Englische*." He paused. "And especially Joe Holgate."

Evan smiled. "I would never have guessed." His mind wandered to the image of Rachel. *I wonder if she would date me?* he thought.

"I got a strange question," Evan said.

Zak turned to face Evan. "What? Is it about stocking the store?"

Evan laughed. "No. I wondered. Do you milk cows?"

Zak burst into a hearty laugh. "Milk cows? Of course, I milk cows. We have a herd of about forty we milk every morning and evening." He drew in a deep breath. "Yes, I milk cows." He paused. "Why?"

"Can you teach me?" Evan asked.

"Why do you want to learn how to milk a cow?"

Evan shrugged. "My grandmother has one cow and somebody comes over to milk her every day." He gazed at Zak. "I thought maybe I could do it."

Again, Zak laughed heartily. "Milking is easy. If you want to learn, come over this Saturday and I will teach you."

Evan nodded. "I will be there. You live just a little way from my grandmother's house. I can use my dad's old bicycle to come over."

"Be at my house by six-thirty in the morning," Zak said. "I will hold Betsy aside to teach you." He watched Evan. "Do not be late. Cows like to be milked early in the morning and again in the evening."

"Zak! Evan!" The intercom sounded above them. "Carryout."

"Sounds like it became a busy Monday morning," Zak said. "Ready?"

Evan nodded and followed Zak to the front of the store to help carry groceries for the customers.

I wonder if Rachel will be there Saturday morning? Evan thought.

#

Saturday, June 28 7:30 a.m.

"As always, breakfast was good, Grandma Addie." Evan munched on the last strip of bacon. He stared at his empty plate with its pancake crumbs and leftover swirls of syrup. Evan leaned back in his chair and watched his grandmother. "Are you okay?"

Adeline leaned against the kitchen counter, her hand dangling into the soapy water of the sink. She inhaled deeply. "I'm fine. Why do you ask?"

"Well, the day I came you were all bouncy when my dad was here and after he left, I noticed you have issues from time to time." He frowned. "Are you okay?" He glanced at the clock. "Oh, I have to go."

"Go?" Adeline asked. "Where?"

"I told you," Evan said. "I'm going to Zak Graber's this morning before work. He is going to teach me to milk a cow."

Adeline grinned. "Milk a cow? Whatever for?"

"So I can milk our lone cow for you. I bet fresh milk tastes good."

Adeline sighed. "When you return, I'll tell you about fresh milk."

Evan glanced at the clock. "Gotta go, Grandma."

Slipping on his shoes, he dashed out the door, grabbed the bicycle, and headed down the lane.

Adeline slowly made her way to the front door to see Evan near the end of the driveway. He turned east and headed toward the Graber farm. She smiled. *Better he spend time with the Amish than that Joe Holgate,* she thought.

#

Evan steered the bicycle into the Graber driveway. He immediately saw Zak sitting on the back porch, waiting. Zak waved.

"You ready to learn to milk a cow?" Zak asked.

Evan rode the bicycle up to him and Zak motioned for Evan to put the bicycle against the big oak tree. "Over there," he said.

As he pushed the bicycle to the tree, he heard a voice singing. He gazed about, trying to locate the source. It was coming from the window in the house. He saw Rachel standing there, singing. She smiled.

Evan smiled and waved at her.

"Follow me, Evan," Zak said and headed for the barn. "Betsy is waiting."

The two walked side by side to the barn and Zak opened the door. "Betsy is still in her stall and probably getting anxious to be outside, grazing." He grinned. "And, she definitely wants to be milked."

Evan listened as the cow let out a loud bellow.

"She doesn't seem happy," Evan said. "Are you sure she'll let me milk her?"

Zak nodded and grabbed a stool and bucket. "First, we put this down so we can sit. Then we place the bucket like this." He moved the bucket under the udder. "Have a seat, Evan. You are about to become a farmer."

Evan attempted to sit on the three-legged stool but found it awkward.

"Like this," Zak said and showed him how to straddle the stool. "Betsy is going to know you have no idea what you are doing, so be careful if she attempts to kick the bucket over."

Evan frowned.

Zak got off the stool and Evan again attempted to sit on it. He succeeded. Zak continued with the instructions of how to apply his hands to utters and milk the cow. Evan felt it awkward but kept at it until he was comfortable with the action and was actually getting milk and aiming it into the bucket.

"Now, you have the idea," Zak said. "Continue until the utter is almost empty."

Evan continued, realizing there was a tempo and he heard it in his mind. Suddenly, a song burst in over the rhythm, matching it. He didn't recognize the song at first until he realized it was the song Rachel was singing when he arrived. Evan didn't know the words, but the tune was soothing.

"That is good, Evan," Zak said, placing a hand on Evan's shoulder. "Betsy has been milked." He removed his hand. "We will take the milk to the house and get us a cold drink of water, sit on the porch and get ready to go to work."

Evan sat on the porch as Zak took the bucket of milk inside the house. He quickly returned with two tall glasses of water. He sat down beside Evan, handing a glass to Evan. In the kitchen, Rachel continued to sing and Evan listened. He liked the words and memorized them as she sang.

"That is a pretty song your sister is singing," Evan said.

"It is one from the production at the Blue Gate Theater," Zak replied. "I think it is called *I Believe*."

The kitchen door opened and Rachel stepped onto the porch.

"That is a pretty song," Evan said.

"Thank you," Rachel replied.

"Could you teach it to me?" Evan asked, hoping to keep the conversation going.

"I know you can sing," Rachel said.

Evan frowned.

"I heard you at Hanson's Garage. I was walking by and heard the music and peeked in the window. You were singing a song." She shrugged. "You have a nice voice."

"Evan, we need to get to work," Zak said. "No time for singing lessons today. Grab your bicycle and I will get mine." He hustled away.

"Maybe next time," Rachel said with a smile and bent to get the glasses. She turned and went back into the house and began to sing *I Believe*, again.

Evan listened, concentrating on the words.

Zak came up with his bicycle. "I have never seen Rachel talk to a stranger before." He grimaced. "Strange."

Evan tried not to smile. *Maybe she likes me*, he thought as he got on his bicycle.

CHAPTER TEN ~ Rachel

Saturday, June 28 6:35 a.m.

Rachel placed the glasses into the sink to wash. She stared out the window, watching Zak and Evan ride their bikes out the driveway on their way to work.

He is cute, Rachel thought, then stopped, frozen. *He is not Amish! Why would I think such? He's Englische!*

She watched as her brother and Evan turned onto the road and rode toward Shipshewana.

He is... No! She thought. *I cannot think about him.*

Rachel immediately put all her energy into cleaning the glasses. To ease her thoughts, she sang, singing *O Gott Vader.*

I will call Grandpa Yoder tonight, she thought. *He will know what to do.*

She smiled, satisfied with her answer, although unsure if he would have the answer to her question.

Rachel placed the glasses to the side to dry.

Why am I infatuated by an Englische boy? she thought and again shook her head to clear her thoughts of Evan.

# # #

Evan and Zak rode side by side on their way to Shipshewana. As the rode by his grandmother's house, he waved, unsure if she would see him or not. He noticed her on the front porch and she waved back. He smiled. Zak waved, also.

"Your grandmother is a strong woman," Zak said. "It is sad she is so sick."

Evan frowned. *Sick? She said she wasn't well, but sick?*

"What do you mean? Sick?" Evan asked.

Zak coasted. "You do not know?"

Evan shook his head.

"I will not be the one to tell you," Zak said. "Talk to your grandmother." He paused. "Soon."

Evan frowned. *I will ask Grandma Addie tonight. If not then, for sure when we go to church. She wouldn't be able to lie to me as we go to church.*

Evan saw the stoplight at the center of town.

"Race you to work," Evan yelled and took off, headed for the lighted intersection.

"As you wish," Zak replied and smiled, letting Evan get a head start. He turned left onto a side street as Evan continued toward Route 5 and the center of town.

Evan approached the light and turned to see where Zak was. He didn't see him. He frowned, unsure where Zak went. He turned south on the main street and pedaled even faster in hopes of beating Zak. He turned into the E & S parking lot and saw Zak putting his bicycle against the building.

Evan frowned. "How did you beat me?"

"Simple," Zak replied. "I took a side street, cut through the campground, through the flea market and..." He spread his arms apart. "Here I am." He grinned.

"You cheated, Zak," Evan said with a grin. "I thought you'd go to the light and then south to the store."

Zak smiled and shook his head. "No, you said race you to the store. I took a different route than you. I cut off an extra block, you did not. I win."

He went in the store. Evan followed.

"Can I ask another question?" Evan asked.

Zak shrugged. "Yes."

"How many cows can one man milk?"

Zak shrugged. "As many as he wishes. Ten. Twenty. More."

"How much would it cost me to buy maybe ten?" Evan put his apron on in preparation of working.

"Cows are expensive, Evan," Zak replied. "You could get calves much cheaper, but it will take longer to milk them since they must mature, be bred, have a calf, then, when the calf is weaned, you can begin to milk the cow."

Evan leaned against the wall, surprised by the answer. "Maybe I should buy one cow at a time."

"I am sure my father would sell you a cow, if you wished." Zak headed into the store. "Shall we see what we need to do today?" He gazed at the aisles. "Look at all the customers. It will be a busy day."

Evan followed Zak into the store and gazed at all the customers strolling the aisles.

"Maybe we should head up to see if we need help at checkout," Evan said.

Zak nodded and lead the way to the front of the store.

# # #

Saturday, June 28 10 a.m.

"Mama?" Rachel called. "I need to call Grandpa Yoder in Centertown."

"Are you sure?" Bethany asked. "You spoke with Grandpa Yoder only a couple of days ago."

"I have questions only he can answer," Rachel murmured.

"If you must," Bethany said. "I am guessing he is working at the U-pick farm." She smiled. "The strawberries are in harvest and he is probably handling the sales for the self-pick customers."

"*denki*, (thank you) Mama," Rachel said and headed out the door for her bicycle. "I will be back shortly."

Bethany nodded and watched as Rachel rode out the driveway. *I wonder what is causing her concern*, Bethany thought, then shrugged. *She acted strange around Zak's Englische friend.*

Rachel raced down to the neighbor to use the telephone.

I hope Grandpa Yoder can help me, she thought.

She knocked on the door.

"Come in, Rachel," Hailey Miller said. "You know where the phone is."

"Thank you, Mrs. Miller," Rachel said and hustled over to the small table holding the black phone. She dialed.

"Aunt Mary?" Rachel asked as somebody answered the phone.

"This is Hannah Mueller," came the response. "Aunt Mary is out in the self-serve area helping the customers."

"Can I talk to Grandpa Yoder?"

"He is not here. He just left to go into town with Jason Muirs."

"Have him call me when he gets home," Rachel said. "Goodbye."

She hung up.

"I am sorry, Mrs. Miller," Rachel said. "My grandpa was not available. He will call back later."

"It's not an issue, Rachel," Hailey said. "Would you like something to drink?"

"Thank you, but no. I need to get back home and help Mama."

Rachel moved toward the screen door.

"Don't worry, Rachel. When your grandfather calls, I will notify you."

Rachel rushed down the steps and grabbed her bicycle to head home. Mrs. Miller came on the porch to wave goodbye.

#

Saturday, June 28 10:10 a.m.

Jason whirled into Daniel Yoder's driveway and honked his horn. Martha came out and stared at the strange black car. Jason stepped out.

"Is Daniel here?" Jason asked, his voice filled with anxiety.

"No," Martha replied. "He is working at the U-pick store at the farm."

"Thank you," Jason said and jumped back into the car.

"Nice car," Martha yelled.

Jason leaned out the window. "Just your run-of-the-mill Jaguar," he said with a smile.

"At least it is black, not yellow," Martha said as Jason turned the car around and spun the wheels as he left.

He certainly is in a rush, Martha thought.

# # #

Jason pulled into the driveway and parking lot of the U-pick operation area. He raced in honking his horn, hoping Daniel would come to check it out.

Daniel appeared at the door of the building, hand over his eyes to see what was going on.

Jason jumped from the car. "Come with me, Daniel," Jason yelled. "We don't have much time."

Mary strolled across the parking lot.

"Take over," Daniel said and headed for the black car and Jason. "What is the rush?"

"It's Ben Hopkins," Jason said. "They don't think he will make it through the day." Jason turned the car around and headed out the driveway and toward the Hopkin's residence.

"Ben is dying?" Daniel asked.

Jason wiped a growing tear from his left eye. "Yes, Daniel." He took a deep breath. "I hope we get to his house in time."

Daniel frowned. "He is not at the hospital?"

Jason shook his head. "No. It is renal failure and the doctor told him to just go home and enjoy his last hours." He shrugged. "They gave him something for the pain."

Daniel bent his head.

Heavenly Father. Place Your mantle of grace over Ben's shoulders. Place Your healing hands on him and give him peace. In Jesus name. Amen.

Jason pulled the car into the Hopkin's driveway.

"C'mon," he yelled as he jumped from the stopped car and headed up to the house.

A young woman opened the screen door to welcome them in.

"Daddy is upstairs in the bedroom," she said and gazed at Daniel. "You must be Daniel Yoder my father has spoken of so many times."

Daniel nodded as he passed her and followed Jason through the house and up the stairs. He entered the bedroom. Ben lay in bed. Alice, his wife sat at his side.

Ben opened his eyes and saw Daniel and smiled.

"You came, my old friend," Ben whispered in a soft voice. "I hoped to see you a last time."

Daniel moved to the opposite side of the bed from Alice. He smiled at her, then grasped Ben's hand.

"May I pray for you?" Daniel asked.

"Reverend Myers has already prayed, but if you wish, I would like that."

Daniel knelt by the bed, still holding Ben's hand.

Dear Heavenly Father. I come to You with my friend, Ben Hopkins. Bless his soul and guide him to his Heavenly reward. Make his passing painless and quick.

"That is quite enough, young man," Alice said. "What type of prayer is that?"

I ask this in Jesus name. Amen.

Daniel stood and gazed at Alice Hopkins. "It was a prayer to make his passing as easy as possible." He gazed at Ben. "Your time is near. Goodbye my dear friend."

Ben closed his eyes, his breathing slowed. It stopped.

"No!" Alice screamed. "Not yet. I love you." She reached over and hugged Ben.

Daniel bent his head. "Ben is gone."

Jason came up and placed a hand on Daniel's kneeling body.

"You did good, Danny-boy," Jason said and helped Daniel to his feet.

For some reason, Daniel wasn't upset at being called Danny.

"It is sad to see a friend depart, but he has moved to accept his reward." Daniel moved to Alice and embraced her. "He was a good man, a very dear friend to me and the Amish community."

Alice sobbed into his shoulder. "He left me," she murmured. "I'm alone."

"You are not alone," Daniel said. "You have many friends in your husband's life. If you need anything, come to me. I will help you any way I can." He paused. "You have my condolences."

Alice leaned up and kissed Daniel on the cheek. "Thank you, Daniel Yoder."

A tear traced a path down Daniel's cheek. "I will also miss him."

Daniel stepped away as Jason and the minister approached.

"I will wait in the car," Daniel said and left the room.

Daniel walked into the house.

"What is wrong, Daniel?" Martha asked.

"Ben Hopkins died today," Daniel mumbled. He sat in his rocker and drew a deep breath. "He will be buried on Wednesday."

Martha nodded. "Mary stopped in. Rachel called you."

Daniel rocked. "I wonder what she wants? I thought she was no longer concerned with the play."

"Perhaps you should go and call her," Martha suggested.

Daniel nodded. "I will harness Arrow to the buggy. Do you wish to go?"

Martha nodded. "Supper can wait." She shrugged with a giggle. "It was leftover meatloaf."

Daniel headed to the barn and harnessed Arrow. He quickly had the buggy in front of the house and Martha came down the steps to join him.

"It is lucky for us it is a short trip to Mary's," Martha said as Daniel turned the buggy to the right out of the driveway.

"I hope Rachel has not been waiting all this time for me to call back."

Martha shook her head. "Nay, my husband. Mary told her you were gone and would be back later." She frowned. "Of course, Mary did not know where you went, so she could not tell me, either."

Mary, Daniel's younger sister, welcomed them into her house. Isaac Wyse, her husband, called Daniel into the main room. "The telephone is in here," he said.

Daniel sat beside Isaac and gazed at the black phone on the table between them.

"I need to call Rachel," Daniel said.

Isaac nodded. "I know." He nodded toward the phone. "Use it. When the bill comes in, like always, we will let you know how much you owe." He grinned like a Cheshire cat. "After all these years, I still cannot believe you graduated me from eighth grade. Was it because of my mother?"

"Your mother is a great teacher, Isaac," Daniel said, picking up the phone and dialing the number. "I graduated you because I did not want to see your face anymore." He laughed and listened for the ringing at the other end.

"Hello?" Hailey Miller said.

"Hello," Daniel replied. "This is Daniel Yoder calling for Rachel Graber. Is she there?"

"No, Mr. Yoder," Hailey said. "She went home. I will drive over and get her. Do you wish her to call you or will you call back?"

"I will call back," Daniel said. He hesitated. "About twenty minutes?"

"That will be fine, Mr. Yoder," Hailey said. "Goodbye." She hung up, "George! Go over to the Graber farm and get Rachel. Her grandfather will call back in about twenty minutes."

George gave Hailey a glaring look. "It would be a lot easier if they put a phone in their home." He shrugged and trudged to the front door and out to the car.

###

The phone rang and Rachel answered it. "The Miller residence," she said.

"Rachel?"

"Grandpa! I do not know what to do." She paused. "Jack Sonner said today that the play is not coming together correctly and something has to be changed."

Daniel thought on her words. "Did he say it was you?" he asked.

"Nay, grandfather," Rachel replied. "He said it was missing something."

"He did not say what it was. Is that correct?"

"I do not remember. He got upset and sent all of us home."

"Is this what is truly bothering you?" Daniel asked.

"I..." Rachel hesitated. "There is... I... I do not know what to do," Rachel blurted. "Zak has a new *Englische* friend and I find myself talking to him."

"*Englische*?" Daniel asked. "Is that the problem?"

"I am Amish, Grandfather," Rachel said. "He is *Englische*. What do I do?"

"Talk with the boy," Daniel said. "There is no harm in speaking with the *Englische;* I do it all the time."

"But..."

"No but, Rachel," Daniel said. "You are seventeen and just realized there are boys in the world beyond your brothers."

Isaac Wyse snickered and nodded his head, knowing.

"He is *Englische!*" Rachel said.

"If it is meant to be, so be it, Rachel. You have not joined the church through baptism. Call it *Rumschpringe.* That is how I met your grandmother."

"Grandma Yoder wanted to be Amish." Rachel shrugged. "I do not think Evan wants to become Amish."

"So," Daniel said with a smile. "You know his name."

Rachel blushed. "Yes."

"Focus on the play," Daniel said. "Maybe this Evan does not want to court you."

"Grandfather!"

"Calm down, Rachel," Daniel said. "Find out what the problem Jack is having with the play and everything else, including this Evan. It will all fall into place."

"*denki,* (thank you) Grandfather," Rachel said. "Goodbye." She hung up.

She turned to the Millers. "Thank you for letting me use your phone."

George stood to take her home.

"Please," Rachel said. "I will walk home." She smiled and shrugged. "I need to think and the cool evening breeze will help me clear my mind."

"I didn't mean to eavesdrop," Hailey said. "Who is this Evan boy? I thought I knew most of the community's youth."

"He is Adeline Kurtz's grandson," Rachel replied.

Hailey nodded. "I will visit with Addie in the next day or two." She grinned. "Gossip, you know."

Rachel again thanked them and left the house to walk the road back to the farm.

Grandfather said things will be as they should be, she thought. *I will work with Jack to find out the problem. Evan...* The image of the young filled her mind. *He is cute and easy to talk to. He... He is Englische!* She shook her head to clear the image.

#

Saturday, June 28 6:10 p.m.

"Grandma?" Evan called from the evening table. "Can we go out on the front porch and talk?" He hesitated. "I mean, now?"

Addie frowned. "Of course, Evan. What do you want to talk about. Something is bothering you?"

Evan took the plate from her hand and placed it in the sink.

"You can do these later," he said and led her to the front porch where their favorite rocking chairs waited for them.

"This is serious," Addie said.

"Yes, Grandma," Evan replied. "I need you to tell me the truth. You said you weren't well when I first arrived. Today, while riding into work with Zak, he said you were sick."

Addie gazed at Evan, silent.

"I'm not giving up on this. Either tell me now or I will ask you at church tomorrow morning and I know you can't lie in church."

Addie smiled. "I will tell you. I have TB. Do you know what that is?"

"TB?" Evan watched her carefully. "Isn't that called tuberculosis or something like that?"

Addie nodded. "It is tuberculosis, Evan."

Evan frowned. "Isn't TB contagious?"

"Yes, and no," Addie replied. "Yes, it is contagious, but no, I've been taking shots and medications to keep it somewhat controlled. If you notice, I turn when I cough so I don't spray you with my saliva." She reached out and touched Evan's hand. "You are my grandson and I don't want to infect you. I'm not contagious."

"How did you get it? Can I ask that?"

Addie nodded. "The dairy farm. We'd milk all the cows and send off the excess to be processed. We'd keep a small amount each day for us to use." She shrugged. "It wasn't pasteurized. The bacteria, called *mycobaterium bovis,* is what I caught from one of our cows."

Evan nodded. "So, that is why you got rid of the cows?"

"Not right away, Evan," Addie said. "Your grandfather tried to continue on, but your father had left for New York, our daughter was dead, and I couldn't help because I was sick. He did what he could and finally we kept selling off the cattle until he passed." She sighed. "Then I sold off everything except for Gertrude."

"So, you won't get well?"

"No, Evan. I'm dying. The Lord will call me when He is ready for me. Until then, I bid my time here on Earth and await that glorious day when I am reunited with Jesus in Heaven." She heaved a heavy sigh. "I only hope my time will last until I have straightened out my young grandson." She smiled.

"I have plans, Grandma Addie," Evan said. "I have plans. I want to make this a working farm again... if you'll let me."

"If you wish, Evan."

CHAPTER ELEVEN ~ The Play

Monday, July 1, 2013 8 a.m.

Evan walked with Zak to the front of the store. Ezra Wyse stepped from his office and motioned to the two of them to come over.

"I have some bad news," Ezra said. "We have five stockers and six checkers." He shrugged. "Too many for a slow Monday and more coming in later." He grinned. "How would the two of you like to be off today?"

"Off?" Evan asked.

"You can work until your first break when the late shift comes in. If things haven't changed, I'll let the two of you go home early."

Evan shrugged. Zak grimaced.

"I can use the money," Evan finally said.

"Fine," Ezra said. "I'll pay you for a half day."

Zak nodded.

"I'm so outta of here," Evan said. "Just watch me boogie down Broadway."

Ezra and Zak frowned, staring at Evan.

"It means watch me leave, I'll be dancing."

Zak shrugged and Ezra turned to go back into the office. "Dance if you wish," he mumbled, entered his office, and shut the door.

"You *Englische* have such strange words," Zak said. "Boogie?"

#

Zak smiled at Zeke. "I will see you at home tonight," he said. "I will help Papa with the fields until you arrive."

Zeke shrugged and nudged his way past Evan to go to the front of the store.

Evan shook his head. "He still doesn't like me."

Zak pushed Evan toward the dock doors. "Come with me. We will go and see my sister at the theater." He grinned. "We will sneak in." He put a finger to his lips. "We need to be quiet, though."

They grabbed their bicycles and Zak led the way to the Blue Gate Theater.

Zak rested his bicycle against the theater and Evan mimicked the action. Zak opened the door of the theater and again put his finger to his lips. "We must be quiet," he whispered and then slipped through the doorway into the shadows of the theater.

Evan followed, unsure.

On stage, Rachel sat on the ladder to one side. A couple walked across the stage and were singing. A man, standing on the floor in front of the stage with his back to them, pointed at Rachel.

"Sing!" he demanded.

Rachel began to sing, lifting her voice into the air. Zak and Evan quietly moved to a table and sat, watching and listening.

"No! No! No!" the man screamed. "This isn't right." He stomped across the floor in front of the stage to a table where another man sat. "This is not working," he screamed at the man then slumped into the chair next to him.

In a dramatic action, he flopped his upper body onto the table, his head turned to face the other man.

"Jack, you'll figure this out," Joshua Beiler said, placing a hand on the man's shoulder with a small rubbing action. "Trust me."

"I can hear it," Jack said. "I just can't see it, so I don't know what is missing." He sat up and leaned against the back of the chair. "A voice. I need a voice. A deep voice."

He stood up and gazed at the stage and the people waiting.

"Jimmy!" Jack yelled. "Get down off of there and come over here and sit with Rachel on this ladder."

Jimmy stood, frowned, and worked his way down the heavenly stairs to the stage.

"This is your chance at being a star, Jimmy," Jack said. "I want you to sing along with Rachel." He glanced around. "Somebody give him the lyrics... sheet music so he has some idea of what is expected."

A young girl ran across the stage with sheets of paper flapping in the breeze. She handed them to Jimmy.

"Now, get your butt up on that ladder." Jack stepped back to evaluate the scene. "About two steps below where Rachel is sitting."

Jimmy moved into position, smiling at Rachel.

"Okay, from the top of *Some Believe*," Jack said. "I want Jimmy and Rachel to sing it as a duet." He nodded to the two sitting on the ladder. "Understood?"

The music started and Rachel began to sing. Jimmy joined.

Jack listened then dramatically placed a hand over his heart in a mock heart attack.

"No! No! No! No!" he screamed. "Jimmy! Where did you get that voice?" He shook his head. "You're singing is..." He waved at Jimmy. "Back to the chorus. Sorry, Jimmy."

Again, he ambled over to the table. "I need a voice; a deep, full voice." He glared at Jimmy. "Not some whiny, nasally voice." He stopped about mid-stage. "Okay, Rachel, take it from the top, but this time, from the very beginning."

The music started and Rachel began to sing.

Evan sat at the table, softly singing the song. Zak frowned at Evan's singing. Then Evan stood, he sang with Rachel, filling the open theater with his voice.

Jack whirled around. "Who is that?" The music stopped. "How do you know the words? The music?"

Evan stopped singing.

"His name is Evan Kurtz," Rachel said from the stage. "He is a friend of my brother." She nodded at the table in the shadows. "He is sitting there."

"We came to listen," Zak mumbled.

Jack waved his hand to dismiss Zak's words. "Evan. You know this song?"

Evan nodded. "Yes, I heard her singing the song at her house."

"Would you please go up on the stage?" Jack asked. "I want you to sing with Rachel on this first song."

Evan shrugged and hustled up the couple of steps setting the stage a bit higher than the dining tables. He smiled at Rachel, unsure what her thoughts were as he took a seat two steps below her as Jimmy had done.

"Now," Jack said. "From the top." He paused. "Yet, again."

Jack strutted in front of the stage as the intro music started and he waved his hands in the air to the tempo. The angels on stage right began their descent down the stairs. Rachel started to sing; Evan joined her.

"That's it!" Jack yelled. "Keep going."

"What are saying?" Joshua Beiler asked. "What's it?"

"What was missing!" Jack exclaimed. "He has the voice I needed. It is what was missing."

Jack rushed onto the stage. "Okay, Evan. You're hired."

"Whoa! Wait a minute," Evan said. "I have a job." He shrugged. "I just enjoy singing."

"I want you in the show," Jack replied. "Joshua?"

"What?"

"Hire this man," Jack said.

Evan stood and walked to the middle of the stage. "Hey! Mister! Like I said, I already have a job at E & S. I'm not looking for another."

Jack strolled over to the table where Joshua sat.

"I will call Ezra and get things fixed. Evan will be able to start tomorrow morning." He shrugged. "At least, I hope I can do that."

Evan stretched out his arms toward the two men. "Is anyone listening to me? I like working at E & S. I don't want another job."

Rachel touched Evan on his shoulder. "Give up, Evan." She nodded at the table with the two men. "Joshua's wife is Ezra's sister."

"Is not Ezra Amish?" Evan whispered.

"He is. His sister married a non-Amish and became *Englische* and left the Amish community. She had not been baptized, so it was accepted." She grabbed his hand. "Come with me." She led him to the edge of the stage. "I told you that you have a beautiful voice. Jack agrees. See if Ezra Wyse will allow you a time of absence from the store so you can participate in this production."

Evan gazed down at his hand which Rachel continued to hold. She saw his gaze and immediately let go.

"It was okay," Evan whispered.

Rachel tried not to blush, but could feel the heat in her cheeks.

Joshua placed his phone on the table and gazed up at the two of them on the stage.

"Evan Kurtz!" Joshua Beiler yelled. "You are now a part of the show. I just finished talking with Ezra and he agreed to allow you absence from work until the play finishes."

Evan glared down at the two men. "Did anyone think to include me in this decision?"

Jack looked up at Evan. "You will sing for the play. Yes?"

"Fine," Evan said. "Maybe I can work at E & S on Saturdays." He paused. "I do get the weekends off?"

"Of course," Jack said. "You will be here from eight in the morning until near five in the evening, Monday through Friday. Remember, that is until we go live; then you will only have Sundays off."

"I better be getting paid," Evan said and watched the two men.

"Of course, Evan," Joshua said. "In fact, it will pay more than you are currently making working for Ezra. Is that satisfactory?"

"Guess I'm a singer on a stage," Evan said, turned and walked toward the ladder. "Guess we need to get started."

Rachel scurried behind him.

"I am going home," Zak yelled from the shadows of the dining room.

Evan nodded and waved as Zak disappeared.

# # #

Saturday, July 6 7:30 a.m.

Evan sliced the ham and added a piece of fried egg to it before sticking it in his mouth.

"As always, Grandma Addie," Evan said. "Excellent breakfast."

"What are your plans today?"

"I was going over to Graber's farm but Zak is working at E & S. I think I'll mow the yard."

Addie grinned. "Too late. I did it yesterday."

"Grandma!" Evan yelled. "You shouldn't be mowing the yard."

"Why?" Addie asked. "I'm too old? I'm sick? I'm a woman?"

"All of the above," Evan replied. "Dad put me out here to help you. Let me help."

Addie picked up the empty plate in front of Evan, along with the leftover ham slices on another plate.

"Want to help? Go collect the eggs."

Evan stood and headed out the back door. "Will do."

He headed for the chicken coop knowing he would get at least four to six eggs.

Maybe I should check the barn, too, he thought.

Five eggs later, Evan headed for the barn.

Probably won't find any here, he thought as he headed into the barn. He gazed at Gertrude and examined her utter.

She can be milked, Evan thought and gazed about the barn for a bucket and stool. He knew there had to be one someplace in the barn. He spotted them.

"I will milk Gertrude," he whispered and grabbed the bucket and stool.

"What is this?" A voice caught Evan's attention and he turned to the main door where a stranger stood.

"You are?" Evan asked.

"I am Leroy Volhaus." He smiled. "I am the neighbor down the road who milks Gertrude each day." He motioned for Evan to continue. "If you wish to milk her, please do so."

"I just learned to milk a cow," Evan said. "I'm not that good."

"I am here," Leroy said. "I will watch to make sure you do it right."

Evan placed the stool near Gertrude and sat. He placed the bucket and began to milk the cow. She bellowed and Evan placed his head against her. She mooed with less voice.

"A wise move, young Evan," Leroy said. "By doing that, you comforted Gertrude and she relaxed."

Evan continued to milk. Leroy nodded approval.

"I think she is milked," Evan said.

Leroy glanced at the utter and nodded. "You have done well. Will you be milking her from now on?"

Evan picked up the pail of milk. "I can do that."

"Twice a day; early morning and again in the evening."

Evan nodded. "Come in and visit with Grandma Addie. I'm sure she would enjoy it."

"I can only stay a little while," Leroy said as they walked to the house.

"I hope to restore this farm back to a fully functioning farm," Evan said.

Leroy glanced at Evan. "I do not wish to intrude, Evan, but you are pushing yourself too much. I have heard; you work at E & S, you are part of the newest play at The Blue Gate Theater, and also, you are part of the Hanson band. Now, you wish to be a farmer, too?"

"I will work at E & S until I can be a full-time farmer," Evan said as he walked up the steps to the back door. "The play is only temporary, as is my involvement with the Hanson band." He grinned. "I don't see myself as a rock and roll idol by any means." He lifted his hands. "I like to work with these. Singing? I'll reserve that for..." He grinned. "For church," he whispered.

Leroy followed Evan into house.

"We have company, Grandma," Evan yelled as he slipped off his shoes.

"No need to yell," she said as she wiped her hands on a towel while standing by the kitchen sink. "Dishes are all done."

"Leroy Volhaus has come to visit," Evan said.

Addie headed for the front of the house. "Let us go out on the front porch and enjoy the cool breeze."

"I can only stay a little while," Evan said as he sat in a rocker, allowing Leroy to sit in the one closest to Addie. "Remember, our band has a gig tonight by the lake." He paused. "I didn't know Shipshewana had a lake."

"I think that is Joe Holgate coming in the drive now," Addie said.

Evan got up. "Guess I'm leaving sooner than I thought." He headed down the front porch steps to meet Joe in the driveway.

# # #

Evan stood on the make-shift stage and watched the people mill closer.

"Who wants to rock tonight?" Evan asked.

The crowd roared in cheers.

Evan stomped twice then clapped his hands. He repeated and the rest of the band joined in sync. The crowd joined in.

Evan grabbed the mike and began to sing.

Buddy, you're a boy, make a big noise
Playing in the street
Gonna be a big man someday

You got mud on your face
You big disgrace
Kicking your can all over the place, singing
We will, we will, rock You.

The mob standing in front of Evan joined in the lyrics surprising him that they knew the words to the *Queen* song. The area reverberated with the final six words as everyone near and far joined in. He continued to sing, realizing this would probably be a good gig. He gazed at Joe who nodded to continue, all the time smiling while playing his bass guitar.

They like this one, Evan thought. *We can slip it in again on the second set.*

Evan spoke a few minutes, taking time to introduce the band and jibe with the crowd.

"You're going to find," Evan started. "Our music is rather eclectic." He saw the frowns. "Varied. Our music is varied and ranges several decades. I hope you find this next song one you like."

Arnold Hanson began to strum the cords of *Hotel California*. The crowd cheered.

# # #

Joe pulled into the Kurtz farm driveway. The house was dark so he drove slowly as to not make too much noise.

"I still can't believe the crowd loved us that much," Joe said. "We had a good night."

"Did we get paid?" Evan asked, unsure if it was a free gig or not. He remembered back in New York City the group he was in had done three gigs for free just to get their name out there. When they began to charge, the gigs faded away.

"Yes, we got paid six hundred dollars. We each made one hundred, but the guys decided since you did such a great job maintaining the crowd and stretching the time so we only had to repeat four songs." He paused. "I... they took only ninety dollars each, so you get one hundred and fifty." He grabbed a folded wad of money from his shirt pocket. "Here."

Evan took the money and knew exactly what he would do with it.

#

Sunday, July 7 12:30 p.m.

Addie placed the roast chicken on the platter and moved it to the table. Evan grabbed the mashed potatoes and green beans. Addie opened the oven and pulled the hot biscuits out, placed them on a plate and poured the chicken gravy into a small boat.

"Shall we give thanks?" Addie asked.

"May I?" Evan asked.

Addie nodded and bowed her head.

Thank you, Heavenly Father, for this beautiful day. Today's word was inspiring. I thank you for a wonderful night last night, and...

He paused. Addie opened one eye to gaze at him.

Give me the strength to do what I plan. Bless my father and...

Again, he paused.

Open his heart to forgive. Bless the food we are about to partake, let it feed both the body and the soul; in Jesus name. Amen.

Addie whispered 'Amen' and smiled at Evan.

"That was a nice prayer," Addie said. "Have you forgiven your father?" She watched Evan from the side.

"Sort of." Evan shrugged. "I know he has a lot on his mind and that is why he probably ignored me." He paused. "But, still..."

Addie reached over and patted Evan on the hand. "Between the death of Alyssa, his sister, and Barb, your mother, his wife." Addie bowed her head and shook it. "Of course, the issue between his father and him. I think it was too much when your mother was killed."

"My mother wasn't killed," Evan snarled. "At least, not during the attack. Dad killed her. He took her off life support."

Again, Addie grabbed Evan's hand and held it in her grasping two hands. "Do you know all the facts about your mother's attack?"

"Yeah," Evan said. "I was told she was attacked by some thug wanting to steal her purse and it want bad. She got shoved, hit her head and went into a coma."

Addie nodded her head. She sighed. "Unfortunately, Evan, there was more. Yes, she was attacked, they think it started as a robbery, but it escalated. Your mother was forcibly raped in a most degenerate way. She fought back, scratching her assailant. He hit her with a rock, several times, knocking her unconscious, and, most likely, causing the coma."

Evan shook his head. "No. Dad never said anything about a rape."

"I'm sorry, Evan," Addie said. "I thought you deserved the truth." She gazed out the dining room window. "I know it hurts. Sometimes the truth does hurt. I'm sorry."

"That explains a few things," Evan whispered. "Dad never told me why he took mom off life support."

"Your mother had less than a ten per cent chance of surviving and an even smaller chance of living a normal life. She was more vegetable and would probably remain that way all the rest of her life, if she had survived."

Evan munched on a chicken leg. "So, what you're telling me is that my father tried to protect me from the truth."

Addie nodded.

"I guess I need to apologize to him for my actions for the last few years."

Addie smiled. "Now you're acting like a young man about to turn eighteen." She paused with a sigh. "Do you realize many Amish young men marry at eighteen?"

"What?" Evan exclaimed. "Eighteen?"

"You met Rachel Graber's father. Yes?" Addie swirled a forkful of mashed potatoes in her chicken gravy. "How old do you think he is?"

Evan shrugged. "I don't know. Maybe fifty? Fifty-five? I mean, he has ten kids."

Addie broke into a full laugh. "Mr. Graber, Rachel's father, is six years younger than your father."

Evan slammed back into his chair, surprised. "Younger than my father?"

Addie swabbed a piece of chicken breast in her gravy then popped it into her mouth to chew. She swallowed. "Most Amish men marry as young as maybe seventeen and sometimes as old as mid-twenties. Most marry between eighteen and twenty."

"Do you mean that Rachel Graber could marry at any time?"

Addie nodded.

Evan winked, leaned forward and shoved a few green beans into his mouth. Holding his fork over the plate, he leaned back in his chair. "I can do that."

Addie raised her eyebrows. "Oh? What can you do?"

"Get married."

Addie nodded. "I am sure you could. What would you do? Continue to be a stockboy at E & S?"

Evan grimaced. "No. I want to be a farmer, Grandma Addie. I want to make this a working farm, again." He paused and stared at the half-eaten chicken leg. "I want to get more cows. You know, like Grandpa John had years ago."

Addie sighed. "That's a a nice dream. Where do you plan to get the money?"

Evan slipped the money from his pocket he'd made the night before and placed it on the table. "Last night I made one hundred and fifty dollars. I make more at the theater than when I work at E & S. I'm saving money. I have over a grand, almost two grand, up in my room from when I worked back in New York City."

Addie put her fork on her plate. "I believe both you and your father have mis-judged each other. Your father thinks you have no work ethic and you think your father works too much and ignores his family."

Evan nodded.

"Tomorrow, on your lunch break, first thing we're going to do is put your money into the bank so it is safe." She grimaced. "Not that my house is not safe, but there is no reason to tempt another human being into thinking they can break the Lord's law and steal."

"Zak said his father would maybe sell me calves for a hundred dollars each," Evan said and grabbed the chicken leg and ate the last of the meat on it. "I want to get some cows, too."

Addie scrutinized Evan, evaluating his words. "Maybe you should talk with Leroy Volhaus. He has cattle and might be willing to help you out."

"Do you think I could talk to Leroy today?" He gazed at Addie. "I know today is Sunday and I'm sure you frown on business on the Lord's day, but..."

"Tomorrow would be soon enough, Evan." Addie reached over and patted Evan's hand. "Tomorrow." She leaned back in her chair. "Today? I think we will just sit on the front porch and enjoy the day the Lord has given us." She gazed at the dishes. "In fact, I think I will just let these soak in the kitchen sink until later."

Evan grabbed up Addie's plate with his and snagged the silverware. "No, you will go out on the front porch and wait for me. I'm doing the dishes. You fixed the meal. The least I can do is clean up."

Addie frowned at Evan. "Are you sure?"

"Grandma!" Evan said. "I learned how to clean a kitchen working for Lin Ho at the Happy Dragon restaurant."

Addie toddled to the front porch, grabbing the staircase banister for support when the pain hit.

Not yet, Lord. Please. Allow me a little more time. Amen.

The pain eased. She wiped the wetness from the edge of her mouth with her handkerchief. There was blood. She gazed back to see if Evan had seen. He was busy clearing the dishes from the table. She stumbled, but continued on her way to the front porch, pushing the hankie into a pocket.

# # #

Sunday, July 7 2:45 p.m.

"Will you ride with me, Zak?" Rachel asked. "I want to take a small bike ride."

Zak gazed at all the people still at the house after church and the meal.

"A ride?" he asked. "Where?"

Rachel shrugged. "I do not know; just a couple of miles." She winked. "Maybe into town?"

Zak nodded and walked with her to get the bicycles. "It is Sunday so no racing. Understood?" Zak said.

Rachel nodded and pushed off on her bike. "Out and to the right," she said.

Zak followed her, letting his sister set the path for the ride. It was liesurely and easy. Slow going. No rush.

Zak took the time to scrutinize the scenery as it passed. The sky was a bright cerulean blue with a multitude of white clouds with lightly grey-colored bottoms.

"Somebody to our east is going to get a storm at some point," Zak said.

"Not us. Not today." Rachel turned and headed west into Shipshewana.

Ahead, Zak saw the Kurtz farm come into view. He smiled.

She is a sly one, Zak thought. *Evan and his grandmother will probably be sitting on the front porch, enjoying the afternoon.*

As they approached the Kurtz property, Zak kept an eye on the front porch. As expected, Adeline Kurtz was sitting in her rocker. Evan appeared at the door and moved toward the nearby rocker.

Zak waved.

Evan waved back and motioned for them to come in.

"Do you want to stop and talk?" Rachel asked. She tried not to show any possibility of wanting to do so.

"He did wave to us and invited us," Zak said. "It would be rude not to."

Rachel turned and started on the long driveway to the Kurtz home. Zak followed, knowing she wanted to do this.

Zeke will not be happy," Zak thought. "This is Rachel's choice, not his."

Rachel jumped from her bicycle and pushed it toward the front porch. Zak followed suit, finally taking the lead. He went up the steps with Rachel following.

"Welcome," Addie said. "Come. Have a seat. Relax. I'll get some fresh lemonade." Adeline got up and ambled to the screen door. "You three sit out and talk."

"Out for a Sunday afternoon bike ride?" Evan asked.

Zak nodded. "Rachel wanted to go on one." He gazed at his sister.

"I thought it would be fun," she murmured, trying not to look at Evan.

"I know the Amish don't do business on Sundays," Evan started. "But I'd like to know if I can buy about five cows from your father."

"We can talk business, but not do business on the Lord's day." He nodded at Evan. "I will tell my father of your wishes tomorrow morning and let you know his response at..." He grinned. "I forgot. You are working at the theater."

"I can let him know," Rachel said and smiled at Evan.

"Here we go," Addie said, coming back onto the porch, carrying a tray of tall glasses filled with lemonade.

Rachel jumped up and crossed over to help her.

"Tell you what," Addie said. "Evan? Move Rachel's chair over beside me so we can have our girl-talk."

Evan stood and picked up the chair to move it beside Addie's rocker.

"No. Not that way," Addie said. "Angle it so we can see each other."

Evan tried not to grin, realizing his grandmother was placing Rachel's chair so he would be able to see her, rather than sitting hidden on the other side.

"There. That's so much better," Addie said. "Now I can see you, and you can see me."

Rachel nodded and gazed at Evan sitting back down in his rocker.

Addie patted Rachel's hand. "Did you have a good sing last night?" She sighed. "My daughter, Alyssa, she always enjoyed those and felt honored when she was invited to participate." She glanced at Evan. "Maybe Zak will invite Evan to join a sing some time."

"These are on Saturday night?" Evan asked.

Zak nodded. "You can come this coming Saturday, if you wish." He drank his lemonade.

Evan shrugged. "If I don't have a gig with the band."

"Oh, Evan, dear," Addie said, watching Evan. "I'm sure you could miss a band gig for an evening at an Amish sing." She nodded ever so slightly toward Rachel. "I'm sure you would have more fun."

"I make money at the gigs, Grandma. I need to buy cows."

"Having even two cows without somebody to help you..." Again, she bent her head toward Rachel who sipped her lemonade. "You need another to help with the farm."

"Grandma!" Evan shouted.

"Perhaps we should leave," Rachel said, stood and began to head for the steps. She gazed back at her brother. "Are you coming, Zak?"

Zak stood. "Stop by E & S when you get a chance." He grinned. "You know, just to have a refresher course in how to stock a store."

"I'm going to be a farmer," Evan said. "A dairy farmer."

Zak followed Rachel down the steps to the bicycles.

"It was nice visiting with you, Mrs. Kurtz," Rachel said pushing off on her bicycle. "See you tomorrow morning, Evan." She waved.

"Have a nice afternoon," Zak said and followed Rachel.

Addie shook her head as the two rode back toward their farm. "Evan Kurtz! You have a beautiful, young lady on the front porch and you're worried about how many cattle you can buy."

"Rachel is Amish," Evan said. "I'm not."

Addie stood. "Honestly!" She shook an index finger at him, scolding. "Yes, she is Amish but that doesn't mean she will remain Amish." She winked. "Maybe you'll become Amish."

Evan slunk back in his rocker. "Me. Amish?" He shook his head. "I like my TV."

Addie broke into a laughter. "Evan, honey. Do you realize you haven't even looked at the TV since you got here? I know you haven't watched it because it isn't even hooked up."

Evan joined her in the laughter. They sat on the porch, sipped their lemonades, and watched the light breeze play within the green leaves of the tress. A perfect Sunday afternoon since the storm clouds Zak fretted about moved north, away from Shipshewana.

CHAPTER TWELVE ~ Monday Business

Monday, July 22, 2013 8:15 a.m.

Rachel sat on the ladder on stage waiting for Jack to make a decision. She leaned down to Evan.

"Papa said he will sell you five cows," Rachel whispered. "He said to come over and discuss the terms."

"Terms? Evan echoed. "Do you know what he means?"

Rachel shook her head. "No."

"I will check with Grandma Addie and try to get over to your father tonight."

"Enough chit-chat up there," Jack said. "This is not working. We have lovebirds on stage and two entities sitting on a ladder from Heaven." Jack stepped back and placed a hand to his chin and rubbed it as he thought, scrutinizing the stage. "The placement is all wrong."

"Tell me, Jack," Joshua said. "Is this production going to be ready by the first week of August?" He sat at the table with Chef Harold going over the new menu ideas for the next week. Joshua pointed at the soup. "Go with the Chicken Couscous. It's something light and it is getting warmer as the summer progresses."

Chef Harold nodded. "I agree."

Jack spread lifted his arms and spread them apart. "The ladder needs to be wider. More impressive. One arm fell to his side while his other arm, with hand spread open, he wiggled his fingers. "Yes, that's it. Evan and Rachel on the same step. They are also lovers."

Joshua frowned. "Are you changing the play?"

Jack lunged over to the table and sat beside Joshua. "Change? No. Director's intuition and creative discretion? Yes."

Joshua stood and stared at the stage. "So, what you want is for both of them to sit together with the white fabric draped in front of them." He grimaced. "Sort of angels, but not angels?"

Jack lifted his hand and wavered it. "Maybe yes; maybe no." He stood and walked to the front of center stage. "Let's have Evan and Rachel walk down the ladder to their positions when the music starts." He turned to the opposite side. "Then the angels start descending." He stepped back. "From the top."

Rachel frowned as Evan offered a hand to help her stand. "I do not act," she said. "I am Amish. I..."

"Just follow my example," Evan whispered. "We're not acting. We're coming onto the stage."

They stood on the platform at the top of the ladder and waited. The intro music started and Evan led the way down, holding Rachel's hand to help her balance. She followed; one step behind. He got to the position, waited for Rachel to join him, and they sat. It was tight.

"Jack?" Evan called. "This ladder isn't designed for two people to sit comfortably together." He grinned. "Right now, my right cheek is barely on the step and I don't want to push Rachel off the other side."

"The carpenters will fix that tonight," Joshua said. "When Jack suggested two on the same step, I realized it was too narrow. Don't worry, Evan, it will be corrected for tomorrow's rehearsal."

Evan nodded. It was then he realized their knees touched. He felt Rachel squirm and move so they didn't touch. He sighed, watched the others come down on the other side, waited for their music to start. Evan sang. Rachel didn't.

"Stop! STOP!" Jack yelled. "What is the problem now?

"I am Amish, Mr. Sonner. I do not act." She hesitated and drew a deep breath. "I was told I would sit on the ladder and sing."

Jack slapped his forehead. A soft murmuring under his breath.

"This is not acting," Evan whispered. "As I said, we are walking and sitting, then we sing. Nothing more."

Rachel shrugged. "I guess it is okay." She turned to Jack. "I am sorry, Mr. Sonner. I will walk and sing as you wish."

"Fine," Jack said, taking a deep breath and slowly releasing it. "So many divas in this business," he whispered. "And I get an Amish one."

Once more Evan led the way down from the platform, holding Rachel's hand. He gazed at her as they went down.

Grandma Addie is right, Evan thought. *She is beautiful, but I knew that the first time I saw her. Maybe I should consider one of their Saturday night sings.*

# # #

Monday, July 22 7:30 p.m.

Grandma Addie pulled the car into the Graber driveway.

"You know, Grandma," Evan started. "I could have driven the car, or if you didn't want to come along, I could have ridden my bicycle." He grinned. "I'm getting good at riding a bicycle around."

"Actually," Addie said getting out of the car. "I thought you should have somebody along who knew something about dairy farming and cattle." She wrinkled her nose at Evan as he got out of the car and looked across the top at her.

"And you're just the person to fill the shoes," Evan said.

"Oh, honey, I'm not going to say anything. I'm just going to sit there quietly and listen to my young grandson do business." She paused and winked at Evan. "Or, make a fool of himself."

They walked up to the door and knocked. Zak immediately answered the door.

"Come in." He held the screen door open and allowed Addie in. Evan followed. "This is my father, Jeremiah Graber," Zak said, introducing his father who sat in a solid chair in the large room.

"Good evening, Mr. Graber," Addie said.

"How are you doing, Mrs. Kurtz?" Jeremiah asked.

Addie took a chair opposite Jeremiah and watched. "Just an observer."

"So, young Kurtz," Jeremiah said. "I understand you want to buy some cows." He grinned. "Are you hoping to begin a dairy farm?"

Evan nodded. "Yes, sir." He sat in the chair beside Addie.

"Getting right down to business," Jeremiah said. "I heard you are looking for five. I have five calves ready for weaning. I can sell each of them for one hundred dollars." He leaned forward. "Five hundred dollars, young man, and you have a starter herd."

"That sounds fair," Evan said. "I was hoping for older ones so I could milk them."

Jeremiah leaned back in his chair and tugged at his beard. "Older ones. Hm?" He eyed Evan and then scrutinized Adeline who was watching him like a hawk. "I have a few old ones I am considering for butchering." He hm-hawed. "I could sell them for... say, maybe one hundred dollars a hundred weight. About nine hundred pounds, that would be nine hundred dollars each."

Evan slumped back in his chair. "I didn't realize they'd cost that much."

Jeremiah grinned.

"May I?" Addie asked.

Evan nodded.

"Let's look at this realistically. You want to sell my grandson some old cows that really aren't producing anymore and you want prime pricing?" She lowered her head and stared sternly at Jeremiah with one eye. "He might be young, but I'm not. I sold you some of my best dairy herd for practically nothing. Do you remember?"

Jeremiah nodded.

"The boy wants to become a dairy farmer," Addie said. "I say give him a break."

"Perhaps I could sell you five dairy cows that I know are pregnant. Are you willing to offer me seven hundred dollars for each of them? Thirty five hundred?"

"Tell you what," Addie said. "He will take the five pregnant dairy cows and the five that are weaned. Four grand. Deal?"

Jeremiah's eyes widened. "Fair."

"I don't have that much money, Grandma," Evan whispered. "I can't afford it."

"I can. I'll write the check and you can repay me with all that money you'll make in those singing gigs you brag about."

"I..."

"Now, hush, Evan. Shake hands with the man. Seal the deal." She grinned. "You're about to be a dairy farmer."

Evan stood and walked across the room to shake hands with Jeremiah. "Thank you, Mr. Graber," Evan said and gripped the older man's hand firmly. "Deal."

Addie opened her purse and pulled out her checkbook. "That is four thousand dollars to Jeremiah Graber. Correct?"

"Aye," Jeremiah said.

Zak stood by the kitchen doorway, listening and watching. "Next thing, you will become Amish," he said with a grin.

Evan gave him a glance. Zak walked over and sat down beside Evan as Addie moved to give Jeremiah the check.

"Do you realize you just basically bought fifteen cows?"

"Fifteen?"

Zak nodded. "Aye. You did. Five calves. Five cows that are pregnant and will have five more calves." He grinned. "That is fitteen."

"I will only need to milk the five older, correct?"

Zak nodded. "Until they give birth, then you can only take a small amount, if any, until the new calves are almost weaned. About five months."

Evan nodded. "Uh-huh." *What have I gotten myself into?* he thought.

"We're done here, Evan," Addie said and headed for the front door. "I'll talk with Leroy Volhaus about picking them up."

"If you wish," Jeremiah said. "I can select and bring them over tomorrow." He paused. "Or, did you wish to pick them, Mrs. Kurtz?"

"I'm an old lady, Mr. Graber," Addie said. "I'm sure you will pick a nice selection of dairy cows for my grandson." She paused. "None too old. And, of course, pregnant, each of the five cows. Plus, five nice well-weaned calves." She turned to Evan. "The boy is learning, but no reason to toss him into the deep end of the pool on his first day."

"I will be fair, Mrs. Kurtz," Jeremiah said.

Rachel strolled into the room. "Would anyone like something to drink?"

Evan smiled at Rachel, ready to nod his head just so he could spend time with her.

"No, thank you," Addie said. "We were just leaving."

Addie opened the door and headed out. Evan sighed and followed. They walked side by side to the car. He opened the door for her then rushed around to the other side and jumped in."

"I hope you realize starting tomorrow night you will be milking six cows. Gertrude and the five new ones."

"Uh-huh," Evan mumbled. "Six cows."

"And you're going to have to watch those calves so they don't attempt to nurse on the the pregnant cows."

"What?"

"The calves might be weaned, but if there is an utter with milk, they will quickly revert back to nursing," Addie said. "We will keep the young calves in a different pasture, away from the pregnant ones."

"Okay," Evan whispered. "Whatever you say."

"You wanted to be a dairy farmer." She glanced at him as she pulled into their driveway. "You're a dairy farmer." She paused and took a deep breath. "I will help you to understand what you need to do." She grinned. "It is not going to be easy, but I know you can do it. Otherwise, I wouldn't have spent four grand."

"Thank you, Grandma," Evan said. "I will get the money to you as soon as I can."

"Don't you fret the money," Addie said. "It will be nice to see the farm back to a working place." She patted Evan's hand as she pulled into the small garage. "I have faith in you."

"Thank you, Grandma," Evan said before getting out of the car. "Do you think Dad will let me stay here on a permanent basis... I mean, if you say okay?"

"When my son shows up, we'll discuss things then," Addie said and got out of the car.

#

Rachel sat the table with Evan in the Blue Gate Theater dining area. Low lighting glowed over the stage.

"Papa went out to the barn last night after you left," Rachel whispered. "He checked the pregnant cows and selected the five for you. Then he examined the calves and pulled aside the five he sold to you."

Evan nodded, happy to be siting at the table with Rachel, talking.

"He said he would bring them to your grandmother's house today." She smiled at Evan. "You will have cows to milk when you get home tonight." She sighed. "Are you sure you want to be a dairy farmer?"

Evan nodded. "Yes. I'm sure." He grinned. "I will have to have Zak come over and teach me more about farming."

Rachel smiled at Evan. "Or, you could come to our farm and Zak could teach you there."

"Yes," Evan replied. "I could do that."

"Plus, we could rehearse our songs." She bowed her head. "If you wanted."

"That would be nice, Rachel," Evan said.

Rachel gazed at Evan. "That is the first time you have ever said my name."

Evan blushed.

"Let's get this show on the road," Jack said, entering the dining room and clapping his hands. "Everyone on stage."

"Guess we need to go to work," Evan said, stood, and helped Rachel to her feet.

Again, she bowed her head. "Thank you," she murmured.

CHAPTER THIRTEEN ~ Cows

Tuesday, July 23 5:20 p.m.

Evan rushed up the back steps, kicking his shoes off, and raced into the kitchen. He immediately smelled something good cooking. Grandma Addie was working at the kitchen sink. She was washing lettuce.

"Did my cows arrive?" He paused. "Wow. Something smells good, Grandma Addie."

Addie turned around. and smiled at Evan. "The answer to your first question is no. Your cows aren't here. MY cows are." She laughed. "The cows are out in the barn. The answer to your second question, it's supper and is called Tater Tot Casserole"

"So Jeremiah Graver brought them over today," Evan said. "Rachel said he would do it."

Addie ripped up the lettuce leaves for a salad. "Now, the question is, do you want to milk the cows before supper, or after supper?"

"When did you and grandpa milk the cows?" Evan asked.

Addie grabbed up her apron and dried her hands. She picked up the bowl of torn lettuce and the bottle of salad dressing.

"When did Grandpa John milk the cows?" She smiled and sat in her chair at the table. "Like clockwork. Six-thirty in the morning, and again at six-thirty in the evening. We'd have supper then head out to the barn to milk the cows and finish the daily chores."

Evan nodded his head. "Six-thirty." He grimaced. "That's sort of early in the morning," he muttered.

"If we plan on eating, I'd best get that casserole out of oven." Addie stood up.

"I'll get it," Evan said and grabbed the two potholders on the oven. He opened the door of the stove and gazed at supper. "It looks good."

"It will taste even better once you have it on the table." She patted the center of the table where a trivet waited. "Place it on this. No reason to ruin the dining table."

Evan pulled the casserole out of the oven and he could feel the saliva building up to a drool. The cheese bubbled up between the tater tots.

"What all is in this?" Evan asked as he placed the dish on the trivet.

"A simple meal," Addie said. "A layer of hamburger spread out evenly in the dish, then I slather it mushroom soup. Next I spread frozen peas over the mushroom soup and then I cover that with slices of cheese." She grinned. "The hard part? Lining up all those tater tots." She shook her head. "Your father usually did that since he thought it made cutting it into pieces a lot easier than just tumbling the tater tots onto the mixture."

"Peas, huh?"

"Don't tell me you don't like peas," Addie said. "I got them frozen and canned." She narrowed her eyes at Evan. "I like peas."

"They're okay," Evan said and sat at the table.

"Do you want to say grace, or should I?" Addie asked.

Evan nodded at Addie. "I'll let you."

Addie gave thanks then picked up the spatula to cut into the casserole. "Since you seem hesitant," Addie said. "I'll give you a small piece." She placed the gooey mess on Evan's plate and smiled. "There's always seconds."

Evan took a tater tot and the mixture below it onto a fork. He watched the steam wisp into the air. "Hot," he mumbled.

Addie nodded. "Let it cool. I do think you'll enjoy it."

Evan blew on the fork of food and when he thought it was safe, he shoved it into his mouth with gusto. It was still a little warm, but the combination of flavors surprised him. He liked it.

"This is great, Grandma Addie," Evan exclaimed. "My dad likes this?"

Addie nodded. "Another one of his favorites."

Evan nodded as he shoved another bite into his mouth and chewed. "Me, too."

# # #

Evan walked into the barn and saw it was empty. He gave Addie a quizzical glance.

"They're out behind the barn," Addie said. "I kept the calves over to the right so they wouldn't nurse."

Evan nodded and moved through the barn to the back where he saw Gertrude and the other five cows grazing. He smiled and headed for Gertrude, hoping when she headed in, the others would follow. They did.

"They're eager to be milked," Addie said as the cattle moved into the barn and she moved them toward the milking area.

Evan grabbed the stool and bucket. He quickly realized that milking a total of six cows, the bucket was going to be filled beyond its capacity. He frowned.

Addie noticed the look. "There is a big cannister over here. I got it from Leroy earlier today knowing we'd need it."

Evan began to milk. He enjoyed it. *I can do this,* he thought. *By the end of next year I could have sixteen cows to milk.* He paused. *That is, if Gertrude lives that long.*

"What are you thinking, Evan?" Addie asked as she leaned against the open barn door.

"For starters, how many cows I can milk." Evan laughed. "But, you know, I think I would rather sing."

"That would be nice, Evan. I've only heard your voice in church. Go ahead. Sing."

Evan broke out with the third song from the play. It was slow and melodic, yet was soothing. A couple of cows bellowed softly. He finished the song.

"That was beautiful, Evan," Addie said. "I've never heard that song before."

"It is from the play at the theater," Evan said. "I sing it with Rachel."

"Oh," Addie said, her voice filled with surprise. "You and Rachel?"

"Grandma!"

"Just pour the milk from the bucket into this container, Evan," Addie said. "Get along with the milking." She paused. "Sing another song."

Once again, Evan thought about what song to sing. He knew most of the songs the band played wouldn't be good to sing since there was no instrumental backup. He grimaced then smiled as he remembered one from his youth.

"Row. Row. Row your boat," Evan started and moved to the next cow.

Addie smiled and joined in, starting her own round.

Four more songs later, the cows were milked and Evan placed the stool up on the post. He rinsed out the bucket, cleaning it, then hung it so it could drain and dry.

Addie leaned over to lift up the canister of milk.

"You let go of that, Grandma," Evan chastised. "I'll get it. Where do you want it?"

"We'll drive down to Leroy Volhaus' place and give it to him. Just put it behind my seat in the car." She walked towards the vehicle. "Now, tomorrow morning when you milk the cows, I want you to save out a small amount for us."

Evan nodded and hefted the canister into the backseat area of the car behind the driver's seat.

"Can I go along?" Evan asked.

"Of course," Addie said. "You might as well learn what you need to do each time you milk." She gave Evan a sly glance. "Do you think you can ride the bicycle and carry this canister?" She paused, waiting for an answer. "Leroy and his sons have been doing it in the past."

"If they can do it, I'm sure I can." He gave Addie a grin. "At least, I'll give it a try." He sighed deeply. "Sixty-thirty tomorrow morning." He shook his head. "So early," he mumbled.

"When we get back, we need to start to enlarge the paddock." Addie started the car and quickly pulled out of the driveway toward the Volhaus residence.

Evan frowned at Addie. "Enlarge?"

"Those cows can survive that small area for a few days, but they need more space. I spoke with James, the man who farms the property and explained what we'd done. He said to take what we need of his planted fields for the cows and he'd deduct it from my profits."

"How much are we going to take?" Evan asked.

"About two acres, for now," Addie said. "That will make the paddock about three and half acres. Not great, but should do until we can enlarge it later after the harvest. We'll put the calves in the front yard." She winked at Evan. "So much for needing to mow the front yard."

"Exactly how do you plan to do that?" Evan asked.

"The same way your grandfather and I did it. Fence in the front yard and put a runway from the barn to it. That way we can move the calves back and forth as needed."

Evan nodded. He had his answer. Grandma Addie was a farmer.

CHAPTER FOURTEEN ~ The Accident

Thursday, July 25 9:10 a.m.

Dan Noble popped the last of his strawberry waffle into his mouth.

"The food is so good here at the 5/20 Country Kitchen," he said between munches.

"Don't talk with food in your mouth," Emma said.

"Will there be anything else," the waitress asked as she walked up with another pot of coffee to pour into the cups.

"Somebody to pay the bill?" Dan asked with a grin.

"Not the first time I've heard that one," the waitress said. "Plus, I've yet to ever find someone to pay it other than the patrons I give the bill to." She placed the small tab on the table. "You can pay at the register on the way out. Thank you and have a great day."

"We will," Emma said. "We're sneaking into The Blue Gate Theater to listen to our great-granddaughter rehearse the play."

"Your great-granddaughter is in the play?" the waitress asked.

"The new one coming out next month," Emma gushed. "We're so excited."

"Again, enjoy your day," the waitress said and left.

Dan glanced at the bill, pulled out his billfold and grabbed the amount of the bill plus a tidy tip. "She was a great waitress," he said. "She kept that fresh coffee coming."

Emma and Dan paid the bill and left the restaurant. Dan stretched before getting into the car. "A beautiful day. Just look at that sky. Gorgeous." He glanced at the traffic on Routes 20 and 5 at the stop light. *Light traffic, almost enough to put one to sleep behind the wheel*, he thought.

Dan drove the car to the west end of the parking so he could get on Route 5 and go into Shipshewana and the Blue Gate Theater. He waited for the traffic.

A screech caught his attention, and a blaring truck horn. He jerked to the left to see what was happening.

In slow motion, a semi-truck on US 20 was veering toward him to avoid a horse and buggy stopped at the light on US 20. The rig careened across the intersection, running the red light to clip a black Ford Escape headed south on Route 5. The semi caught the car on the driver front side of the hood, spinning it around. It slammed against the trailer wheels of the semi and the impact was enough to send it ricocheting into a ditch along US 20. The semi continued toward the Noble car.

Dan watched in horror as the bright chrome grill of the semi grew in size, getting larger and larger. Emma screamed. Dan sat frozen, unable to move.

The sounds of grating metal and smashing glass was all Dan could hear as the semi smashed into their car, hitting his door straight on.

# # #

Thursday, July 25 10 a.m.

Zak rushed into the Blue Gate Theater.

"Rachel!" he yelled. "We have to leave. There was an accident."

"What?" Rachel asked, standing and coming down the remainder of the ladder.

"Grandma and Grandpa Noble were killed in an auto accident at the corner of 5 and 20. Come on!" He headed back out toward the door. "Zeke was coming into work with the buckboard when he heard it. He saw the car and ran to the intersection. It was Grandma and Grandpa Noble's car. They were killed instantly."

Rachel stumbled at the words and Evan raced to her side, grabbing her before she totally collapsed on the floor.

"Zak!" Evan yelled. "Your sister."

Zak turned and saw Evan holding Rachel in his arms. He frowned, but rushed up to the stage to help.

"What is going on?" Jack Sonner bellowed. "I step away for a minute. In case anyone was wondering, there is a rehearsal going on."

"Rehearsal got canceled," Zak said. "We have a family emergency."

"Well, somebody had best be dying," Jack said.

Zak glared at Jack. "In fact, our grandparents were just killed. So, yes, somebody is dead. Are you happy now?"

"I will not be back," Rachel mumbled. "This is not right."

"Whoa, hold up," Jack said. "I was out of line and a bit hasty. Go."

Evan helped Zak get Rachel out the door.

"I'm going along," Evan said. "I'm not related, but you're my friends and this is important. I'm here to support you."

"*denki*, (thank you)" Zak said. "Do you think you and Zeke can get along?"

Evan shrugged. "We can go to my grandmother's house and make any phone calls."

Rachel sighed. "We need to call Grandma Yoder in Centertown. I do not know where Uncle Alexander and Aunt Bethan are, but they need to know."

Zeke glared at Evan as he climbed into the buckboard. "Why is he coming?"

"Because we are going to his grandmother's house to make the phone calls," Zak replied. "It is closer and easier."

Zeke shrugged and mumbled Amish under his breath.

#

Evan rushed up the back steps with Rachel, Zak, and Zeke following. He kicked off his shoes and dashed into the kitchen. Grandma Addie wasn't there.

"What is all the noise?" Addie asked as she ambled from the living room.

"There was a horrible accident in town, Grandma," Evan gushed. "They need to call family to let them know."

Addie pointed to the telephone on the wall. "You can use that one, or the one in the living room." She paused. "Just call. Don't worry about the charges."

Rachel picked up the phone and dialed the number for the Yoder U-Pick Farm. She leaned against the wall and Evan grabbed a chair for her to sit on.

"Give me the phone," Zak said. "Let me talk to them."

Rachel handed the phone to Zak.

"Hello?" he said. "I need to talk with Daniel Yoder. Is he there?"

"He is helping a customer. This is Mary. Can I help you?"

"This is Zak Graber. I need to talk with him, and only him."

"I will get him," Mary said and Zak heard the phone thunk on the table when she set it down.

Zak winced.

Zeke frowned.

"She put the phone on the table," Zak whispered.

"This is Daniel Yoder," Daniel said.

"Grandpa! I am calling you. The Nobles, Grandpa and Grandma Noble, were killed in an auto accident about an hour ago. Will you tell Grandma?"

"Killed?" Daniel echoed. "How?"

"Here Zeke," Zak said and handed the phone to his brother. He wiped a building tear from his eye. "Grandpa wants to know the details."

Zeke grabbed the phone. "A semi almost hit a horse and buggy, but turned left to avoid it and ran the light at US 20 and Route 5. Grandpa and Grandma Noble were coming out of the restaurant parking lot and he hit them straight on the door. They were both killed instantly."

"Grandma and I will be there as quickly as possible," Daniel said. "Have you notified Alexander or Bethan?"

"We do not have their numbers," Zeke said. "Maybe Mama has them."

"If not, we will contact them when we arrive, if the police have not already notified them."

"Goodbye, Grandpa," Zeke said and hung up the phone.

"Would you like some fresh lemonade?" Addie asked. "It's cold and in the refrigerator."

"That would..." Rachel started.

"We leave," Zeke said and headed out of the kitchen to the back door. "We must get home to Mama."

"If you need to make any other calls," Addie said. "You come back here. You hear me?"

Zak nodded as he slipped on his shoes and left.

"See you tomorrow?" Evan asked Rachel.

She shook her head. "Nay."

# # #

Tuesday, July, 39 10:00 a.m.

Daniel sat behind Martha staring at the two coffins. He still couldn't believe that his in-laws were gone, even though they were in their 90s, it was still a shock. Beside Daniel was Thomas, Bethan's husband. Beside Bethan was Alexander. He was the odd one out of all those in attendance. Sitting quietly, he was obvious wearing his Hare Krishna robes of white and orange, the shaved head except a small tuft of hair that was braided and about fifteen inches long. He sat on the chair with legs folded up Indian-style, hands on knees, thumb and index finger making a circle.

Alexander kept watching all the people in the room, noting the Amish. For some reason he had forgotten his mother was Amish before she married.

Daniel stared around the room at the mixture of English and Amish. They had considered closing the Yoder U pick farm, but the cousins picked up the slack and kept the business running while most of Daniel's family was at the funeral. Paul Hershberger and all his family were in attendance. Daniel figured there had to be almost two hundred people.

The Noble's minister moved to the podium and began the funeral service. This was not Daniel's first *Englische* funeral, so he had some idea of what was going to happen. It had been decided that after the funeral, everyone would go to Paul Hershberger's farm since it was the only place that could handle such a large group. Evan sat to one side with his grandmother. He watched Rachel, wondering if there was anything he could do to console her. Zak and Zeke sat on each side of Rachel, the protective brothers.

Zak noticed Evan sitting with his grandmother and acknowledged him with a nod.

The minister finished with his service and then gazed at the assembled people.

"Would anyone like to say something?" he asked.

Paul Hershberger stood, as did Alexander Noble. Paul waved a hand at Alexander. "You go first," he mumbled and sat.

Alexander strode to the front, standing in front of the podium, not behind it. He lifted his arms into the air and began to dance. He chanted.

Hare Kristna, Hare Kristna
Krishna, Krishna, Hare, Hare.
Hare Rama, Hare Rama,
Rama, Rama, Hare, Hare.

Daniel stared in disbelief at the action. He gazed about the room and noticed others stared in shock, watching, silent.

"That is quite enough," Paul said, standing and walking toward Alexander. "This is not the place."

"I dance and chant to move my parent's spirits to the next reincarnation. I have released them from the grip of Kali by calling out the sixteen names."

Paul shook his head. "Sit. Your parents were Christians and have no need of reincarnation. They have gone to meet their

Maker." He pointed at the empty chair. "You can do your charlatan singing and dancing at a later time." He moved behind the podium as Alexander glared at his uncle before taking his chair, again. Alexander once more took his Indian sitting position, hands on his knees and fingers in circles. He began to softly hum/sing. "OM."

Paul glared at his nephew, but shook his head and ignored the sound.

"My sister, Emma was born and raised Amish. She met and married Dan Noble, an *Englische* man who made her happy. She had three children. My sister..." He broke down and started to cry. Shaking his head, he walked back to his seat.

"Any others?" the minister asked as he once more stood behind the podium.

Several people took turns telling tales and anecdotes about Dan, Emma, or both.

Once more the minister stood behind the podium. "We will be going to the cemetery and anyone who wishes to join the family there, that is fine. For others, please go to the Paul Hershberger farm where the Amish community has some fine food prepared and we all can spend time together remembering and rejoicing in the life of Dan and Emma Noble."

Daniel stood and stretched; his aching bones needed to move to ease some of the pain. Martha came up beside him and locked her arm in his. "Are you ready to go to the cemetery?"

Daniel nodded. "It was nice of your uncle to get extra buggies for the family to use for the funeral."

Addie patted Evan's hand. "We'll go to the farm and allow the family some private time together for their final goodbyes."

Evan shuffled behind Addie, all the while keeping an eye on Rachel. He wanted to go over and comfort her, hold her, tell her he... Evan's eyes opened wide. *I what?* screamed in his mind. He stumbled at the thought. *I think I love her*, he thought.

Martha watched people get into their cars and buggies and head east toward the Hershberger farm. "Not that many people going to the cemetery," she mumbled. "Sad."

Daniel embraced Martha. "It is better. This part should be family, not a show."

He watched as Alexander strolled behind Bethan and Thomas. He still wasn't sure about his brother-in-law. This was his first time meeting him. Daniel wondered what Alexander would do when they arrived at the grave site.

Martha and Daniel walked to the buggy and Daniel helped her up into it. Sarah and her husband, and Ezra and his wife joined them. Daniel watched as his other children and their spouses got into the remaining buggies behind them. He gazed at the lineup: Alexander, Bethan, and Thomas with Faith and Hope rode in the small limousine. Daniel and Martha were next with Paul Hershberger and his remaining sister, Mary, in the next buggy. The rest of the family followed with a mixture of buggies and cars.

# # #

The immediate family, Alexander, Bethan, and Martha sat in chairs closest to the grave sites for their parents. Spouses and family sat or stood behind them.

Daniel watched Alexander, waiting.

The coffins were carried in with a mixture of *Englische* and Amish pallbearers.

The minister began his graveside service. As he finished, he turned to Emma's coffin. As it was lowered into the ground, he said "In sure and certain hope of the resurrection to eternal life through our Lord Jesus Christ, we commend to Almighty God our sister, Emma Noble; and we commit her body to the ground; earth to earth; ashes to ashes, dust to dust. The Lord bless her and keep her, the Lord make His face to shine upon her and be gracious unto her and give her peace. Amen." He reached over, grabbed a handful of dirt and gently filtered it through his hands onto the coffin.

The minister then turned to Dan's coffin and repeated the action. He turned to the family. "Any last words?" he asked.

Once again, Alexander stood and chanted his Hare Krishna as he danced between the two grave sites. Bethan and Martha silently watched their brother. This time Paul sat patiently to the side and did nothing.

Alexander finished and took his seat with hands spread. He hummed "OM."

"This concludes the graveside service," the minister said. "Again, you are all welcome to the Hershberger farm." He turned and headed for his car.

CHAPTER FIFTEEN ~ The Play

Wednesday, July 31 7:20 a.m.

Joshua Beiler sat at the table in the dimly lighted dining room of the Blue Gate Theater. He sipped his coffee as he waited. Sitting the coffee cup down, he softly strummed his fingers on the table. Patience was not his forte.

"Good morning, Joshua," Jack said as he strolled into the dining room.

"Sit," Joshua commanded. His voice was cold and authoritative.

Jack eased into a chair opposite Joshua and studied the man on the other side.

"Is there a problem?" Jack asked as he poured himself a cup of coffee.

"Today is July 31," Joshua said. "We open the play on August 9." He leaned in over the table toward Jack. That is exactly nine - NINE - more days."

"Uh-huh," Jack mumbled. "Your point?"

Joshua slumped back into his chair. "My point? MY POINT?" He jabbed a finger toward the stage. "The play, Jack. The play. Will it be ready? Where is your ladder angel? Are the props finished?"

Jack blew over the lip of the cup, then sipped his coffee. "Hm? Hot." He gazed at Joshua and shrugged. "If my singing ladder angel doesn't appear, I will adjust the play. I still have Evan and I know he can carry the part." Again, he shrugged. "Okay, not what the original play called for, but I can make it work." He sipped more coffee. "We will open on the ninth of August?" He paused. "F'sure."

Members of the cast started to amble in, heading for the table with the large coffee urn and the three toasters. Jack watched as Madeline made herself a slice of toast and spread a meager amount of honey on it. He smiled. *That will keep her voice in good tone*, he thought, remembering the first day when the restaurant chef, Harold Abbott had filled the table with an assortment of donuts, sweet rolls, and other munchies. Jack had squashed that quickly, informing Abbott that the sweets coated the throat and compromised their singing capability.

"You're sure about this," Joshua said, once more grabbing Jack's attention.

"I'll know more when we begin rehearsal and I see who all is here," Jack replied.

Hoping Joshua didn't notice, Jack kept an eye on the arriving cast. He was getting concerned; no Evan, no Rachel. He glanced at his watch. It was three minutes to eight. Jack again surveyed the cast at the table and those taking positions on the stage. Two were missing. Two very important people.

"Okay," Jack said. "Everyone in position." He hoped Evan and Rachel would show. They didn't. The ladder was empty. He glanced back at Joshua who sat in the chair, arms folded over his chest. The whole visual impression was one of 'and now what' as Joshua cocked his head to one side and grimaced.

"Jimmy!" Jack called. "Get over to the ladder. "And... and... Miriam. The two of you on the ladder. If you don't know the songs, grab sheet music from the piano so you can sing the parts."

Jimmy and Miriam stepped down from the angel stairs to the piano. Both watched each other with questioning looks.

"Are you ready for this?" Jimmy whispered as they walked across the stage to the ladder.

"Not really," Miriam replied. "But I'll give it my best."

They walked up the enlarged ladder to the platform above the stage.

"Begin," Jack yelled.

The music started and Jimmy and Miriam walked down the ladder toward their destination. The angels began their descent.

Jimmy and Miriam began to sing *Some Believe.* Jack cringed, listening to Jimmy's nasally high voice. Miriam's voice wasn't too bad. Jack didn't want to, but he turned in Joshua's direction to see what he thought.

Joshua sat at the table, hands over his ears, and his face scrunched up in mock pain; at least, Jack hoped it was mock.

"We're here," Evan said as he and Rachel walked into the dining area.

Relief flooded Jack. "Jimmy! Miriam! Back to the angel side," he bellowed. *If I need, I can use Miriam,* he thought and shook his head. *But I definitely need to find another to replace Evan if need be; Jimmy is not the man.*

Jack again glanced back at Joshua who now eased back in his chair, sipping his coffee.

"Sorry we're late," Evan said. "Bicycles are not the fastest mode of transportation and... well... it took a little convincing to have Rachel come back."

Rachel continued her walk to the stage and up and onto the ladder.

"I am here," she said and glared at Jack. "Can we start?"

"Definitely," Jack said. "From the top... again!"

Evan jumped on stage and rushed up the ladder to the platform. He leaned in toward Rachel. "I think the word is *denki,*" he said.

Rachel smiled, grabbed his hand and gave it a squeeze. "You are correct."

# # #

Wednesday, July 31 3:50 p.m.

Jack strutted in front of the stage, waving his hands in sync with the music.

"Perfect. Perfect," he mumbled. "This is what I could hear in my head."

The music stopped, abruptly. He turned to see what had caused the sound system to malfunction. Joshua Beiler stood over the mixing board.

"As I stated earlier this morning, Jack," Joshua started. "We have only a week left to go. I have yet to see a real play. When do I see the costumes? The props?"

"Tomorrow," Jack said. "We will start full dress rehearsals... tomorrow."

"Evan!" A voice called from the darkness of the dining room.

Evan turned to see Joe Holgate coming toward the stage.

"Good news, dude," Joe said. "We got a gig for Saturday." He lifted in hand into the air and rubbed his thumb against his two first fingers indicating money.

Rachel gave Evan a surprised glance.

"I can't, Joe," Evan said. "I have another obligation this Saturday. Sorry."

Joe stopped in his steps. "What? You can't bail on us."

Evan shrugged. "I'd loved to help out, but I've got cows to milk and I promised Zak I would join him for the sing this weekend."

Joe smiled. "The gig is for Saturday afternoon. Do the gig, milk the cows, and go off on your Amish singy-thing."

Evan grimaced, clenched his hand and slowly counted. "It is not some Amish singy-thing."

Rachel came up behind and slipped her hand in his and gripped. "It is nothing," Rachel whispered. "Come. We need to rehearse." She pulled Evan back toward the stage.

"What time on Saturday?" Evan asked.

"The gig is at two in the afternoon for two hours." He paused. "That should give you plenty of time to milk your cows. We'll rehearse things Friday night. I'll pick you up at seven. Will you have your cows milked?"

Evan was sure it was a slur at him trying to be a daily farmer, but ignored it. He followed Rachel, enjoying the fact she held his hand as she towed him back to the stage and up the ladder to the platform.

"It is not the Amish way, but I do not like that man," Rachel whispered. "He does not like the Amish."

Evan grinned. "That's okay, Grandma Addie doesn't like him, either." *And, now I'm wondering if I like him,* Evan thought. *I may be dropping out of the band real soon.*

# # #

Friday, August 2 7:30 p.m.

Joe Holgate pulled into the Kurtz driveway and honked his horn. Addie gazed at Evan with raised eyebrows, then shrugged, all the while shaking her head. Evan knew she was silently muttering her disapproval.

"I'll be back later, Grandma," Evan said, leaned over and gave her a kiss on the cheek. "Unless the guys want to go out afterward, it will be an early night."

Addie coughed and immediately grabbed her hankie to cover her mouth. She waved Evan to head on out.

Evan jumped into the car, surprised to see Tobias Snyder in the backseat.

"Hi, Tobias," Evan said. "Another gig. Exciting. Yes?"

"What's this I hear you want to quit the band?" Tobias asked.

Evan froze and stared at Joe. "You told him?"

"I told the band," Joe said. "I don't want you getting a swell head or anything, but you're the best thing to happen to this band. Our first gig and you had the audience eating out of your hand."

Evan felt the heat in his cheeks. "I did what I do."

Tobias leaned forward and placed a hand on Evan's shoulder. "You probably don't remember seeing that cute blond named Jessica in the front of the mob at the stage..."

"I remember her," Evan said with a grin as the memory of the young girl in the red gingham blouse and cut-off shorts with the short blond hair and cutest smile came to mind. *Jessica*, he thought.

"Anyway," Tobias continued. "She is a friend of my sister's boyfriend and they fired the band they'd hired and want us." He paused. "Why?" He paused again. "Because of you. You worked that mob into a frenzy. She loved it."

Evan shook his head as the car headed to Shipshewana. "Anyone can do what I did. Peter has the ability. Put his keyboard out there, a mike, let him sing and talk with the crowd." Evan shrugged. "It's not that hard."

"That's why we're talking to you now," Joe said. "Sure, Peter can do it, but Peter doesn't have your charisma. If you walked off the stage and mingled with the crowd, they'd separate like the Red Sea before Moses to let you pass."

Joe continued through the intersection and out to the west of town.

"Where we going?" Evan asked.

"Just driving so we can talk," Joe said. "Peter is good, but he's not you. We need you. Sure, Peter will take over again if you leave, but..."

"We'll be back where we were before you came," Tobias said. "Nowhere. Just a bunch of guys playing instruments in a garage, hoping to hit a gig."

"In case you didn't know it, we've been asked to do another three gigs in addition to this one on Saturday afternoon."

"THREE?!" Evan yelled. "When did this happen?"

"Wednesday night, Thursday afternoon, and this morning," Joe said.

"All because of Jessica and you," Tobias said.

Evan shook his head. "I don't know. I now have a small herd of dairy cows that need my attention."

"When the band has a gig, maybe your grandma can milk the cows?" Tobias offered.

"No," Evan said. "Her health won't allow it."

"Yeah," Joe said. "I heard the ladies of the church talking and praying for your grandma. I guess she doesn't have long to live according to what I heard." He paused and glanced at Evan.

Evan stared out the front of the car, "Let me out. NOW!"

Joe slammed on the brakes; the car skidded to a stop. "What's the problem?"

"I quit. I'm done." Evan opened the door and got out. "No more band." He shut the door with more force than was needed. Evan leaned in the open window. "My grandmother is fine. She has TB. Yes, she is dying, but that is none of your concern." He started to stand then leaned back down into the open window. "Don't bother trying to contact me. I'm not coming back. It's over."

Tobias sat in the backseat, eyes with disbelief.

Evan stood and looked around. A business was about another hundred yards away. He was sure there was a phone there he could use.

Joe spun the car around, throwing gravel into the air.

"That didn't go as planned," Tobias mumbled from the back seat.

"Shut up," Joe snarled.

Evan walked up the steps to the business. It was closed. There was no phone outside. He gazed back toward town and estimated he was at least three, if not four miles from town center. Stepping back down and out to the road, Evan gazed back at the business; and the large yellow sign: *Guggisberg Cheese Factory*.

Best get hiking, Evan thought. *It is a long trip home.*

#

"You got home early," Addie said.

"Yeah," Evan mumbled. "Won't have to worry about the band anymore. I quit."

"You quit?" Addie questioned.

"Joe is a jerk, Grandma." He wanted to say more but he saw no reason to upset her. "How are you feeling?"

"Fine, dear. I'm fine."

He gazed at her. "Are you sure? How is the TB?"

"Why the sudden interest?" Addie sat in her easy chair with just the one light on in the living room.

Evan decided it was all or nothing. "Joe said the women at church were praying for you."

Addie nodded. "They have been doing that for several years now." She smiled. "No big issue."

"And..." Evan paused. "Well, that you don't have long to live." Again, he paused. "Is that true?"

Addie shrugged. "Only the Lord knows the day I go to meet Him."

Evan gazed at her. "That's not the answer I was looking for."

"That's the answer I have, Evan. I have no idea how long I will get to live. None of us do. I take each day as a blessing. If I wake up in the morning, I thank the Lord for that blessing. If I make it to bed that night, again, in my evening prayers, I thank the Lord for a beautiful and full day."

Evan nodded, knowing this was the best answer he was going to get.

CHAPTER SIXTEEN ~ Saturday Surprise

Saturday, August 3 6:30 a.m.

"Oh, Suzanna, don't you cry for me," Evan sang as he milked the first of the cows.

It was early, but he figured the cows enjoyed the music and he needed to sing to let off steam. He was still upset over Joe's comments, but he was adamant, he wasn't going back to the band.

His mind wandered and he thought about the evening and joining Zak for the sing with the Amish. He knew Rachel would be there and he would see if she had eyes for another. He remembered her putting her hand in his earlier in the week. He felt his heart rush.

She is Amish and I am what they call Englische. He shook his head. *There is no way she is going to be interested in me.*

Evan moved to the next cow and began another song.

Hm? he thought. *Maybe I should have a separate song for each cow.* He grinned. *That way each cow will think they are special.*

"How's it going, Evan?" Addie asked from the barn door. "I have breakfast ready to go anytime you come in." She turned to head back to the house. "By the way, I'm sure the cows enjoy your singing. I do." She left.

"It's going to be a great day," Evan said to nobody in particular. "Yes, a great day, indeed." He smiled. "The sing will be fun tonight."

Evan moved to the third cow and wondered what song to sing, all the while making sure he remembered the sequence of songs he was singing.

Cows like to be contented, he thought. So, definitely no rock and roll.

Without thinking, he broke into the next song, completely out of season.

"Sleigh bells ring, are you listening? In the glen..." He broke up, laughing. "I'm sorry..." He leaned back to get a good look at the cow. "Yeah, Henrietta. You get a Christmas song." He began again and finished the song and milking her.

Evan finished milking the remaining cows and lugged the big container onto the back porch.

"I'm going to take this to Mr. Volhaus and then come back for a yummy breakfast."

"It'll be ready," Addie said and turned the burners on the stove. "Get a hustle on, boy."

Evan grabbed the container and his bike and headed for the Volhaus residence down the road.

This seems a lot heavier than usual, he thought. *Are the cows giving more milk? I will need to ask Zak.* He started to whistle in the early morning and decided after breakfast he would visit the Graber home about his cows. He wanted to make sure he was doing the right thing.

#

Evan headed out the back of the house, slipping his shoes on.

"I'll be back later." He paused. "More than likely I'll be back for lunch. Okay?"

Addie turned from the kitchen sink. "You're going to the Graber's. Is that right?"

"Yes," Evan said. "I need to talk with Zak."

He rushed down the steps and grabbed the bicycle. Evan shook his head. *Who'd have thought I'd be riding around on a bicycle to go anywhere?*

He headed down the lane and turned right to go to the Graber farm.

Evan placed his bicycle against the large maple tree and rushed up the steps, taking them two at a time, to the back door. He knocked.

Rachel answered. "Come in, Evan." She stepped aside to let him in. "Today is haircut day." She grinned. "Zeke is getting his cut now. Zak is next, followed by Peter and Adam."

Evan pulled at his hair. "A haircut, eh?" He smiled. "I haven't had a haircut since I arrived in Shipshewana. I must look ragged."

"Your hair is fine," Rachel said while gazing at his dirty blond hair.

"If you want," Zak started. "Mama can cut your hair."

Zeke glared at Evan from under the bowl on his head as his mother cut the hair that showed.

Bethany Graber snapped the scissors in the air. "If you wish, Evan Kurtz, I will cut your hair to match my boys."

Once more Evan reached up and tugged at his hair. *It is long*, he thought. *If she wishes to cut it, I will let her.*

He nodded. "I will wet my hair so it is straight to cut. Will that make it easier?"

"I will help you," Zak said, getting up.

"No, you will not," Bethany said. "You will sit right there. I am almost done with your twin. You are next."

"I will help," Rachel said, picked up a comb, and headed for the kitchen door.

Evan followed her outside and to the hand pump.

"Stick you head under and get it wet," Rachel said. "I will comb it so Mama can cut it."

Evan did as he was told and then squeezed as much water out of his hair as possible. Rachel dried his hair with a towel then carefully combed it straight, parting it down the middle. She grinned.

"Not quite the length necessary for a good Amish cut, but Mama will make it work." She hesitated. "Are you sure about this?"

Evan nodded. "Yes."

They headed into the house.

"You are next, Evan," Bethany said.

Zeke glared at him. "Are you trying to be Amish?"

"No," Evan replied. "I am... as you say, *Englische* but I have found the Amish lifestyle to be of my liking. I think it is what I have searched for."

"Sit," Bethany said and placed the bowl on his head. "I will do my best."

Evan watched as locks of hair fell to the floor.

"Done," Bethany said. "I hope your grandmother recognizes you."

"Next thing you will be wearing dark pants, blue shirts and suspenders," Zak said.

"I could," Evan said. "But I fear you would think I am mocking you."

"There are many in the stores of Shipshewana who pretend to be Amish," Zeke said with disgust. "They may fool the *Englische* customers, but not the Amish."

Zak slapped Evan on the back. "You almost look like an Amish man on *Rumschpringe* in your *Englische* clothes."

"Why did you come?" Zeke asked.

"Ezekiel Graber!" Bethany blurted. "Keep a civil tongue about you."

Evan shrugged. "I came because it seems my cows are giving more milk right now and I wondered if there was a reason I should be aware of."

"A real dairy farmer would know," Zeke started. "A cow gives more milk after... AFTER the birth of the calf."

"That is what I learned in my studies," Evan said. "Yet, today, I know I took more milk than usual to Leroy Volhaus." He shrugged. "Just wondering."

Zak grinned. "Some days cows give more than usual. I would say today is one of your lucky days and all your cows gave extra."

"I guess I should get home to my grandmother," Evan said and headed out the door. "Thank you, Mrs. Graber, for the haircut." He paused. "*denki*. (thank you)"

"Now you are learning Amish?" Zeke sneered.

"Is it wrong for the *Englische* to learn the Amish language?" Evan asked.

Zeke shrugged and walked away.

"Forgive my son," Bethany said. "He is leery of the *Englische.*"

"Not all *Englische* are bad," Evan said and opened the kitchen door to leave.

He grabbed his bicycle from the tree and got on it.

"Give Zeke some time," Zak said. "See you tonight for the sing? Be here about six. You can ride with us."

"I need to milk my cows at six-thirty," Evan said.

"Milk them early," Zak said. "We do. The cows will enjoy it."

"See you tonight," Evan said and pushed off to head home.

# # #

Evan pulled into the driveway and rode his bicycle up the long lane. He scrutinized the dark blue car parked by the house.

I wonder who is visiting Grandma? he thought.

He leaned his bicycle against the house and headed up the stairs onto the back porch where he took off his shoes and carefully placed them by the other set of wing-tip shoes on the small carpet.

Wing-tips? A male visitor? Evan's mind ran rampant in thought wondering who this stranger might be. *A doctor? NO!!*

Evan raced into the living room. He stopped and stared.

"Dad!" he yelled. "You're here?"

"Hello..." He hesitated. "Evan?" Nathan stared at his son. "A new haircut?"

"How long are you here for?" Evan asked.

"I can only stay..." He glanced at his watch. "Maybe for about an hour longer." Nathan replied. "Mom has made us lunch and I'll probably leave shortly after that."

"So, what do we owe for your visit here? " Evan asked "School will be starting soon. And, I thought maybe you should come back home to New York now."

Evan stared at his father, unsure of exactly what to say or what to do.

"Is there a problem?" Nathan asked.

"No" Evan replied "It's just that I don't plan to go back to New York City or, to go anywhere. I plan to stay here and be a dairy farmer."

"A dairy farmer. You?"

"Yes, Dad," Evan replied. "I purchased five calves and also five cows that are pregnant, and with luck next year, I will have fifteen cows. Okay, sixteen with Gertrude." He paused. "I plan to bring this farm back to the dairy it was years ago under Grandpa John"

"So, you're telling me you're not going to finish school?" Nathan asked

"That's right, Dad," Evan replied.

"So, I'm just supposed to sit here and accept the choice of a seventeen year old with no questions asked?"

"Let's not be hasty, Nathan," Addie said. "If Evan would like to stay here, I have no issue with that. He can go to school here and finish his senior year."

Nathan stared at his mother. "Evan is my son. I will decide what he can do until he is eighteen."

"I am happy here, Dad."

"You can be happy in New York City, too." He reached out and stroked Evan's hair. "So, what's with the new haircut? Why an Amish cut?"

"Zak's mother cut my hair today," Evan said. "I kind of like it"

"Zak. Zak, who?"

"Zach Graber," Evan replied. "He lives about a mile and a half away from here."

Nathan repeated the name, trying to place it. He frowned. "Is he related to Paul Hershberger?"

"Paul?" Addie questioned. "He is related to the Grabers." She paused for a few minutes. "In fact, your father talked with Mrs. Graber's mother before she married Daniel Yoder in Centertown." Addie sighed. "That was when John and I were dating back in college." She paused. "In fact, they just buried, Emma Noble Paul Hershberger's *Englische* married sister earlier this week. That is Mrs. Graber's grandmother."

"Don't forget, Grandma," Evan said. "I'm in a play that opens next week. I can't leave."

"Fine," Nathan said. "I'll come back... in what, a week? You can come home with me then. Your little play should be done by then."

"No, Dad," Evan replied. "This play will probably go for maybe three months, maybe longer."

Nathan stared at his son, then glanced at his mother who sat, smiling, slowly rocking in her favorite chair.

"He's in a play at the Blue Gate Theater," Addie said.

"Blue Gate? How?"

"There are things about your son... well, you just don't know, Nathan." Addie stood. "I best get lunch around so you can leave..." She paused. "I know you want to leave soon, but I think it would be good if you stayed the night." Again, she paused. "If nothing more than to learn about Evan."

Nathan glared at his mother. "I know my son."

Addie turned at the kitchen door and glared back at Nathan. "No, you don't." She headed into the kitchen. She raised her voice. "Nathan. Come help me."

"I'll help you, Grandma," Evan said.

"No, Evan," Addie yelled back. "I want your father to come help me and I want you to go out and make sure the cows have proper food and bedding for the night."

"But..."

"No buts, Evan," Addie replied. "Now, skedaddle."

Evan frowned, unsure, but did as he was told and headed out the door to the barn.

"Okay, Mom," Nathan said as he stood beside Addie. "What do you want to talk about?" He nodded at the back door. "Evan is gone. He's almost to the barn."

"Evan is a good boy, but I don't think you see that," Addie said. "What do you remember of the mirror incident?"

"You mean the one he broke in the apartment building?" Nathan nodded. "Yes, I remember."

"He didn't break it."

"Oh?" Nathan said with a voice of curiosity. "Who did?"

"The gang who was chasing him and scuffling with him in the lobby. One of them broke it, but Evan took the blame." She paused. "And, you let him, never giving him a chance to explain."

Nathan shrugged. "He still has no work ethics. All he wants to do is sit around and goof off."

"Do you know how much money Evan put in the bank shortly after he got here?"

"Money?" Nathan grabbed an apple and bit a huge chunk out of it. "Where? How?"

Addie grabbed two slices of bread and put them in the toaster.

"Has he ever mentioned some Chinese restaurant?"

"You mean Happy Dragon?" Nathan asked and bit another chunk of apple. "What of it?"

"The night you called me? He worked for the owner's relative and made over one hundred dollars. What did he tell you? He worked out?"

Again, Nathan shrugged.

"You don't know your son. He bought these cows. I paid for them, and he took his money out of the bank the next day to pay me." Addie pointed at the barn. "That boy is out there with HIS cows; not mine. HIS."

"I didn't know," Nathan mumbled.

"Of course not, Nathan, dear," Addie said and placed a hand over his heart. "You have been wallowing in the death of your wife, Barbara. You've ignored your son and he has grown up to be a strong, young man in spite of you."

"You learned all this in two months?" Nathan asked.

Addie smiled. "When you sit on the front porch, enjoy a nice evening, and talk. Well, you learn a lot."

"You can learn a lot by just looking," Nathan said. "When were you going to tell me about your illness?"

"Illness?" Addie echoed.

Nathan nodded at the pocket at her hip where the hankie dangled precariously from it. "You don't have any cuts."

"I have TB." The toaster popped and she place another two slices of bread in.

"How long, Mom?"

Addie shrugged. "Maybe a year? A couple of months? Maybe a week?" She shook her head. "Only the Lord knows. Could be tomorrow?"

"So, what do I do about Evan?"

"The boy is doing good here, Nathan." Again, the toaster popped up and she put two more slices of bread in. "I know you want him in New York with you, but he is coming into his own here in Shipshewana." She paused and moved the finished slices of toast to a plate. "Maybe we can convince him to attend school here." She grinned. "Of course, his best friend stopped his schooling after eighth grade, so it could be an uphill battle."

"Eighth grade?" Nathan asked.

"Zak Graber. Amish." She opened the mayonnaise jar and spread some on each slice of toast. The next two slices popped up and she added them to her assembly line.

"Yeah, an uphill battle." Nathan moved to the table and sat down. "If I leave him here, I..." He paused. "You have to convince him to go to school this fall." He smiled. "Okay, Mom, you have the upper hand on this one. I place the ball in your court."

"Fine," Addie said. "I will take him under my wing and see what I can do. Can you come back next weekend? I mean, Evan is in a play at the Blue Gate. Do you want to miss that?"

Nathan stood, walked over to Addie and kissed her on the cheek. "You win, Mom."

Evan opened the back door. "Can I come back in, now?"

Addie and Nathan laughed.

CHAPTER SEVENTEEN ~ The Sing

Saturday, August 3, 2013 2 p.m.

"Let's go sit on the front porch," Addie said. "The weather has changed and it's a lot cooler out there."

"It looks like rain, Mom," Nathan said, opening the front porch screen door for her.

"Don't worry," Addie replied. "If it storms, it's coming from the southwest and we'll be nice and dry."

The three sat on the rockers and watched the darker clouds fill the sky.

"So, Evan, you want to stay here and not come back to New York," Nathan said.

"If I can," Evan replied. "I have the play, plus the cows to milk."

"So, you go to school, do the play and play farmer." Nathan shrugged. "Is that what you want?"

"Yes, Dad," Evan said. "Can I?"

Addie laughed.

"What's so funny, Mom?" Nathan asked.

"Evan didn't mention the real reason he wants to stay here."

Nathan glared at Evan. "What? Tell me."

Evan frowned and stared at his grandmother.

"Her name is Rachel," Addie said with a grin.

"Oh," Nathan said with a knowing nod. "Rachel," he muttered.

"If you're wondering," Evan started. "She is Amish, so nothing is going to happen."

"Uh-huh," Addie whispered and rocked.

Nathan looked Evan in the eye. "Okay. If I let you stay here with my mother, you agree to go to high school and get your degree. You're a senior, it's your last year." He paused. "None of this crap of skipping classes, not doing your homework, or getting kicked out of school and need to go to another school." Nathan cocked his head to one side. "There isn't another school for several miles and I am not having my mother drive you to school elsewhere." Again, he paused. "So, you agree and if you break this agreement, no matter what, you are back in New York City so fast you won't have time to look both ways. Am I understood?"

"Yes, Dad," Evan said and stuck his arm out, offering his hand to shake. "I agree."

Nathan momentarily caught off-guard, wasn't ready for the handshake. He shook his son's hand.

Rain began to pitter-patter on the roof and a light mist covered the front yard. The wind picked up and swept around the corner of the house onto the porch, filled with a light moisture caressing each of them.

"That feels good," Nathan said. "Reminds me of when Alyssa and I would play on this porch as kids when it was raining." He sighed and gazed at Addie. "Sorry, Mom."

"That's okay, Nathan," Addie replied. "I've sat out here many times and thought the same when the wind catches me off-guard like that."

"I hope it stops before the sing tonight," Evan said. "Zak said it was going to be at the bridge over by the Hoffmeyer farm." He shrugged. "Wherever that is."

"A couple of miles away," Addie and Nathan said together then laughed.

"If it is raining," Addie added. "They will go in the barn and sing." She hesitated. "They do the sing on Saturday nights as it is one of the only times the young can get together so they get to know about each other."

"Huh?" Evan asked.

"Call it group dating," Addie said. "The Amish youth gather together and get to know each other and finally begin courtship. It's a simple process; the boy will ask to take the girl home and if she agrees, they start a courtship and if all goes well, it leads to marriage."

Evan nodded, then grinned. "I seem to be missing one buggy to start dating."

"Well, if we want to have supper tonight, I'd best get into the kitchen and start something." Addie stood.

"I'll help you, Mom," Nathan said.

"No, you won't," Addie snapped. "You sit out here with your son and the two of you talk."

Nathan gazed at Evan. "Guess we'll talk." He grinned. "What topic?"

"How about mom's death?" Evan asked.

Nathan sighed. "I guess I should have told you all the truth."

They began to talk.

Evan stuffed the last bit of sauerkraut from his plate into his mouth. "This is good," he mumbled as he chewed.

"Yes, Mom," Nathan said. "You know how I love this food and I don't think I've had it in several years."

Addie gazed at the bowl that had held the sauerkraut and ribs. It was empty. "Maybe I should have made more."

Nathan sat back in his chair and patted his bloated stomach. "No, I don't think so, Mom. This was plenty and I ate too much."

"Well, I've got to milk the cows," Evan said. "Especially if I want to make it to the sing tonight."

Nathan stared at his son, surprised that he actually was doing dairy farming.

"You mind if I help you?" Nathan asked.

Evan stared at his father in disbelief. "Do you know how to milk a cow?"

Nathan grinned. "I have milked a couple of cows in my lifetime."

"Headed to the barn, Grandma," Evan said. "Do you need any help before I leave?"

Again, Nathan stared at his son, surprised he was offering to help.

"Go and milk the cows," Addie said. "Before you take it to Leroy, make sure I get a quart so it will be cold in the morning."

Evan nodded and slipped on his shoes, watching his father put on the wingtips.

"Kinda fancy for the barn," Evan said.

"Only shoes I have," Nathan said. "I had planned on being back in New York City by tonight. I didn't even bring a change of clothes."

"Maybe you can fit some of mine," Evan offered. "You know tomorrow is Sunday and we will be going to church."

"Church?" Nathan asked.

Evan grinned as he opened the barn door. "Every Sunday, like clockwork." He gazed at the cows as they sauntered into the barn. "I'll start at the other end. You can start here." He paused. "Oh, and they like to be sung to, in case you didn't know."

# # #

The cows were milked and Evan carried the canister to the back of the house. He poured out a quart of milk and handed it to his father.

"Take this in for Grandma," Evan said. "I'll take the bicycle and get the canister to Mr. Volhaus down the road."

"If you can wait," Nathan said. "I'll drive you."

Evan shrugged. "Sure."

# # #

Evan raced for the back door. "I'll be home later," he yelled, slipped on his shoes and grabbed his bicycle.

Nathan and Addie watched him cycle to the end of the driveway and turn right to head to the Graber farm.

"He seems excited about this sing tonight," Nathan said.

"I don't think it is the sing that he's all excited about," Addie said. She smiled. "I think the name you were looking for is Rachel."

Nathan nodded. "Yes, I forgot about her." He paused. "Is he really serious?"

Addie rocked. "Serious?" She gazed at the lowering sun to the west and then looked at the moving clouds to the east as they continued on their way. "Did you see his haircut?"

"So, it is serious," Nathan mumbled. "Do you think he will... No, he wouldn't do that. He's too... what's the word?"

"*Englische?*"

"I know my son, Mom, and he won't give up the conveniences."

"Evan has changed since he came here," Addie said. "His first day here I was sure I'd bitten off more than I could chew." She shrugged. "Then he got the job at E & S and well, he changed." She paused. "When the shunning started..."

"Shunning?" Nathan stopped rocking to stare at his mother.

"Your grandfather, James Kurtz, married Eliza Waldvogel and his family shunned him, hoping he would return to the Amish community. He didn't. They then invoked ex-communication and in anger, he changed the spelling of the last name from Kertz to Kurtz."

"Huh?"

"I'm sorry, Nathan," Addie said and patted his hand. "That's a lot of information so late in life, but we were originally Amish and became *Englische* for the last couple of generations." She smiled. "Maybe the circle will complete and your son will become Amish."

Nathan shook his head. "Not Evan."

#

Evan pulled into the Graber driveway to see Zeke, Zak, Rachel, their older brother, Daniel, and their younger siblings, Peter, Adam, and Elizabeth headed for the buckboard.

"Here comes Evan Kurtz," Adam yelled and waved.

"Why is he coming?" Zeke snarled.

"I invited him," Zak replied. "I know he likes to sing and I thought he would enjoy the experience."

Rachel stood quietly to the side, watching Evan put his bicycle against the tree. She had secretly hoped he would come.

"Sorry," Evan said. "My dad showed up today and I was visiting with him."

Zeke shrugged. "You could have stayed home."

"Join us," Zak said and waved him into the gang getting onto the buckboard. "We will be at Hoffmeyer farm in no time." He slapped Evan on the back. "I think you will have fun tonight."

Evan glanced at Rachel. *Yes, I hope to*, he thought. *Perhaps Rachel will join me on the ride back home.*

Zeke snapped the reins and the horse began its plodding way out of the driveway. Zeke turned it left at the road and another mile and a half down the road, he pulled the horse into the Hoffmeyer farm.

Evan noticed several buggies and buckboards already tied around the barn. Young Amish strolled the farm, talking and laughing. Evan stood and helped Rachel to stand and he quickly jumped from the buckboard. He offered his hand to allow her to step from the buckboard to the ground.

"Thank you," Rachel whispered as she passed Evan.

Zeke stepped between them. "Go. Be with Zak." He nodded toward a group of young men where Zak made his way. "Hurry."

Evan headed the way Zak had gone and noticed a few of the men who he knew from E & S among the group. Joining them, they were surprised to see Evan.

"You have come to join the sing?" Benjamin asked.

Evan nodded. "Zak asked me."

"Look! Here comes the Zooks and Klopfensteins. We are all here and can now begin."

The group split into two sections; girls on one side, boys on the other.

Evan frowned. *Exactly how does one date while staring across the open space at each other?*

Songs began and Evan was lost. He didn't recognize it. The song was slow and somewhat melodic.

"We are singing *O Gott, Vater,* hymn 131. Next we will sing *Das Loblied.*" Zak shrugged. "It is our Amish way. He smiled at Evan. "After that we will sing songs maybe you will know."

Evan sat, listened, and watched Rachel who sat at one end of the girls on the other side. He was sure she was glancing at him from time to time, but would quickly bow her head and hide beneath the bonnet.

Zak nudged Evan. "See that beauty over there?" He pointed at a young girl sitting three to the left of Rachel. "That is Leah Beiler. We have been courting for two weeks now. Next week I hope to come in my own buggy so I can escort her home."

Evan nodded.

Zak stood. "Now we go and talk with the girls and then we will sing again."

Evan watched Zak make a direct line to Leah. They held hands, sat together on a bale of straw, and waited. Evan waited. He didn't know any of the girls other than Rachel.

"Come. Sit with me," Rachel whispered and held her hand out to him.

Zeke glared at them, stood, but the girl he was with pulled him back down to sit on the bale with her. Zeke continued to glare.

"You probably will not know most of the songs we sing," Rachel said. "The songs we sing we have learned since we were born. Most of them are our hymns." She grinned. "Still, we do sing a few of your *Englische* songs."

Evan nodded.

"We can sit here," Rachel said and grabbed his hand to pull him down to sit on the bale.

Evan was surprised, but sat and watched as a young man started a fire in the pit they all sat around. A voice began to sing and all the others joined in, except Evan who didn't know the song.

# # #

Evan helped Rachel into the back of the buckboard with her other siblings. Zeke and Zak sat up front. Evan and Rachel sat beside each other, holding hands.

"Zak, you go back and sit with your friend. Rachel. You come up here and sit."

"I will stay back here," Rachel said.

"No, Rachel. You will sit up here with me. Now." Zak glared at his sister.

Zak moved over the buckboard's bench to join Evan. He helped his sister to stand and get on the front bench with Zeke who continued to turn back and glare at Evan.

"I don't think Zeke likes me, yet," Evan whispered to Zak as the young Amish boy sit down beside him.

"He is protecting our sister from the *Englische.*" Zak shrugged and leaned in close. "I think Rachel likes you."

Evan tried not to grin. He liked her, too.

CHAPTER EIGHTEEN ~ Monday Problems

Monday, August 5 8:20 a.m.

"Hold it!" Jack bellowed. "What is this?" He glared at Evan. "Are you trying to be cute, or what?"

Evan frowned, unsure what Jack was upset about. He shrugged.

"No. No shrugging allowed," Jack blurted. "Who told you to look Amish?" He held up his hand. "Before you even attempt to tell me this is an Amish play, I know that."

"I'm not trying to be Amish," Evan said.

"The haircut. That haircut." Jack raced onto the stage and up the few steps to where Evan and Rachel sat. He tugged at a lock of Evan's hair. "This!"

"I got my hair cut this weekend," Evan mumbled.

"Now you look Amish. I need you to look *Englische.*"

Rachel reached up and ruffled his hair, pushing locks this way and that way. The Amish look disappeared. "Is that better?" she asked.

Jack stepped down and back across the stage. He nodded his approval. "It will work."

"Now," Jack started. "The next issue." He gazed at Evan and Rachel. "With the costumes on, coming down the steps doesn't work." He fussed his hand in the air. "What I want... Yes, I want both of you already sitting in your positions on the ladder when the light comes on. The draped cloth works when sitting, but when you are moving, it looks like you have a sheet on, pretending to be a ghost but with your head showing." He shook his head. "No. That just isn't what I see in my head."

Jack walked off the stage and about three tables back from it.

"Lights off," he yelled. "Everyone off stage and in their starting positions. Evan and Rachel, you stay seated." He paused. "From the top. Lights!"

Rachel leaned over. "I think that is the first time Jack has called us by our names," she whispered.

The lights came on and the music started.

# # #

Monday, August 5 4:30 p.m.

Rachel and Evan headed home, each riding a bicycle. Dark clouds loomed in the west, rolling eastward at a quick pace. Rachel glanced back at the storm.

"I do not think I will make it home before it begins to rain. I need to call my grandfather and let him know the show opens this weekend," Rachel said as they pedaled side by side in their hurry to beat the storm.

"You can call from my grandmother's house," Evan offered.

"Only if you tell me how much when the bill comes in," Rachel said. Again, she glanced behind at the closing storm and nodded agreement.

"Deal." Evan leaned and turned right into the lane up their house. "Follow me."

Evan placed his bicycle against the house, as did Rachel. Drops of rain began to fall.

"Come on in," Evan said and led the way up the back steps. He slipped off his shoes then noticed Rachel untying her shoes.

"You don't need to remove your shoes, Rachel," he said.

"If you do, so do I," she replied and removed her shoes.

Outside a bolt of lightning danced across the open area between the house and barn. It was immediately followed by thunder.

"That was close," Rachel said, glancing outside at the sheeting rain.

"Good afternoon, Miss Graber," Addie said coming into the kitchen and seeing the two of them in the backroom. "Come in. Come in."

"Rachel would like to call her grandfather," Evan said.

"In Centertown?" Addie asked.

"Yes, Mrs. Kurtz," Rachel said. "If that is okay with you. I will pay."

"You can use the phone and don't worry about the expense." She gazed at Evan. "It will be taken care, I'm sure."

Evan nodded.

Rachel finished her call and put the phone back on the wall and frowned. She gazed at Evan.

"Is there a problem?" Evan asked.

"I spoke with Grandpa Yoder and he said he will be here tomorrow." Again, she frowned. "He didn't say why. He just said that he would be here. I wonder what is going on?"

"Would you like to join us for supper?" Addie asked.

Rachel shook her head. "I better be going," she said. "I need to get home."

Addie cocked an eye in Rchel's direction and shook her head. "Not in this weather," Addie said. "I'm not about to let you go out in this rain. You'll get drenched, my dear." She led Rachel into the dining room. "Sit here and let me get another setting. You'll join us for supper tonight." She toddled into the kitchen and came back out with another setting. "When the rain lets up, I will drive you home."

"It is only a little water, Mrs. Kurtz," Rachel said. "I will get wet, but my clothes can dry."

"That's true, my dear" Addie said. "But there is lightning and I don't want you to be struck by it."

Rachel sat at the table across from Evan and Addie brought out the food. There were pork chops smothered in mushroom gravy, scalloped potatoes, and green beans with almonds. Addie poured fresh lemonade into each glass then took her seat.

"Let us give thanks to the Lord," Addie said and bowed her head.

Heavenly Father. We thank you for the beautiful day you gave us earlier and for the rain which we now receive which the farmers are in need of. Let this bounty of food strengthen both our body and our soul. Thank you for allowing Rachel Graber to join us for this meal. In Jesus name, Amen.

Addie handed the plate of pork chops to Rachel who frowned.

"I have never eaten with an *Englische* family before," Rachel said while taking the plate.

"Nothing to fret about," Addie said. "Some families say grace, some don't. But we all pass the food around to eat." She grinned. "I am sure that is how it is at your house."

Rachel nodded. "Papa will say a silent prayer and when he is done, he clears his throat and we then know to eat." She gazed out the window. "It looks like the rain is easing up."

Addie turned to look out the windows. "Yes, I believe it is. We'd best hurry and eat so we can get you home."

Evan took a bite and glanced out the window. He frowned. The buckboard passing he was sure was the Graber one. Evan attempted to see who was in the buckboard but the big umbrella hid the people. He shrugged. The buckboard was headed into Shipshewana.

They sat in the silence eating. Finally, Addie could take it no longer.

"How is the play coming along?" she asked.

Rachel gazed at Evan. He realized she wasn't going to say anything.

"The play will go live this Friday night, barring any unforeseen problems," Evan said.

Addie popped the last of her pork chop in into her mouth, smiled, and chewed.

"Well, it appears I have something to do this Friday night." She gazed at the plates of Rachel and Evan and realized they were finished eating.

"If you wish, the two of you can go out on the front porch." She gazed out the window. "It appears the rain is letting up and you should be able to sit without getting wet."

Evan stood and Rachel picked up her dish. " Let me help you, Mrs. Kurtz," Rachel said.

"That's nonsense," Addie said. "I'll just place these in the sink to soak for a while. Then I will join you. Plus, I have dessert for us. I hope you like rainbow sherbet ice cream and homemade sugar cookies."

Rachel continued to put the plates together. "You fed me a wonderful meal, Mrs. Kurtz. I cannot just walk away and not help you clean up."

Addie shrugged. "If you must, just help me bring the dishes into the kitchen. I will get all the dishes into the kitchen, scoop out the ice cream, and we'll all go out and sit on the front porch."

Addie grabbed a towel. "Don't just stand there," she said as she threw it at Evan. "Go out and dry the chairs for us."

Evan caught the towel and headed out to the front porch. He wiped the chairs down so they were no longer damp from the mist of the earlier downpour. Rachel carried a tray with three bowls of sherbet and a plate of cookies. Addie followed behind with three large glasses of lemonade. Evan glanced out at the road where a buckboard headed to the east, coming from Shipshewana.

"That looks like my brothers," Rachel said.

Evan whistled and waved his hands. The buckboard slowed to a stop and the two passengers stared back at them from under the large black umbrella. The horse turned and headed back toward the driveway.

"It is Zeke and Zak," Rachel exclaimed and rushed to the west side of the large front porch. She watched as her two brothers approached. "Why are you coming from Shipshewana?"

"We were looking for you," Zak yelled. "Mama was concerned."

"You need to come home," Zeke added and glared at Evan. "Now."

"I'll get your bicycle," Evan said and headed into the house.

Rachel followed, stopping at the door. "I need to put on my shoes." She bent down. "I will be out shortly."

Evan slipped on his loafers and headed out the backdoor. He grabbed Rachel's bicycle and walked it to the front of the house. He started to lift the bicycle into the back of the buckboard.

"I will do that," Zeke said and grabbed the bicycle from Evan's hands.

"I can do it," Evan said, still holding onto the bicycle.

Zeke pulled the bicycle from Evan's hands. "I said I would do it." He glared at Evan. "My buckboard."

Evan stepped back and raised his hands now that the bicycle was no longer his. "My bad," he whispered.

Zeke slung the bicycle into the back of the buckboard. Rachel approached from the back of the house.

"Get in," Zeke commanded. "We need to leave."

"What is the rush?" Rachel asked. "I stopped here to call Grandpa Yoder and Mrs. Kurtz offered me supper since it was storming so badly."

"Grandpa Yoder will be here tomorrow," Zak said.

Zeke climbed into the front of the buckboard. "Get in. We need to get home."

"There's no rush," Evan said. "Come sit with us on the porch and enjoy some sherbert and cookies."

Zak held the umbrella over Rachel.

"I said we need to go," Zeke snarled. "We are leaving."

Rachel got on the buckboard and Zak followed. He gazed at Evan and shrugged.

Zeke snapped the reins and the horse began a trot toward the road.

"See you tomorrow, Rachel," Evan yelled as Zeke turned the buckboard onto the road.

###

"Where have you been?" Bethany asked as Rachel came into the house. "I see the twins found you."

Rachel walked across the kitchen and sat at the table. "I was at Evan Kurtz's grandmother's house. She fixed us supper and we ate while the storm passed." She paused. "It started to rain just before we got to his driveway and I wanted to call Grandpa Yoder."

"He will be here tomorrow," Bethany said and sat down at the table beside Rachel.

"I know," Rachel replied. "He said that when I called." Again, she paused and frowned. "Then he hung up."

Bethany reached out and held Rachel's hands. "Uncle Paul passed away today."

Rachel nodded. "That is why Zeke was so rude to Evan and why Grandpa Yoder hung up on me."

Bethany shrugged. "Probably," she whispered. "But Zeke is rude to all *Englische* and I do not understand why."

"Uncle Paul did not like the *Englische,* either, and I think it was because Grandma Noble married *Englische.*"

Rachel shook her head. "Is it because Grandma Yoder was *Englische* that Zeke is angry with them?"

Bethany held Rachel's hands tightly in hers. "Nay, my daughter. Zeke is upset because his best friend, an *Englische* man, tormented him when Zeke quit school after eighth grade. I think you know him, Joe Holgate."

Rachel pulled her hands back, surprised at the information. "Joe and Zeke were friends?"

Bethany nodded.

"But Joe Holgate does not like the Amish," Rachel said. "Everyone in town knows that."

Once more Bethany nodded. "Who was Evan friends with when he first came to town?"

Rachel's eyes widened. "Joe," she whispered.

"Now you understand why your brother does not like Evan." She sighed. "Give Zeke time and he may change his mind." She paused. "Have Zak invite Evan to Uncle Paul's funeral." Bethany shrugged. "It will allow Evan to learn more of our Amish ways."

"Can Evan bring his grandmother?" Rachel asked.

Bethany nodded. "Tomorrow you will need to let whoever is in charge of the play that you will be attending your uncle's funeral."

Rachel frowned, having forgotten that small detail.

"I will let Mr. Sonner know," Rachel mumbled. "And Evan," she whispered.

CHAPTER NINETEEN ~ Tuesday Problems

Tuesday, August 6 7:50 a.m.

Evan strolled into The Blue Gate Theater, immediately noticing Jack Sonner at the table with Joshua Beiler. Evan didn't recognize the third gentleman at the table who was wearing a white jacket. Still, he approached.

"Get rid of the pork medallions," Joshua said and pointed at the sheet of paper the strange man held.

"In its place?" the man asked.

"You're the chef, Harold. Use your imagination... perhaps Pork Milanese."

Harold nodded. "I will see what I have in my magic box of recipes."

"Mr. Sonner?" Evan called.

"What is it, Evan?" Jack turned in his chair while placing his coffee cup on the table.

"My father only allowed me to stay in Shipshewana if..." Evan paused. "If I finished my last year of high school. My grandmother will be picking me up at nine for me to enroll in the local school."

"School?" Jack screamed. "Three days before opening and now you decide to let me know that you're a student?" He slammed his fist on the table, rattling the coffee cups on it. "School?" He sat there shaking his head.

"Is there a problem?" Joshua asked. "You assured me the play was on schedule."

Jack scanned the stage. "It is. No problems." He shrugged. "I'll just find another person to replace Evan." He stretched to see around Evan then sighed. "Kevin! You will replace Evan."

"I can still do the play," Evan said. "I just have to go to school during the day. I should get out mid-afternoon and can be here for a final rehearsal each day."

Jack eyed Evan. "You can do that?"

Evan nodded, noting Rachel entering the theater. She approached.

"Mr. Sonner?" Rachel said.

Jack hung his head and shook it. "Why me?" he mumbled.

"My uncle passed away yesterday. I will be attending his funeral on Thursday."

Jack leaned back in his chair and rubbed his forehead with his open hand. "Three days. Three lousy days." He shook his head. "Leave Broadway. Tour the nation." He sighed. "They said it would be good for my career." He slumped forward in the chair. "I guess when I get back to Broadway, if I do, things should be much easier."

Jack gazed up at Rachel. "Will you be able to do the play?"

Rachel nodded. "Yes, Mr. Sonner. I will do the play. I will be gone all day Thursday."

Jack sighed relief and grabbed the coffee cup. "I need this," he said and gulped the last of the dark liquid down. Slamming the cup down on the table, he gazed at the two young people in front of him and shook his head. "Days before opening," he mumbled. "Why? Why? Why?"

Standing, Jack glanced at his watch. "Let's get busy." He clapped his hands. "We only have less than an hour and then people will start disappearing and I want to get as much rehearsal done as possible." He paused. "Chop. Chop."

Evan glanced at Rachel and nodded toward the stage. "Best get up there," he said, grabbed her hand and led her to the steps onto the stage and then up the ladder to their positions.

"I'm sorry to hear about your uncle," Evan whispered.

"If you wish," Rachel whispered back. "You and your grandmother are welcome to attend the funeral on Thursday."

"I will tell Grandma Addie," Evan replied. "I might be in school, but I will see if I can attend."

"School?" Rachel leaned back to scrutinize Evan.

Evan shrugged. "Last year. I'm a senior and my staying in Shipshewana was on the condition I finished my senior year." Again, he shrugged. "It was either that or I go back to New York with my dad and finish school there."

"I thought you were done with school," Rachel whispered.

"Enough chit-chat," Jack yelled. "Music! Let's get this show on the road."

Rachel frowned. "Why does he continue to say that? The play is here. It is not on the road."

"Just a funky *Englische* phrase," Evan said, surprised at his usage of the word, like he wasn't *Englische.*

Rachel smiled and squeezed Evan's fingers while nodding.

The music started and Rachel began to sing the first line of the song. Evan joined in the second line and together they finished the song as the angels on the opposite side of the stage descended down their stairs. The Amish peasants toiled in the make-believe field between the two ladders.

During the third song, Evan glanced up to see the door closing and the dark image of Grandma Addie come into the shadows of The Blue Gate Theater dining room. She took a seat and watched.

The song finished and Evan glanced at the area in front of the stage for Jack.

"I need to leave now," Evan said and walked down the ladder to leave the stage. "My grandmother is here."

Jack shrugged. "Whatever." He glanced at the other actors. "Come back when you can and if we make any changes, I'll let you know."

#

Addie got in the driver's seat and started the car.

"You know school starts next week," she said, gazing at Evan. "Your father will be happy you're enrolling."

Evan sat in the front seat and stared out the window.

"Tomorrow, I turn eighteen," he mumbled.

"You didn't think I know that?" Addie grinned. "I was wondering if you'd play that card."

"Huh?" Evan snapped around from looking out the window to staring at his grandmother.

"You promised your father you would go back to school and get your degree." Addie continued to stare at the road before them. "But, we all know when a person turns eighteen, that person has the right to quit school." She pressed on the brakes as she neared the corner of US 20 and Route 5. "This is a dangerous corner." She paused. "This is where Rachel's grandparents were killed." She nodded to the left. "And just down the road, not even a mile, is where Alyssa's accident was."

Evan gazed to the left and saw where the road curved. He nodded, understanding how it could be hazardous, especially with new truckers unfamiliar with the area and the Amish horse and buggies.

"So, are you saying you're not going to go to school?" Addie asked.

"I promised my father I would complete my final year of school," Evan mumbled. "Should I?"

Addie giggled. "Oh, honey, that is your decision; not mine." She turned right. "Should I continue or head back to the theater?"

"Continue to the school. I promised my father." Evan leaned back in the seat and sighed heavily. "I promised," he muttered.

#

"That certainly was a surprise," Addie said. "Imagine. Only going to school for half a day."

Evan grinned. "I guess transferring credits from school to school worked to my advantage even if my father didn't like it."

Addie shook her head. "I still can't believe it. Only three classes to graduate." She paused. "English. Algebra 2. Government." She sighed. "It was nice of them to fore-go the physical education. Imagine. Sitting in study hall until the last class of the day?" She gazed at Evan who stared out the window. "It is a good thing you mentioned you farm." She shrugged.

Evan looked back to his grandmother. "I'm trying to figure out what I'm going to do? I can ride the bus to school in the morning, but..."

"Never you fear, Evan," Addie said. "I will be picking you up for the next couple of days or weeks." She grinned. "I'm getting things around for you to be on my insurance and you can drive the car to school and then back to the theater each day." She glanced over at him.

Evan's eyes widened. "Really, Grandma?"

"You've shown me you have accepted responsibility." She paused. "And, I've noticed you are no longer hanging around with that Joe Holgate."

"He's a jerk," Evan mumbled. "Did you know he doesn't like the Amish?"

Addie nodded. "Quite aware of the fact. I bet you didn't know that Zeke Graber and Joe Holgate were the best of friends back in grade school?"

"Huh?" Evan jerked around to stare at his grandmother.

"Give me a minute to get my facts in order. I think it was right after eighth grade. Joe wanted to start a band. Zeke was his best friend. Zeke, of course, being Amish, had completed school. That irked Joe. Then the fact Amish don't play music instruments became an issue. Anyway, Joe started to call Zeke a dumb Amish farmer who didn't know anything. I think it was jealousy of Zeke no longer having to go to school, but there might have been other issues. Anyway, things escalated and it became a well-known community gossip about their feud."

"Feud?"

"When Joe got his driver's license, he began to hassle Zeke. He would follow the buggy and honk his horn to startle the horses. Rumor says Joe would pass the buggy, honk, and then cut back in front sharply." She shrugged. "Joe got in trouble for it and lost his license. He blamed Zeke for it"

"Why didn't you tell me this when I first met Joe?" Evan asked.

"Would you have listened to me?" She reached over and patted Evan's hand. "I love you, but some things you have to learn on your own."

Evan nodded. *So that is probably why Zeke doesn't like me*, he thought.

Addie pulled the car to the side of the road, grabbed her hankie, and let the coughing spell envelope her.

"Are you okay?" Evan asked. "Do I need to drive us to the hospital?"

Addie waved her hand to pacify Evan. When the coughing spell was over, she carefully wrapped the hankie and stuck it in her pocket.

"I'm fine, Evan." She inhaled deeply. "The Lord is knocking on the front door and I keep telling Him to come back tomorrow." She sighed. "I don't think He is going to wait much longer."

"Let me drive you to the hospital," Evan said, opening the door. "You slide over."

"I'm fine, Evan. Now, close the door and I'll drop you off at the theater and then finish up a few things I have to do. I'll see you for supper. Promise."

Evan frowned and scowled at his grandmother. He hesitantly closed the car door. "If you say so, but..."

"There is no but, Evan." Addie put the car in gear and pulled back onto the highway. "Next stop, The Blue Gate Theater."

CHAPTER TWENTY ~ Paul's Funeral

Tuesday, August 6 5:30 p.m.

Rachel walked into the kitchen, seeing Grandma Yoder at the kitchen sink helping her mother, Bethany, with fixing the evening meal. In the next room she heard Grandpa Yoder talking with her father. She hugged Grandma Yoder then raced into the main room to see Grandpa Yoder.

"Grandpa!" Rachel said as she entered the main room.

Daniel stood and opened his arms to embrace Rachel.

"How is my favorite songbird granddaughter?" he asked.

"The play opens this Friday," Rachel gushed.

"Will you be ready?" Daniel asked. "I mean, with Uncle Paul's funeral the day before..." He shrugged.

"I can do it," Rachel said. "Evan will be there to support me."

Daniel raised an eyebrow. "Evan?"

"The *Englische* boy," Jeremiah Graber said. "He is learning to be a farmer." Jeremiah snickered. "A dairy farmer."

"He is doing very well, Papa," Rachel said, not realizing she was defending Evan.

Daniel nodded. He understood. "Is this the one from the play?"

Rachel nodded. "He has a very nice voice. I think you will enjoy it."

"Perhaps tomorrow, while Grandma Yoder and the others help prepare for Uncle Paul's funeral, I will come to the theater with you and speak with Jack." He sighed. "It has been many years since I last saw him."

"Rachel?" Bethany called from the kitchen. "Could you help with the carrots and green beans?"

"We can talk later," Daniel said as Rachel slipped away to the kitchen. He waited then turned to Jeremiah. "An *Englische* boy?" he asked.

Jeremiah raised an eyebrow. "You married *Englische*," he whispered.

"Grandma Yoder became Amish."

"There is history with young Evan," Jeremiah said. "His great-grandfather was James Kertz - that is with an "E" not the "U" Evan uses today. James was a cousin to Paul."

Daniel nodded, surprised by what he was hearing.

"You see why Uncle Paul had issues with the *Englische*. Anyway, James dated a strong German woman, Eliza Waldvogel. The family shunned him. They broke up and James was brought back into the Amish community. Later, not quite a year, they met again and picked up their romance. Once more the community shunned James, but he did not back down and finally married Eliza. James was ex-communicated. In his anger, James changed the spelling of his last name from "E" to "U" and they had a son, John, who married Adeline Jones. They had two children; a son, Nathan, and a daughter, Alyssa. Alyssa embraced the friendship of the Amish and we, the community, turned our heads and allowed it. There was an accident and she was killed along with several Amish. Once more, the ex-communication was reinforced and it was not until Evan came to town that it became an issue. Addie, Evan's grandmother called Bishop Zwyer to the carpet when my son, Zeke, called *Meidung* on Evan at work." He paused. "There is a chance Mrs. Kurtz will attend Paul's funeral."

Daniel nodded.

"To be honest, Papa Yoder," Jeremiah continued. "I see a strong Amish man rooting within Evan. He comes here quite often and learns of our ways from Zak. They are good friends." He paused. "And, as we both could see, Rachel is quite taken by the young man."

"If Evan's great-grandfather was ex-communicated, Evan would not be allowed to join the Amish," Daniel said.

"Since Bishop Zwyer has removed the *Meidung* on Evan, I feel we can use Ezekiel 18:20 to bring the young man back into our community." He shrugged. "Only time will tell."

Wednesday, August 7 6:45 a.m.

Evan came in the back of the house and slipped off his shoes. He heard Grandma Addie singing in the kitchen. He inhaled the scents of fried eggs, sliced ham, and... He frowned. It was a new scent. He inhaled, again. There was onion and something else frying. Evan came around the corner to see Grandma Addie adding more sliced potatoes to the cast iron skillet.

"That smells great, Grandma," Evan said.

"Well, something special for the birthday boy. Did you forget?"

"Totally, I did," Evan replied with a sheepish grin. "I'm eighteen today."

Addie gazed at the clock. "Best get a move on, Evan. The school bus will be here soon."

Evan carried the platters of potatoes and ham to the dining table. He frowned. A white box with a blue ribbon was beside his table setting.

"What is this, Grandma Addie?"

"A birthday present. Afterall, you only turn eighteen once." Addie giggled. "Open it."

Evan ripped the package open. He lifted the blue denim bib overalls.

"Just what I wanted," Evan blurted.

"Every good farmer needs at least one pair. But, I've always said, the more, the better. There're two more pair in the living room. Happy birthday, Evan."

Wednesday, August 7 7:50 a.m.

Jack looked over the top of this coffee cup and noticed two people walking in. He recognized the one as Rachel; the other confused him. The gentleman was older, but definitely Amish. The graying beard and the salt and pepper hair indicated the man probably was in his mid-sixties. Jack was sure this was Rachel's father, and he feared something was up. He was concerned.

"Mr. Sonner," Rachel said as she approached the table. "Do you remember Daniel Yoder from New York City?" She grinned. "It has been many years."

Jack dropped his coffee cup, catching it before it hit the table, spilling what little coffee was left in the cup.

"Daniel Yoder?" Jack whispered. "Is that truly you?"

"You have changed, also," Daniel said and grinned. "Neither of us are the young men we were back in New York."

Jack leaned back in his chair and grabbed at his chin with his fingers. "Whiskers? A beard?"

"I am a married man," Daniel replied.

Jack nodded. "Whatever happened between you and that young blue-haired girl?"

Rachel frowned. "Blue hair?"

"What was her name? It started with a "M"... I think..." His eyes widened. "Yes! It was Marti." He sighed. "I was going to ask her to go out with me and she disappeared."

"Her name was Martha Noble," Daniel said with a sly grin beneath his beard. "I married her."

"Married her!?" Jack sprawled out on the chair. "How'd you manage that?"

"Blue hair? Grandma?" Rachel asked.

"Never you mind," Daniel said. "Go rehearse." He waved his hands at her to shoo her away.

"Grandma got upset when Mama wanted to come to Shipshewana to date," Rachel said. "She had blue hair?"

"It was *Rumschpringe* so it was okay,' Daniel said then turned to Jack. "Martha... Marti as you knew her, left New York to come back home to Shipshewana. She knew I was from Centertown. Seems my Uncle Mark, my father's brother, married Martha's mother's sister." He shrugged. "Yes, Martha is... was Amish. Actually, she was *Englische* because her mother married *Englische,* but her Uncle Paul whose funeral is tomorrow is Amish."

Daniel reached out and held Rachel's shoulders, turned her toward the stage, and gave a gentle push. "Jack and I will talk..." He gazed about. "When stray ears are not listening."

Evan rushed up beside Rachel. "Grandma said we will go to your Uncle Paul's funeral."

Jack glared at Evan. "What? Both of you? Gone? Tomorrow?" He leaned back in his chair and placed a patting hand over his heart to mimic a stroke or heart attack. "The day before going live." He winked at Daniel. "Now I know how Peter felt when you walked away that day." He turned to Rachel and Evan. "Up on stage. We rehearse."

"Did..." Daniel frowned in thought. "Oh, yes, Donald Humphrey. Did he take my place?"

"Indeed, he did," Jack said. "There was all kinds of screaming and yelling between Preston and Peter. Seems Peter wanted the costume to have a visual appearance that Preston found obnoxious." He gazed at Daniel. "That's why you left, right? The appendage? I saw it when Donnie walked on stage." He started to laugh. "Poor Donnie. He could barely walk with that thing between his legs." He paused. "Is that why you left the play?"

Daniel shook his head. "Partly, Jack. I am Amish and I realized I was Amish and could not do the play."

"Well, the play was off-Broadway for about four months, then moved onto Broadway and was a hit for about a half-dozen performances." Jack grinned. "Seems Peter was adamant about the costume and kept making adjustments to it. Preston discovered the tactic and ripped the appendage off, ruining the costume. The show closed that night. Peter was disgraced. Preston did that Australian play and it was a roaring success." He shrugged. "I really felt sorry for Adam Brown; that kid had talent."

"I am glad they found his murderer," Daniel whispered then cocked an eyebrow toward the stage while nodding in that direction. "I think they are waiting for you."

"Sit here. Get a coffee. Water. Anything," Jack said. "We'll do lunch and have some time to catch up."

Daniel nodded, reached over and poured black coffee into an empty cup.

# # #

Thursday, August 8 7:30 a.m.

Bethany handed the different items - breads, cakes, pies, beans, chicken - to the children as they headed out the kitchen door. Everything was ready and needed to be taken to the Hershberger farm for the funeral.

Daniel and Martha walked down the steps toward the black buggy waiting for them. Zak waited for his grandparents. Daniel helped Martha into the buggy and Rachel and Peter scampered into the back of the buggy. Zak snapped the reins and the horse gently trotted to the end of the drive and onto the road. Behind was Jeremiah and Bethany with Zeke, Daniel, Adam and Elizabeth. The older three married children would meet them at the farm.

Everyone rode in silence.

# # #

Thursday, August 8 9 a.m.

Mary Hershberger, with the aid of her two eldest sons, walked by the casket to view Paul. They helped her to a chair and sat on each side of her. The rest of the Hershberger family filed by to give their last respects.

Evan followed his grandmother, imitating her to make sure he made no mistake. He glanced at the body of Paul. *This is the man who wanted me shunned*, he thought. *I forgive you, Paul Hershberger.*

Bishop Zwyer started the funeral with a prayer.

Evan watched with awe. This was slightly different than he remembered of his mother's funeral.

As sun continued to climb in the sky, Evan squirmed in his place on the bench and fingered the band of his watch. He glanced at it: 11:37. Evan sighed.

Addie reached over and patted his arm. "Soon," she whispered.

Moments later, the casket was sealed, the family stood, and the funeral service was over. The family strolled from the barn and headed for the family plot where Paul would be buried. Evan stood with the rest as Paul was carried out.

Addie leaned over. "Now, we eat." She grinned. "You have no idea what you're in for. The Amish know how to cook and if you leave here hungry, that is of your own doing." She walked away. "Follow me."

The scent of cooking food attacked Evan's nostrils. All around him, there was a flurry of activity. People were sitting up tables and moving benches around them.

"I really need to get to the theater," Evan said.

"Nonsense," Addie replied. "First, you eat, then I'll take you and Rachel to the theater. You have plenty of time. Tomorrow, you open. Exactly how much more rehearsal do you think is necessary?"

Evan snickered. He could hear Jack's voice screaming about rehearsals, but he knew his grandmother was correct. He shrugged. *At this point, everything is done*, he thought.

"Evan!" Rachel stood on the porch of the house with a tray. She started down the steps toward them. "I made us plates of food and glasses of fresh lemonade." She gazed at Addie. "I hope you like chicken, Mrs. Kurtz."

Addie grinned. "I love chicken, dear. Thank you." She reached up and took the tray from Rachel and gazed around the area. "There's a table right over here." Addie handed the tray to Evan. "You carry our food, Evan."

Evan grabbed the tray and headed for an empty table.

"We need to hurry," Rachel said. "I am sure Mr. Sonner is fuming."

"We'll eat," Addie said, grabbing up a chicken leg. "Then I'll drive the two of you to the theater."

"I hope you like cherry pie, Evan," Rachel said. "I made it."

Evan smiled. "I love cherry pie."

Addie frowned momentarily then gave a small shrug. *Hm? I thought his favorite was Dutch apple pie.* She grinned. *Cherry pie, who knew?*

CHAPTER TWENTY-ONE ~ Thursday Afternoon

Thursday, August 8 1:30 p.m.

Addie pulled the car in front of the theater.

"The two of you hustle inside," she said. "I'll be back to pick you up at five. Okay?"

"That will be fine, Grandma," Evan replied.

Inside, there was hustle and bustle which they didn't expect.

"What is going on?" Evan asked as they approached the stage.

"Finally!" Jack yelled. "Okay, everyone back to their original places." He glanced at the newcomers. "Evan! Rachel! Take your places. I want this rehearsal to be exactly what we will do tomorrow night and every night until the final production."

Holding Rachel's hand, Evan led the way up to the stage and onto the ladder where they would sit.

Jack stood, hands on hips and glared at the couple. "Is this what you plan to wear tomorrow night?"

"Sorry," Evan said and began to stand.

A stage hand hustled across the open area with two folded pieces of material. He rushed up the ladder and unfurled the shimmering fabric. He quickly spread and draped the fabric over Evan's shoulders and then Rachel's shoulders. Another woman quickly came up the ladder and fussed with the draping to make sure everything was pinned and adjusted just right.

"Better," Jack mumbled from in front of the stage. "Okay, kill the lights and let's take it from the top." He glanced to the other side of the stage. "Are the angels ready?"

A voice from the upper recesses of the stage said 'yes' and everything went dark.

The intro music played, the light came on Rachel and Evan. Rachel waited for the first bar of music to play then she began to sing. Evan joined in on the second verse.

Jack strode back and forth in front of the stage, keeping time to the music and listening, watching.

Joshua Beiler came into the theater and took a seat at a table to watch the production. He nodded his approval at Jack.

Angels began to descend on the opposite side of the stage. The song ended. A light brightened in the center stage and from both sides, the cast ambled onto the stage to work in the field, all of them singing the second song, "*Believe In The Faith*."

# # #

Thursday, August 8 5:10 p.m.

Rachel leaned against the wall of the theater. Evan kept walking to curb to gaze down the street toward the east.

Grandma Addie should be here, Evan thought. *She is never late; always early.*

Once more he gazed down the street. No bright red 1967 Chevrolet Nova to be seen.

Where is she? Evan questioned.

"Look!" Rachel pointed across the street at the intersection. "There is... Zak? Zeke? We can get a ride with him." She waved to get the young man's attention.

Zak. Okay, Evan thought. *Hm? Zeke? That could be interesting.*

"Okay," Evan said and glanced one more time down the street, hoping Grandma Addie would be coming. She wasn't.

Zeke pulled the buckboard up to the curb. "Get in, Rachel," Zeke said and glared at Evan.

"Evan needs a ride home, too," Rachel said.

"He is *Englische* and his grandmother will pick him up," Zeke said and raised the reins to snap.

"No," Rachel said. "His grandmother brought us here and said she would pick us up." She shrugged. "Mrs. Kurtz has not come." She frowned. "I hope she is okay."

Until that moment, Evan hadn't given it a thought. Now, he was concerned since he knew she was sick. All her trips to town to 'take care of business' now seemed contrived and out of place.

Evan climbed into the back of the buckboard.

"I did not invite you, Evan Kurtz," Zeke sneered. "Get out."

"Actually, Zeke," Evan started. "We need to talk. Yes, I'm *Englische* but I come from Amish stock." Evan reached up and put a hand on Zeke's shoulder. "What my great-grandfather did might have been wrong, but it was for love. To shun and despise me as you do, well, it is a waste of energy. So, now, tell me, why you really don't like me?" Evan motioned at the reins. "We can go and we'll talk."

Zeke snapped the reins and the horse began to trot on the way east.

"You are *Englische* and that is sufficient," Zeke said.

"No, Zeke, it is not sufficient," Evan countered. "You are Amish and I hold nothing against you. So, tell me, why my being *Englische* is the reason."

"Your great-grandfather deserted the Amish to become *Englische.* He even changed the spelling of his last name to make the break even stronger."

"Again, Zeke, none of that was of my doing." Evan paused. "Let's talk about Joe Holgate."

"Joe Holgate," Zeke whispered. "He is not my friend. He does not like the Amish. He is..." Zeke left the sentence unspoken.

"Because you think Joe and I are friends, you immediately put me in the same box as Joe? Yes, Joe is *Englische* but, trust me,

Zeke, he is not my friend. Joe was the first person I met. In fact, I met him at church." Evan snickered. "Imagine that. Anyway, I thought he would be a good person to know. I was wrong. Joe and I parted ways weeks ago. I don't want to be around him or anyone like him."

Zeke road in silence, thinking. Rachel watched him and then glanced back at Evan and shrugged.

"You have seen the darker side of Joe Holgate?" Zeke finally asked.

"If you mean the ugly side. Yes, it is really, really ugly." Evan snickered. "He even told me when I attended the first sing that I should go play with my Amish friends."

Zeke nodded. "That sounds like Joe." He glanced back at Evan.

"Yes, you are playing Amish. You mock us." Zeke leaned back and tugged at Evan's shirt. "A blue shirt? Dark pants? Even an Amish haircut?" He shrugged. "I think you make fun of us."

Evan shook his head. "No, I'm not making fun of you, or mocking you. Zeke, I envy you and the Amish. Life is simple. Until I got here to Shipshewana, I was a loser, drifting. I mean, sure, I could do hard labor. I wasn't afraid of that, but I had no direction. Until I got to Grandma Addie's house, I had no idea what I wanted. Now, I know."

"So, what do you want, Evan Kurtz? To be Amish?"

"Would that be so bad?" Evan asked.

Zeke slowed the horse. "We are at your grandmother's place. Do you wish us to stay to help, if needed?"

"That would be nice, Zeke," Evan replied.

Zeke turned the buckboard into the driveway and pulled behind the house. Evan rushed inside calling for his grandmother. She didn't answer. All the rooms were empty. He rushed back out to the back porch. Zeke and Rachel stood by the buckboard. The car was in the garage. Evan frowned.

Where can she be? he thought.

A loud bellow from the barn caught their attention.

"You have a cow in labor," Zeke said, and headed toward the barn.

Evan followed. When they entered the barn, Addie was in a stall with a cow in the midst of labor. She was pulling on the front feet of a calf.

"You arrived just in time, Evan," Addie yelled. "Your herd is about to grow." She noticed Zeke and Rachel. "When we bought these cows, I didn't realize they were all going to deliver on the same day." Addie laughed.

A cow bellowed from a nearby stall.

"That's Caroline," Addie said. "Evan named them all. She should be okay but you may want to check on her." She wrangled the legs and suddenly had the head showing. "Now, Antoinette here, she is having issues and needed my help."

Zeke rushed over to Caroline's stall. She was in the throes of delivery and everything seemed to be proceeding without a problem.

"All is fine here," Zeke said.

Evan checked the other stall where AnnaLu was already nursing her calf.

"All is okay with AnnaLu," Evan said and went to help Addie. "What can I do?"

"As Antoinette contracts, pull gently to help her," Addie said, handing the legs over to Evan. "I'm going to check the other cows and see if any others are ready to deliver."

"I just checked, Mrs. Kurtz," Rachel said. "The others will probably deliver in the next day or two."

"I'm sorry I wasn't there to pick you two up when you finished," Addie said.

"That is okay," Rachel replied. "Zeke brought us home." She leaned in to Addie. "It allowed Evan and Zeke to talk and I think they are friends..." She paused. "Maybe." Rachel shrugged. "One can hope."

"If you haven't noticed, Evan is slowing moving toward the simple life." Addie smiled at Rachel. "He is learning to be a dairy farmer, but not like my husband and I, but more like your father." She smiled. "I think it is a good thing."

Rachel blushed. "I have seen it."

"We have another calf," Evan yelled. "It has to nurse." He helped it to find an utter and drink that first milk so important to a calf.

"Caroline just gave birth to twins. Two heifers," Zeke yelled. "That is good."

Zeke walked over to Evan and slapped him on the back. "I think you will make a good farmer." He paused, then grinned. "In time and with proper training."

Evan placed an arm over Zeke's shoulders. "I am willing to learn, if you and Zak are willing to teach me."

Zeke nodded. "We had best be home. Mama will have the evening meal almost ready." He gazed about the barn. "You have the start of a good herd, Evan. I will have Zak stop by tomorrow when he is finished work to check. I will come by on my way home and also check." He gazed at Addie. "There is no reason for you to burden yourself with calving with all us young to aid."

"I thank you, Mr. Graber," Addie said.

"Please, call me Zeke."

Evan helped Rachel onto the buckboard and Zeke jumped up on the other side.

"We will see you tomorrow," Zeke said, snapped the reins and trotted the horse out to the road.

CHAPTER TWENTY-TWO ~ Opening Night

Friday, August 9, 2013 9 a.m.

"Tonight, we open," Jack said. "I want to go through rehearsal one... ONE more time and then everyone can go home, rest and come back at five for the show at six-thirty." He strutted in front of the stage. "Any questions?"

He paused and clapped his hands together. "We go live tonight. Questions? Now is the time because tonight will be too late."

Still, silence reigned within the room.

"Fine," Jack said. "Taking it from the top, all the way through, no stops. You make a mistake, move on. The audience won't know."

"So, you've given me a task," Joshua Beiler said with a grin as he sat at the table behind Jack.

"What?" Jack said, turning to see the man sitting down at the table.

"I'm going to watch and see if I can figure out when a mistake has been made." He winked at Jack. "I mean, you've established a challenge."

Jack shrugged. "Go for it."

Rachel gazed at Evan. "This is it," she whispered.

"I hope we get done soon," Evan replied. "I'm not sure what Grandma Addie is doing but I don't need her out in the barn helping with the calving process."

# # #

Evan raced home on his bicycle with Rachel keeping up beside him.

"I wonder if any more cows have calved," Evan asked as he pulled into the driveway.

He rushed to the barn, hearing a cow bellowing. He realized she was in labor. A quick scan of the area revealed his grandmother wasn't there.

"Grandma Addie is in the house," Evan said.

It was then he noticed the car in the driveway.

My father must be here, he thought and checked on Clara. She had things under control and didn't need any help.

"Come in and get some lemonade," Evan said, grabbing Rachel's hand and pulling her toward the back door. "You can meet my father."

"Is he coming to the play?" Rachel asked.

Evan nodded. "Yes."

"I will meet him then," Rachel said. "I need to get home and talk with my Grandpa Yoder. He wants to come tonight."

Evan let go of her hand. "I understand." He helped her get her bicycle and watched as she rode down the driveway and onto the road. He raced into the house, slipping his shoes off on the carpet by the back door.

"Dad?" he called.

"I'm in the living room with my mom," Nathan said.

Evan strolled into the living room and immediately realized things weren't well.

"Is Grandma Addie okay?" Evan asked.

"Her TB has grown stronger," Nathan said. "The doctor just left a little while ago." Nathan shook his head. "It is not good," he whispered.

"Speak up, Nathan," Addie snapped. "No need to whisper around me. I may have TB, but my hearing is excellent. I heard what the doctor had to say and I know something he doesn't." She paused then coughed. Nathan wiped away the bloody spittle. "The Lord isn't ready for me. At least, not yet." She eased back in her chair. "I have a play to see tonight."

Nathan grimaced. "A play, eh? I don't think the doctor had that on his list of things for you to do."

"Well, he may or may not have it on a list, but I know what I'm doing. I'm going to a play to see my grandson." She eased forward in her chair. "Exactly how many grandmothers can say that? So, unless the Lord decides to take me right this minute, I'm going to the play." She glared at Nathan. "Do you understand?"

"Yes, Mom," Nathan mumbled, knowing he had lost the battle, as if he had a chance of winning at any time during the discussion.

"Did you have anything to eat for lunch?" Evan asked. "I'm famished."

"There is some leftover meatloaf in the frig," Addie said. "Make a sandwich."

Evan slipped from the room.

Addoe waggled her finger for Nathan to come nearer. "Did you notice? He is even more Amish than when you were here last week." She smiled. "The boy is coming into his own."

"Amish, eh?" Nathan rubbed his chin in thought. "Did he sign up for school?"

"You do realize that Evan is eighteen and if he didn't want to go to school, you can do nothing about it."

Nathan frowned and narrowed his glare at his mother. "Did he sign up?"

"Yes, Nathan, he did," Addie said. "He said he promised you that and he signed up for classes." She paused. "Just enough to get his degree. He will only go a half day starting next Monday." She coughed.

"Are you sure about tonight?" Nathan asked.

"Try and keep me away," Addie whispered, closed her eyes and fell asleep from sheer exhaustion.

Nathan eased from the room to join Evan in the kitchen and have a meatloaf sandwich with his son.

# # #

Friday, August 9 6:00 p.m.

Nathan drove the red Nova up to the front door and let his mother out.

"Wait for me," Nathan said. "I'll park the car and be right there."

Addie nodded, turned and watched as others entered The Blue Gate Theater.

Nathan appeared, startling her. "I found a spot real close. Shall we go in?"

Addie pulled two tickets from her purse. "I bought these almost a month ago. I wasn't taking any chances of not seeing Evan on opening night."

Nathan handed the tickets to the usher who guided them to a table that was in the front and almost center stage. They had great seats. Next to them was a group of Amish at the next table. Addie immediately recognized them - the Grabers.

"Good evening, Jeremiah and Bethany Graber," Addie said. "You're here to watch Rachel?"

The Amish couple nodded. "This is Rachel's grandparents, Daniel and Martha Yoder from Centertown," Bethany said with a snicker. "I guess I should have said they are my parents." Bethany pointed at Addie. "That is Adeline Kurtz; Evan's grandmother."

"This is Nathan, my son, Evan's father," Addie said. "I can't wait to hear Rachel and Evan singing."

Two women sitting at the table on the other side of the Grabers listened to the conversation.

"You know Rachel Graber?" the one woman asked.

Bethany nodded. "Yes, I am her mother."

"We..." The woman pointed at the two of them. "We worked with her in the kitchen at the restaurant when Mr. Beiler heard her singing and wanted her for the show." The older woman sat up a little straighter. "My name is Viola Stubbe." She pointed to the younger woman. "This is Katy Hack." She shook her head. "We always enjoyed working with her and listening to her sing. She has a beautiful voice."

"Thank you," Bethany said and watched as a waiter appeared at their table with plates of food.

"Your dinners," anither waiter said and placed plates in front of Addie and Nathan.

The lights dimmed in the room and the harsh lights that had been on the stage went completely dark. The curtain opened and a spot flashed on Evan and Rachel. The music started and Rachel began to sing.

"She has a beautiful voice," Nathan said.

Evan joined in.

Nathan's facial expression dropped. "I didn't know Evan could sing like that."

Addie leaned over and whispered. "You really need to take the time to get to know your son. He was in a band here... and, from what I heard later, he really knows how to work an audience and I knew he could sing, just listening to him in church."

"Church?" Nathan questioned.

Addie nodded. "As I said, get to know your son."

The angels appeared and suddenly the whole stage was alight and the rest of the cast ambled in from the sides.

Daniel Yoder listened to the second song. He enjoyed it and bobbed his head to the tune and tempo.

This play has caught the essence of the Amish, Daniel thought.

During song four, Daniel remembered it from watching the rehearsal on Tuesday. He loved this song.

In the quiet fields where the sun sets low,
Where the simple life and the virtues grow,
With hearts of faith, we choose to follow the way,
In God's embrace, we find our stay.

(CHORUS) Believe in the path we're to pursue,
In the Amish way of our faith true.
With every step, with every prayer,
In God's loving arms, we find solace there.

Through the rolling hills and the meadows green,
In the peaceful calm of this tranquil scene,
We trust in the Lord, His word our guide,
In His presence, we'll never hide.

Believe in the path we're to pursue,
In the Amish way of our faith true.
With every step, with every prayer,
In God's loving arms, we find solace there.

In the rhythm of life, we find our song,
In the bonds of community, we all belong.
With hearts united, we sing and pray,
In God's light, we find our way.

Believe in the path we're to pursue,
In the Amish way of our faith true.
With every step, with every prayer,
In God's loving arms, we find solace there..

In the simple days, and the quiet nights,
In the faith that burns like candlelight,
We live our lives with gratitude and grace,
In God's love, we find our place.

Believe in the path we're to pursue,
In the Amish way of our faith true.
With every step, with every prayer,
In God's loving arms, we find solace there.

In the Amish way, we'll steadfastly stand,
In God's embrace, we'll walk hand in hand.
With faith unwavering, our spirits rise,
In His love, we'll find paradise.

Daniel listened to the verse - *In the rhythm of life, we find our song, In the bonds of community, we all belong. With hearts united, we sing and pray, In God's light, we find our way.*

Yes, Daniel thought. *My life in so few words. Song has been my life and I brought it to my community.*

Suddenly, the play was over and the dimmed dining room lights brightened.

"Your daughter's voice is amazing," Addie said to Bethany. "Did she inherit it from you?"

"Nay, Mrs. Kurtz," Bethany replied. "She got that from her Grandpa Yoder. He is the singer in our family." She paused. "Did you know he was in a Broadway show when he was on *Rumschpringe* in New York City?"

"Please, Bethany," Daniel said. "Tonight is Rachel's night. Let us not talk about me." He turned to Nathan. "You must be very proud of your son, Evan. He has a wonderful voice. Has he considered singing professionally?"

Nathan shrugged. "I don't think so." He paused. "We don't talk a lot, but that is about to change."

Saturday, August 10 9:30 a.m.

"Well, I'd best get a move on," Nathan said.

"Do you have to leave already?" Addie asked. "You got here yesterday and we've only had a short time together to talk."

"I really need to get back to New York," Nathan said.

"Why, Dad?" Evan asked. "Is your work that important?"

"To be honest, Evan. Yes." He shrugged. "I'm to meet with two new clients at nine tonight." Again, he shrugged. "If I can secure them as clients, I've been assured I will make partner." Nathan paused. "Have you any idea how long I've worked for this?"

"Ignoring everyone," Evan sneered. "As usual."

Nathan expected nothing less as Evan stormed out of the room.

"Are you sure about this?" Addie asked.

Nathan nodded silently.

"Think heavily on what we discussed yesterday," Addie said. "I believe it to be the answer you seek; not necessarily what you want."

"Your idea is..." Nathan searched for the word. "I can't," he finally blurted. "Let me go back and head out." He gazed at the doorway where Evan had disappeared. "I probably won't see him before I leave."

"Again, Nathan," Addie whispered. "Think long and hard on my words." She coughed.

"Do I need to call the doctor back?" Nathan asked.

Addie shook her head and waved him from the room. "I'm fine," she mumbled behind her hankie.

CHAPTER TWENTY-THREE ~ School

Monday, August 12 8:00 a.m.

Evan waited at the end of the driveway for the school bus to pick him up. He wasn't sure, but decided to go in on the bus so he could meet some of the other students. He shrugged. Most of his friends were Amish and they didn't go to high school. There were a few young people he'd met at the church with his grandmother, and then he'd see a few in town. Still, other than the Grabers, he didn't have a lot of friends.

The bus stopped and Evan got on. He was tempted to turn and run back up the lane to the house and call it quits, but he heard his father mocking him. Standing there by the school bus driver, Evan scanned the bus.

"Welcome aboard, Mr. Kurtz," the bus driver said. "The name is Sam Wyse." He paused with a silly grin. "Not to be confused with the character of Tolkien's 'Lord of the Ring' novel."

Evan frowned then quickly caught the innuendo. "Good one," Evan said and headed to an empty seat.

"Hey, Evan!" The voice called from the back of the bus.

Evan quickly searched for who called him and saw Tobias Snyder waving a hand from the very back seat of the bus. He was surprised Tobias would talk to him. Evan ambled on to the back and sat. The bus driver waited until he was sure Evan was seated, then began to drive.

"I didn't know you were going to be coming to our school," Tobias said. "I thought you were only here for the summer and then back to the big city."

"I convinced my dad to let me stay," Evan mumbled.

"Cool. I'd tell you to come back to the band, but, well, there isn't a band anymore. Joe decided he could sing and do better by himself. He left the band. Peter tried to do what you did, but..." Tobias shook his head. "He failed miserably. My buddy from Middletown asked me come help them with sound..." He looked sheepishly around. "I guess that was the end of the band. The Hanson brothers are trying to put together a new group, but..." Tobias left the sentence unfinished.

"I'm sorry to hear that," Evan said, unsure of what to say. "I and Joe just didn't see eye to eye on a few things."

"Joe doesn't see eye to eye with anyone, Evan. You were right to leave." He paused to gaze out the window as the bus slowed. "Ah, we're at Kathy Simons' house." He grinned. "You'll like her; she's a knockout."

Evan watched as the tall, slim girl with long blond hair got on the bus. She gazed about, stopping to stare at Evan momentarily before smiling and joining another girl in a seat about midway in the bus.

Tobias nudged Evan. "She saw you, dude. Try to catch up with her at school and you might even have a date for Friday night."

"I can't," Evan said. "I'm in a play at The Blue Gate Theater. Unless it is a very late date, I can't go out."

"Dude!" Tobias yelled. "I wondered what you've been doing all this time. Blue Gate!?"

Everyone turned to stare at Evan.

Tobias stood. "Evan is in a play at Blue Gate."

Evan felt his cheeks warming, unaccustomed to being singled out.

Tobias sat down, noticing the scowl from Mr. Wyse in his overhead mirror. He leaned into Evan. "By the way," he started.

"Kathy was smiling and staring at you when I said you were in a play at Blue Gate."

Evan nodded.

"Maybe if you asked," Tobias said. "She'd be willing to go to the theater to watch you and then out somewhere else after."

Evan shrugged. *Do I need a girlfriend?* Evan thought. *I mean, I've sort of been seeing Rachel and I know she likes me.* "Actually, I'm seeing somebody right now so I don't need a new girlfriend."

Tobias frowned. "Rachel?"

Evan nodded.

"She's Amish, Evan." He gazed at the seat where Kathy sat. "That one is *Englische* and available." Tobias shrugged. "Your call."

Evan shook his head. "Right now, I have five new calves and one more on the way. My dairy herd is growing and I need to put my energies there. Of course, there is the play and when it ends, I will go back to E & S to work there,"

"Your loss, dude," Tobias said, gazing out the bus window. "We're here."

The bus pulled into the parking lot of the school.

"Enjoy your first day," Sam Wyse yelled. "Everyone out."

# # #

Evan stood outside the school, waiting. He kept watch for the red Nova. Finally, the red car zipped into the parking lot. Evan got in.

"Angel gave birth to a young bull," Addie said as she put the car in gear. "Not sure what you want to do with him." She grinned. "I named him, if you like it."

"What'd you name him?" Evan asked.

"He's solid black so I named him Midnight. When it gets dark, you'll never see him."

Evan leaned back in the seat. "I like it. Midnight. I might keep him around. He can breed with the original five cows." He grinned. "I might even be able to use him as stud service for my neighbor's cows."

Addie glanced over at Evan.

"I didn't mean the Grabers. I was thinking perhaps Volhaus."

Addie nodded. "You might make a good dairy farmer, yet." She began to cough and immediately slowed to the car to pull off the side.

"Do I need to take you to the hospital?" Evan scrutinized his grandmother.

"Give me a minute to get my breath back and I'll be fine," Addie said. She knew better, and saw no reason to worry him, but decided now was the time to tell him the truth.

"If anything happens to me, go into town and visit Mr. James Smith. He's a lawyer and will know what to do."

"Grandma, you..."

"Listen to me, Evan," Addie snapped. "I mean it. The Lord is calling me and at some point, I'm going to have to answer. I've set everything up and, as my attorney, Jimmy knows my last wishes."

"Well, Grandma, that time won't be for a long, long time away." Evan stared out the front of the car. He knew better and he knew she knew it, too. His mind wandered.

"Grandma?"

"Yes, Evan."

"Would becoming Amish be a bad thing?"

Addie tried not to show any reaction; she kept driving and tried not to show her hands tightening on the steering wheel. "Being Amish is not a bad thing, Evan. May I ask why?"

"I like Rachel. I might even be in love with her. She's Amish and definitely won't become *Englische* and well..." He let the sentence dwindle away.

"Your great-grandfather was Amish. He became *Englische* to marry. Don't be too hasty. Find out if Rachel likes you and if she is willing to become *Englische*."

Evan continued to stare out the front of the car; he knew better not to look at his grandmother. "Uh-huh."

# # #

"I'm done milking the cows, for what it was worth. I set the milk in the frig. I'm going for a bike ride. Do you need anything before I leave?" Evan stood at the doorway into the kitchen.

"Enjoy the ride," Addie said. "It's a beautiful evening." She paused. "Say hello to Rachel... I mean, if you see her." She grinned.

"I will," Evan replied and rushed out the back of the house.

He raced down the long drive and turned right toward the Graber household... and also toward Bishop Zwyer's home. He turned into the driveway of the Zwyer home.

"Evan Kurtz is here to see you," Mrs. Zwyer said at the doorway of the main room.

"Send him in," Bishop Zwyer said.

Evan walked into the room where Bishop Zwyer sat in a chair, a newspaper folded in his lap.

"What can I do for you, young Evan Kurtz?"

"How do I become Amish?" Evan blurted.

Bishop Zwyer straightened in his chair and took a deep breath. "You cannot, I fear. Your great-grandfather was excommunicated and therefore shunned."

Evan gazed at a chair opposite the bishop. "May I?"

Bishop Zwyer lifted a hand toward the chair. "Please."

Evan sat. "Because of my great-grandfather?"

Bishop Zwyer nodded.

Evan grimaced and stared at the floor. "That doesn't seem fair to me."

"It is the Amish way," Bishop Zwyer replied. "The Kertz family has been banned from the Amish community because of your great-grandfather."

Evan nodded.

"In Exodus 20:5, it is written, *Thou shalt not bow down thyself to them, nor serve them: for I the Lord thy God am a jealous God, visiting the iniquity of the fathers upon the children unto the third and fourth generation of them that hate me.*"

Again, Evan nodded. "I'm not here to fight Biblical verses, but I don't hate God. I've accepted God." He grinned. "Grandma made sure of that. In fact, Grandpa James loved God, but he also loved Eliza Waldvogel and married her."

"She was not Amish, and your Grandfather James was a member of the community."

"Can I ask a question?" Evan gazed at Bishop Zwyer.

"You can speak freely here, Evan Kurtz. What is it?"

"In Ezekiel 18, verse 20, it says, *The son shall not bear the iniquity of the father, neither shall the father bear the iniquity of the son.* Would that not clear me of my great-grandfather's transgressions with the Amish community?"

Bishop Zwyer leaned back in his chair and tugged gently on his beard as he thought.

"You wish not to banter Biblical verses but you have stumped me with this one. It has caused me to think deeply on your questions."

Evan shrugged. "It was a Bible verse the minister at the Shipshewana United Methodist Church spoke about last Sunday and it got me to thinking."

"Allow me time to review what we have spoken of today," Bishop Zwyer said. "I will discuss this with the elders." He smiled. "I will be talking to you shortly." He paused. "May I ask why you are wanting to become Amish?"

"I am friends with Zak and Zeke Graber. I have come to enjoy their lifestyle. I think the simple life is what I've been seeking all these years since my mother's death."

"Friends with Zeke Graber?" The old man faintly shook his head. "Truly?"

"Zeke and I have spoken and cleared the air of the problems why we did not get along."

Bishp Zwyer nodded then gazed up with innocent eyes. "And Rachel?"

Evan shrugged. "Yes, I like her." He stood. "Let me know what I need to do to become Amish."

"If such can be done, I will," Bishop Zwyer said and shook hands with Evan.

# # #

Tuesday, August 13 6 a.m.

The alarm rang loudly, louder than Evan remembered.

Ugh, he thought. *Today is the thirteenth. Friday the thirteen falls on Tuesday.* He grinned, remembering the character, Churchy from the *Pogo* strips he'd read in his grandfather's scrapbook. It wasn't until then he realized both he and his grandfather had enjoyed those strips.

He sat up in the bed and stretched then threw back the blanket and kicked his feet over the edge.

Best be about, he thought. He sniffed the air. No breakfast scents yet. *The cows are waiting,* he thought. *Wait! I get to drive the car to school today.*

He jumped out of the bed and practically jumped into the bluejeans. He grabbed a shirt and dashed down the hallway and toward the back stairs. Slipping his shoes on, he leaned back toward the kitchen.

"Going to feed and milk the cows, Grandma," Evan yelled and dashed out the door to head to the barn.

The sun was just breaking the horizon, a growing yellow in the east. The dark blue and lavender clouds broke the rays of light, allowing a golden glowing edge to the bottom of the clouds.

"Okay, ladies," Evan said as he opened the barn doors. "I feel good about today. I hope you're ready to give a little milk." He paused. "Not much." He grinned. "I don't want to steal from the young." He stepped on the lowest rung of the ladder. "But, first, something fresh to eat." He raced up the ladder and using the pitch fork, he tossed fresh hay down.

Evan jumped down and began his inspection of the cows.

"It would appear the little ones have been eating healthy during the night." He shrugged. "No milking at this time."

He opened the barn door leading out into the pasture they'd created for the cows and calves.

"When you're ready," he said and headed back toward the house. Visions of fresh fried eggs, crispy bacon, and warm buttered toast filled his mind.

He glanced at the garage where the 1967 red Nova sat, waiting for him. He turned and hastened his steps to the garage. He opened the door and gazed inside the mint car.

I get to drive you today, he thought and ran his hand across the hood of the car. *Now, I wonder that Grandma Addie is fixing for breakfast?*

He continued to the house, slipping his shoes off and stepping into the kitchen.

Addie was not there. Evan frowned. There was indication of anything being prepared for breakfast. He ambled to the dining room, and then into the living room. Addie was not to be found.

Evan ambled to Addie's bedroom. She was asleep on the bed.

"Grandma?" Evan called softly.

She didn't respond.

"Grandma?" He called again, louder.

Still no response. Evan stepped into the bedroom and placed a hand on her shoulder.

"Grandma Addie?" Evan whispered.

She didn't move. He gently pushed her shoulder.

It was then he realized her body was cold. He stepped back, startled, but not afraid. His knees buckled and he fell beside her bed.

Evan placed his head on the edge of her bed, closed his eyes, and folded his hands together.

Heavenly Father. You now have the spirit of my grandmother. Embrace her in Your arms so she may have eternal life with You in Heaven.

He sighed. "I'll miss you, Grandma," he whispered as a tear rolled down his cheek.

In Jesus name. Amen.

"First things first," Evan whispered into the air. "Too early to call the school, but I'm not going today." He shrugged. "Maybe never, again." He gazed at the clock. Ten after seven. "Too early for the lawyer." He sighed. "Guess I'll call Dad and let him know."

Evan picked up the phone and dialed the apartment.

"Hello?" Nathan said as he picked up the phone.

"Hi, Dad," Evan said. "I thought I'd let you know; I quit school."

"You what?" Nathan screamed. "You're on the next flight back to New York, young man."

"No, Dad," Evan replied. "You're on the next flight to Shipshewana. Grandma Addie died in her sleep last night."

"What?"

Evan broke. Tears flowed. "Grandma is dead. What am I supposed to do?"

"I'll be there as soon as I can, Evan. You stay home from school and wait for me." Nathan paused. "I'll be there, son."

Nathan hung up the phone.

Evan put the phone on the hook by the bed then slumped beside the bed. His stomach growled, but he wasn't hungry.

# # #

Nathan charged into the house.

"Evan! Evan? Where are you?"

"In here," Evan replied. "In Grandma's bedroom."

Nathan burst into the room and saw Evan on the floor beside the bed. His mother was lying on her side.

"It's almost four in the afternoon," Nathan said. "Have you ate anything?"

Evan shook his head.

Nathan reached down and helped Evan up from the floor.

"You look terrible," Nathan said. "Let's get you something to eat."

"I'm not really hungry," Evan replied and looked at his grandmother on the bed. "What about her?"

"I called the coroner when I arrived in Chicago," Nathan said. "He should have been here by now."

Evan shrugged. "Somebody knocked on the door, but I didn't answer."

Nathan picked up the phone and called. It was a quick conversation.

"Let's go to the kitchen and wait," Nathan said and led Evan from the bedroom. "I think you might be in shock."

As Evan stumbled from the bedroom toward the kitchen, he shook his head. "I don't want to go to school, Dad."

"We'll discuss that later. Right now, I want you to eat something." He sat Evan at the kitchen table. "Let me see what I can find."

Nathan rummaged through the frig and cabinets.

"Not wanting to cook," Nathan said. "I found orange juice to drink and I'll make us some peanut butter and jelly sandwiches." He paused. "Does that sound good to you?"

Evan shrugged. "It's okay, I guess."

Nathan poured the juice and placed the two glasses on the small table. He quickly made a couple of sandwiches and sat opposite Evan.

"Eat up."

Evan took a gulp of the orange juice. "Grandma always made a good breakfast," Evan said absently staring at the sandwich. "Today, I think she was going to make fried eggs, bacon, and toast."

"Well, it is a little after four in the afternoon, Evan," Nathan said. "Too late for breakfast. Eat the sandwich and after the coroner visits, we'll go into town, find a restaurant, and get something to eat."

Evan's eyes widened. "Restaurant! I need to get to The Blue Gate Theater." He paused. "Mr. Sonner is going to be mad at me."

"I think he can give you a little slack, Evan. I mean, your grandmother passed away."

"But I was to be at rehearsal this afternoon," Evan mumbled.

"After the coroner leaves, we'll go talk to Mr. Sonner," Nathan said.

"I need to let Rachel know," Evan whispered. "Grandma Addie liked her."

"We can do that, too." Nathan nodded at the plate with the sandwich. "Eat."

"Grandma told me we have to—"

The knock at the door interrupted Evan's words.

"I'm Doctor Wilson, the coroner. I'm here about Adeline Kurtz."

"Come in," Nathan said. "She was my mother."

Nathan led the way to the bedroom.

# # #

"That took longer than I expected," Nathan said. "A lot of paperwork."

"Paperwork!" Evan exclaimed. "We need to see grandma's lawyer, a... a.. James Smith."

Nathan nodded his head. "I remember the name." He gazed at his watch. "He probably has gone home for the day. We'll talk to him tomorrow."

Evan grimaced. "Grandma said he would know her last wishes."

"Let's get you to the restaurant and see Mr. Sonner," Nathan said. "One thing at a time."

# # #

"Just where have you been all day?" Jack screamed as Evan walked into the theater.

"My grandmother died today," Evan said and glared at the yelling man.

"I'm sorry," Jack said and eased into a chair. "When is the funeral?"

Evan shrugged. "I guess maybe Friday?"

Jack bent his head and scratched his scalp. "Friday, huh? Will you be able to perform that night?" He gazed at Evan. "I know. I know. That's a lot to ask, but I need to know."

"I guess I can," Evan said.

"You don't need to," Nathan said. "It will be a long day for you. Plus, the viewing will be on Thursday and will more than likely start in the early afternoon and finish up in the evening." He paused. "I'm guessing the ladies of the Shipshewana United Methodist Church will offer to serve a meal after the funeral."

Jack shook his head. "So, no Evan on Thursday night's performance." He gazed at the stage. "Tom!"

A young man turned to gaze out into the darkness of the dining room. "Yes?"

"Thursday night, you will take Evan's place since he won't be here." Jack paused. "Do you want to rehearse?"

"Yes, please," Tom said.

Jack turned to Evan. "If you want, you can take off until Friday... or, even Friday if you want." He offered a weak smile.

Nathan offered a hand to shake. "As Evan's father, I would like to thank you, Mr. Sonner."

Jack offered a hand to shake and nodded. "No problem."

Rachel ran down from up on the ladder. "Evan! Did I hear right? Your grandmother passed away? Grandma Kurtz is gone?"

Evan nodded. "Yes," he whispered, a tear tracing a path down his cheek. "She is gone."

Rachel stepped on tiptoe to whisper in his ear. "I will come to the funeral,"

"Thank you," Evan said, turned, and headed out of the restaurant.

Nathan followed.

# # #

Wednesday, August 14 9:50 a.m.

"Your ten o'clock has arrived, Mr. Smith," the secretary spoke into the intercom.

"Send them in."

Nathan and Evan strolled into the inner office of Addie's lawyer, James Smith.

"You have my condolences," James said. "Have a seat."

"Evan said my mother told him you have her last wishes. Is that correct?"

James smiled. "One lawyer to another. Right to business." He straightened the papers on his desk and set them aside. He pulled a file from the drawer. "Your mother has been a very busy woman the last few weeks. She has adjusted her last will and testament at least three times." He pulled out a stack of papers, grabbing the top one. "This is the final as of last week. Everything is written down, but she made a video for the both of you to watch." He picked up a disk and slipped it into the player. "Do you wish me to leave the room?"

Evan shrugged and Nathan grimaced. "No need," Nathan said. "You know what's on it."

James pushed the play button and the large forty-inch screen TV came to life with an image of Addie.

My name is Adeline Kurtz, maiden name Jones. I am of sound body and mind. These are my last wishes.

To my son, Nathan, I, again, urge you to consider my words. I know you have made a life for yourself in New York City, but I feel you will find yourself and what you want here in Shipshewana. My lawyer, James Smith, is wanting to retire and is in search of one who will take over the business. If you decide to join him, he assures me you will be a full partner, the name will change from James Smith, Attorney at Law, to Smith and Kurtz, Attorneys at Law. Knowing James, he will probably hang in for at least a year and then it is your firm. In addition, I bequeath you one hundred thousand dollars. If you decide to return to New York, the sum of money will go to Evan.

To my grandson, Evan, I give you the farm house, and the whole farm of three hundred and seventy-five acres. You must wait for the farmers to harvest their crops and then you can do as you see fit with the land. In addition, I leave all my household goods, the car... yes, the 1967 red Nova is yours Evan. Also, I leave the remaining sum of two hundred thousand and some odd amount from my checking and savings accounts. If Nathan goes back to New York, the sum is well over three hundred thousand. You want to be a dairy farmer. Be one.

I love you both.

James will make sure all this is done according the law. If you have any questions, talk with him.

She leaned in and frowned at the camera.

"How do I turn this stupid thing off?"

The TV went blank.

"Questions?" James sat in his chair; hands folded in front of him on the desk.

"So, my mother is blackmailing me into staying in Shipshewana," Nathan said. "If I stay, I inherit a hundred thousand dollars." He paused. "Where did she get that kind of money?"

"Not blackmail, Nathan," James said. "Call it an incentive." He gazed up at Nathan. "I really would like somebody to take over the business. I've wanted to retire for years, but nobody wants to be a lawyer in a small country town."

"Shipshewana isn't that small of town." Nathan countered.

"I do a good business, Nathan. The next closest lawyer is in Middlebury and Elkhart to the west and LaGrange to the east."

Nathan nodded. "So, if I go back to New York, I get nothing."

James shrugged. "Basically, that's it."

Nathan glanced at Evan who had been silent.

Evan sniffed and wiped the tears from his eyes. "Grandma left me the farm," he whispered. "I can be a real dairy farmer."

"No, Evan, you're coming back with me to New York," Nathan said.

Nathan glared at his father. "You seem to have forgotten one little detail, Dad." Again, the sneer of dad wasn't missed by the other two men in the office. "I'm eighteen. I can do what I want." He paused. "I'm staying here. Grandma Addie showed me how to be a dairy farmer and that's what I'm going to be."

"Exactly how do you plan to do that?"

"I'm going to become Amish," Evan said with a defiant glare at his father. "The community will help me."

"Amish? You?" He shook his head. "Never going to happen. Grandpa Kurtz made sure of that. We were ex-communicated and that is that."

James nodded. "The Amish way."

"Right now, Bishop Zwyer is wrestling with Ezekiel 18 verse 20. I threw that at him and he is discussing the ramifications with the elders of the community."

"You what?" Nathan asked.

"I am going to be Amish, Dad. There is nothing you can do to stop it."

"If I drag you back to New York, you won't be Amish." Nathan stood and glared down at his son sitting in the chair next to him.

"At eighteen, you're not dragging me anywhere," Evan said. "Uh, ask Mr. Smith. I mean, he's a lawyer and knows the law." He paused. "As you should, too."

James sat quietly watching the unfolding scene.

"Mr. Smith?" Evan started. "May I retain you as my lawyer?"

"Certainly, Mr. Evan Kurtz. It would be my honor."

Nathan glared at James.

"Now, if Evan would like to step outside and wait there..." He gazed at Nathan. "Perhaps we can discuss your mother's wishes."

Evan stood and left the office, sitting in the outer office, watching the secretary and scanning the magazines on the table.

"I am not about to discuss the possibility of my moving to Shipshewana, Mr. Smith. I am a junior partner in a prestigious law firm in New York City. I am up for full partnership in mere weeks."

"Hm? Weeks for full partnership... maybe, or days to be a full partner of a prosperous law firm. Such a decision to make." James paused. "And, of course, there is the money to consider."

"Exactly where did my mother get all that money?" Nathan asked. "It's quite a large sum."

"Your mother invested. When she sold the dairy cows, the money was used to invest in some hedge funds. She did well, cashed out, and kept her lifestyle very simple. Her true luxury was giving to the church and cooking meals for others." He shrugged. "Then she rented out the farmland and earned a percentage of the profits there."

Nathan shook his head. "I always saw my mother as a simple woman who was content to stay at home, unaware of the business world around her. My father, he was the one I figured had the head for business." He shrugged. "Guess I was wrong."

James smiled. "Your father, John, was a good businessman. But, your mother, she was shrewd businesswoman.

She could take a dime and turn it into a dollar with a blink of an eye. I do believe that is why your father married her."

"Why is my mother so insistent on me coming back to Shipshewana?"

James shrugged. "Come home to your roots, perhaps?"

"You seem like a fair man, Mr. Smith," Nathan said. "Is there enough business in this town to keep the two of us busy?"

"Maybe," James said. "I've had to turn away clients because I can't handle every person who comes into the office."

Nathan nodded. "Let me think on the position, Mr. Smith."

"As you wish, Mr. Kurtz," James said. "You decide positive on the proposition, the new sign will be up in two days."

CHAPTER TWENTY-FOUR ~ Addie's Funeral

Thursday, August 15 7 p.m.

"Good evening, Nathan," the strange woman started. "You probably don't remember me. I'm Gladys Holgate from the Shipshewana United Methodist Church. I'm here as a representative of the United Methodist Women. I thought I'd let you know, your mother has made all the preparations for the luncheon, including the payment which was quite sizable. The ladies have already begun preparations and will be ready tomorrow after the funeral service. The church fellowship hall will be ready for everyone to enjoy a meal and remember your mother."

Nathan nodded absently. He knew there would be a meal, but he wasn't aware that his mother had made all the arrangements.

Evan sat by his father, listening, while at the same time innocently gazing about to see if Mrs. Holgate's son, Joe, was anywhere to be seen.

As if in answer, Mrs. Holgate leaned down, and grabbed Evan's hands in hers. "Joe couldn't make it. He's in Chicago with some big-time record producer."

Evan nodded. "That's okay," he mumbled and stared at the line still waiting to see them. *There has to be over one hundred more people*, he thought.

Some he recognized from church, others he'd seen at the store when they came shopping. What he didn't expect was the number of Amish in the line.

Rachel!

She stood in line with her father, mother, Zak, Zeke, and the other siblings.

Evan smiled at her and she blushed.

Finally, the Grabers were standing in front of Evan and Nathan.

"Your mother was a fine woman," Jeremiah said to Nathan. "She was a wise business woman."

Nathan nodded. "So I am learning. How much business did you do with her?"

"She bought the cows for Evan," Jeremiah said. "I understand he reimbursed her."

Nathan gazed at Evan who nodded. "I paid her back every cent."

"Where did you get that kind of money?" Nathan asked.

"I worked for it," Evan said. "Remember that night we fought and you had a deal to handle and I went to get Chinese food? I worked for Lin Ho's brother than night and made a few hundred dollars. I'd done it many times before." He shrugged. "I saved my money. I had over two grand."

Nathan nodded. *A chip off of grandma*, he thought.

"Your mother," Jeremiah continued. "Made sure the cows Evan bought were all pregnant so he could increase his herd. Plus, Jedidiah, my brother, farms about one hundred acres of your mother's farm."

"I am sorry to hear about your grandmother," Rachel whispered to Evan. "I truly loved that woman. She was always nice to me and the Amish."

A tear welled in Evan's eye. "I only knew Grandma Addie for a few months, but I loved her, too."

"Are you going back to New York?" Rachel asked.

"No," Evan replied. "I am staying here. Grandma Addie gave me the farm and a tidy inheritance. I will become a full-time dairy farmer."

Jeremiah leaned down and whispered in Evan's ear. "That is a mighty big aspiration young man. Can you do it?"

"With proper guidance," Evan replied. "I am hoping there are those who will aid me in my ambition."

Jeremiah nodded. "I am sure Zak, and even maybe Zeke, will help you learn the ropes of being a proper dairy farmer."

"I will enjoy their help," Evan said. "They are very knowledgeable."

"Still, it is a lot of work for one person," Jeremiah said.

"I hope not to be alone too long," Evan said.

Jeremiah raised an eyebrow. "Oh?"

"We had best move along," Bethany said. "There are others waiting."

"Thank you for coming," Nathan said.

"See you tomorrow, Rachel," Evan said. "I'll be there for the play."

Rachel leaned down. "Tom is a nice guy, but he doesn't have the voice you have."

# # #

Friday, August 16 10 a.m.

Evan sat in the front pew of the Shipshewana United Methodist Church beside his father. The organist, Hazel Singer played different hymns. He really didn't pay attention to the music as he stared at the open coffin of his grandmother.

She's gone, he thought. *What will I do?*

Reverend David Long stepped to the pulpit. He cleared his voice.

"This morning we gather to say farewell to our dear sister, Adeline Kurtz. She was a member of this church for over forty years. The church knew her, the community knew her. She was a woman to be reckoned with and we all loved her dearly."

Evan inhaled deeply, trying to keep the tears from gathering in his eyes.

The minister continued. "She has selected three songs to be sung. We will begin with the first one - *Amazing Grace.* Please stand."

The congregation stood and Hazel played the opening stanza to get everyone ready. Voices lifted into the air.

Again, Evan paced his breathing to control his emotions. He gazed at his father who stood beside him, singing. He'd never heard his father sing. Every so often Nathan's voice broke as his emotions surfaced.

I need to keep a strong image for Evan, Nathan thought. Memories of his wife's funeral blasted into his mind. He broke.

Evan noticed his father's body shaking and quickly realized he was crying. He reached over and placed a hand on his dad's shoulders.

"It's okay, Dad," Evan whispered.

"No, it's not," Nathan replied. "I'm remembering your mother's funeral. I didn't even invite my parents to it." He sobbed and crumbled, sitting on the pew.

Evan joined him. "That was then," Evan whispered. "Let it go."

"I can't believe I've held a grudge over a stupid thing for so long. My dad and I constantly fought. You and I constantly fight. To me, it seems normal, but I know it's not." He bent over, placing his elbows on his knees and bowing his head. "I need forgiveness."

Evan gazed up at the cross on the wall behind the altar. "You're in the right place, Dad." He pointed at the cross. "Ask God for the forgiveness you seek."

Nathan wiped the tears away and gazed at the cross. He closed his eyes and prayed.

Reverend David Long once more stood at the podium. "Be seated. I will now read from the Gospel of John about everlasting life."

When he finished, Reverend David paused. "Our next hymn is *In The Garden.* Please stand."

Again, Gladys played an opening bar and everyone joined in.

Evan and Nathan clutched hands and sang.

Once more Reverend David stood at the podium. "Be seated. Today's sermon is about the resurrection."

Evan tried to pay attention, but his mind wandered and his eyes gazed at the coffin of his grandmother.

Suddenly, Evan heard Reverend David asking if anyone would like to say any words about Adeline Kurtz. A microphone was passed around by the usher as members of the church shared special moments about Adeline.

Evan listened, amazed at how she had endeared herself into the community.

Nathan sat, silent, eyes wide, listening, shaking his head, realizing all the lost time that had passed. He gazed again at the cross.

"Is there anyone else?" Reverend David asked.

Evan stood. The usher handed him the microphone.

"Adeline Kurtz. I knew her as Grandma Addie. I hadn't known her long, only a few months, but they were months filled with love and learning. I didn't know I had a grandmother until May of this year. The last few months with her were some of my best times."

A tear welled and traced a path down his cheek.

"I love you Grandma Addie." His voice choked. "I will miss you."

Evan handed the microphone back to the usher.

"We will now sing one last song. Any who wish to view Adeline Kurtz may come up during the song. The song is *Abide With Me*. Please stand."

Gladys played an opening bar, her fingers running riffs. She held the final note before starting the song for the congregation to sing.

A few people wandered up and gave their last respects. Evan waited. When no others came forward, he walked up to the casket. Gazing down at her, she appeared only to be asleep and he felt if he tried, he could wake her. He knew different, but he wasn't ready to let Grandma Addie leave his life.

"I love you, Grandma Addie," he whispered. "You were the best thing to happen to me after my mother died. Thank you for showing me my future." He shrugged. "Maybe dad will see his, maybe not." He grinned. "You knew I was going to become Amish, didn't you?" He knew she wouldn't answer, but he knew the answer. She'd guided him toward his new life. "Rest with the Lord, you deserve your reward. Thank you."

He stepped back and once more took his place by his dad at the pew.

Reverend David stood in the middle of the sanctuary before the coffin.

"There will be a short graveside service for those who would like to attend. The ladies of the church have a light luncheon prepared for those would prefer to stay and wait the return of the family. All are welcome."

He moved from the sanctuary to in front of the coffin and closed it.

"The pallbearers will now come forward. The family will follow and then each pew will follow in order, right then left. Please allow the coffin to be placed into the hearse before going to your cars for those going to the cemetery."

Reverend David led the way down the long church aisle, the pallbearers lifted the coffin.

Nathan and Evan walked side by side behind the coffin. They were the only family.

Evan took a deep breath, hoping he could make it to the exit before breaking down. He hoped the fresh air would calm his emotions.

They watched as the coffin was lifted into the hearse and then they headed to the limousine Addie had hired for the occasion.

Evan got in and then Nathan followed. They sat momentarily in silence, allowing time for those who were going to the cemetery to get to their cars.

"Can I ask a question?" Evan asked.

"What do you want to know?"

"Have you made a decision? New York or Shipshewana?"

"What do you want me to do?" Nathan asked.

"It's not what I want, Dad," Evan replied. "It is what you want. But, for me? I want you to be here in Shipshewana."

"Why?"

"Because you're my father," Evan mumbled.

"But you want to become Amish," Nathan responded.

"Yes," Evan answered. "Is that a bad thing?"

Nathan grinned. "I'm not becoming Amish. Is that understood?"

"So you are staying?"

"Yes," Nathan replied. "I told James Smith this morning and the new sign will be up on Monday morning. I even called the New York office and told them I was done."

"What of the apartment?" Evan asked.

"The super said there is a waiting list of those wanting to move in, so he was easy to persuade to let me out of the lease."

"We can go to New York this Sunday after church," Evan said. "Get our stuff and be back here by mid-day Tuesday."

"Actually, Evan, things are being packed as we talk and should be here by mid-week."

Evan nodded.

"So, we're not going to New York?

"Why?" Evan asked.

"Thanks, Dad."

# # #

The graveside services were short. Reverend David said words of peace and Adeline Kurtz was laid to rest beside her husband, John Kurtz.

Evan picked a rose and dropped it on her coffin as it was lowered. He took another to keep as a memento.

Nathan led the way back to the limo and the group headed back to the church and the waiting meal.

CHAPTER TWENTY-FIVE ~ Bishop Zwyer

Wednesday, August 21 7:30 p.m.

The knock startled Evan who sat at the dining room table reading Grandma Addie's Bible by a small kerosene lantern. He answered the door.

"I hope I have not come too late, Evan Kurtz," Bishop Zwyer said. "May I visit?"

"Come in," Evan said. "My father is working, getting to know the clients of the firm. He will be here shortly."

"I have come to see you," Bishop Zwyer said. "You have caused a stir within the community. The Amish have lived by the rules and none have questioned them." There was a pause. "Until now."

"Have a seat," Evan said and led the bishop into the living room.

"We, the elders, have studied your Ezekiel verse. We found others to match."

"Would you like some lemonade?" Evan asked.

"Nay. You have brought up a valid question and it was decided by the elders that the ex-communication should only apply to the person. As you stated, the sins of the father should not be born by the son."

Evan smiled. He liked what he was hearing.

"If you wish to join the Amish community, it is allowed. You will need to see me for lessons, training, and finally baptizing."

"I'm already baptized," Evan said.

"Baptism is the final step in joining the Amish community. It is where you vow to live by the rules and laws of the community." He paused. "It is not like an *Englische* baptism. Do you understand?"

"I think so," Evan replied.

"I would like to see you one day each week so we may begin the process," Bishop Zwyer said.

Evan gazed around the room. "I have Monday's free," he said then paused. "You know I am in the play at The Blue Gate Theater."

"Yes, with Rachel Graber," Bishop Zwyer said. "After some deliberation, it was decided to allow her to participate since it did not involve her wearing a costume."

Evan nodded.

"When will you be done with the play?" Bishop Zwyer asked.

"I think it is sometime near Thanksgiving," Evan said.

Bishop Zwyer nodded. "That will be fine. You will learn and by next spring, if you still wish to join the Amish community, you will be baptized." He grinned. "The water could be bit cold, but the Amish deal with it."

Evan nodded and heard the back door open.

"Evan?" Nathan called.

"In here, Dad," Evan replied. "I have Bishop Zwyer here with me."

"Oh?"

"I am discussing the possibility of Evan joining the Amish community," Bishop Zwyer said.

Nathan grimaced and nodded. "Uh-huh."

"I had best be headed home," Bishop Zwyer said. "My wife will be worried if I am out too late after dark." He grinned, the whiskers spreading.

"That was your buggy out there?" Nathan asked.

"Yes, Mr. Kurtz," Bishop Zwyer replied. "Good evening."

Nathan and Evan saw Bishop Zwyer to the door. "Have a good evening," Nathan said.

# # #

Nathan ambled back to the living room. "Join me, Evan."

Evan followed, knowing there was going to be a long conversation and lecture.

"I want to discuss two things with you," Nathan said.

Evan's shoulders slumped. He knew. *School. Amish,* he thought.

Nathan sat in the easy chair. They both looked at the rocking chair that Addie always sat in. They wouldn't consider it.

"I want to talk about this school issue," Nathan said. "You quit school. Yes, I know you're eighteen and can do that, but, Evan, I really would like you to have at least a high school degree."

Evan was silent, thinking. "What if I got my GED?"

"A GED?" Nathan repeated. "Why not complete your last year of school?"

Evan shrugged. "Because I don't want to. I can take the GED exam, if I pass, I will have my high school degree." He paused and saw his father was about to say something. Evan lifted a finger to hold his father off. "I only take a couple of courses that were needed to graduate; English, a math course, so I took Algebra 2, and a government course." He drew in a deep breath. "If I take the GED, and I pass, I don't need to complete school."

"Fine. Take the GED," Nathan mumbled, realizing he was losing the battle.

Evan waited.

"Now, about this Amish foolishness," Nathan started.

"It isn't foolishness, Dad." Evan glared at his father.

"Why do you want to be Amish?"

"Grandpa James, your grandfather, was Amish. He was ex-communicated when he married Eliza Waldvogel because he was already baptized and she wouldn't become Amish. He left the Amish." Evan paused, watching his father. "Did you know our name was spelled with an "E" but Grandpa James changed it to a "U" when the Amish ex-communicated him and the family shunned him."

"Interesting history lesson, but one I've known," Nathan said. "Do you think Alyssa and I could hang out with the Amish and not know about that? In fact, we should have been banned, but..."

"Therefore, my going back to the Amish is no big deal," Evan said.

"Yes. Yes, it is. I..." Nathan was lost for words.

"I haven't become Amish, yet," Evan said. "I'm looking into the possibility."

Nathan sat in silence, debating his words.

"I think the only reason you're doing this is because of Rachel Graber. Am I right?"

"Yes. Rachel Graber is involved in my choice. I love her, Dad."

"Have you asked her if she would consider being *Englische?*"

"She is Amish, Dad," Evan said. "Zeke would have my hide if I was to take her from the community."

"So, what are you going to do?" Nathan asked.

"First, I will go to the school and check about taking the GED exam. Secondly, I will visit with Bishop Zwyer and learn about the Amish and their lifestyle and rules." He took a deep breath. "I have until next spring to make a decision."

Nathan nodded. "Fine. You have a plan. See to it."

# # #

Monday, August 26 3 p.m.

Evan pulled into the driveway of Bishop Zwyer's residence. He closed the door of the red Nova and scurried up the steps of the front porch. He gazed back at the car and shook his head.

Probably not the best decision you've made, Evan thought as he stared at the car.

Mrs. Zwyer opened the door, gazed at the car, made a small grimace then stepped aside to allow Evan entrance.

"The Bishop is in the main room," she said, wiped her hands on her apron, and headed back toward the kitchen.

"Come in, Evan Kurtz," Bishop Zwyer called. "Have a seat."

Evan walked into the room and took a seat across from the bishop.

"So, you wish to learn about the Amish; become Amish," he said

Evan nodded.

Bishop Zwyer tugged at his beard, gazing at Evan, evaluating.

"First, the Amish do not use modern conveniences." The bishop nodded toward the driveway. "I see you have a car."

Evan nodded. "It was my grandmother's car. She gave it to me."

Bishop Zwyer eased back in his chair. "What will you do with it when you become Amish?" The bishop shrugged. "Amish do not have cars."

"I will give the car to my father," Evan said, shaking his head. "My father does not wish to become Amish."

"And, your house? It has electricity?"

Evan nodded. "It does, but I've started to not use it. In fact, the night you came to the house, I was reading the Bible by the light of a kerosene lantern."

Bishop Zwyer nodded. "That is good." He cocked an eye in Evan's direction. "Would you consider attending our church this Sunday?" He paused, but not too long. "You could come with the Graber family and the twins could show you what to do."

Evan frowned. "I attend church in town."

"If you become Amish, you will attend with the community. We sing our songs from memory. There is the *Ausbund* but a child is brought up singing the songs and learns them. You probably will not recognize many of the songs." He paused and gazed at Evan. "We sing *O Gott, Vader* and *Das Loblied* every Sunday. Are you familiar with them?"

Evan shook his head.

Bishop Zwyer grinned. "You will."

Evan nodded.

"I see you are already wearing the traditional blue shirt and dark trousers." The bishop cocked his head back to survey the hair. "Almost an Amish haircut."

Evan grinned. "Mrs. Graber cut my hair a while back. It did look very Amish... almost, but Jack Sonner, the director of the play got upset. He wants me to look *Englische* and not Amish. Rachel was able to move the hair so I didn't appear Amish."

Bishop Zwyer nodded. He held up his index finger. "I am thinking," he whispered.

Evan sat in silence, waiting.

"Would you like something to drink and perhaps a cookie?" Mrs. Zwyer stood at the entrance to the room.

"Water will be fine," Evan replied.

She nodded and disappeared, only to reappear with a platter with two glasses of water and a small assortment of cookies.

"*denki*, (thank you)" Bishop Zwyer whispered as she leaned in to offer him a drink. "Our guest, first."

With a small shrug, Mrs. Zwyer walked across the room to allow Evan to select a glass and cookie. She ambled back to the bishop who took the remaining glass and a cookie to match.

Evan munched on the chocolate oatmeal cookie. "This is very good, Mrs. Zwyer," Evan said, his mouth full.

"Thank you," Mrs. Zwyer said then under her breath, barely a whisper, she added. "Don't choke." She continued to the kitchen.

Evan frowned. "Will I be met with a lot of opposition to becoming Amish?"

"Nay, young Kurtz," Bishop Zwyer replied. "We welcome any who wish to embrace the Amish lifestyle..." he paused. "If they truly want to be Amish and are not just enamored with the romanticized image of the novels. Yes, it is a simple life, but it is a life filled with manual labor." Again, he paused. "Most Amish get up before the sun, and work until sundown, then spend time with the family before going to bed early in the evening."

Unsure, Evan nodded. He understood that aspect of the Amish life.

"What do you plan to do as an Amish man?" Bishop Zwyer placed both hands in his lap and studied Evan.

"I want to be a dairy farmer," Evan said.

Bishop Zwyer nodded. "Your great-grandfather was an excellent dairy farmer before..." He took a deep breath.

"Before he left the Amish," Evan finished.

"Aye," Bishop Zwyer mumbled, nodding. "Would it not be easier to be a dairy farmer as an *Englische* than Amish."

Evan shrugged. "Probably. It would be a lot easier with all the modern conveniences."

"Then why do you wish to become Amish?" Bishop Zwyer shrugged. "I know, I keep asking the same question, but I have yet to get a proper answer."

"I love Rachel Graber," Evan blurted. "I want to marry her. She is Amish and I know she will not become *Englische* and I can become Amish."

Bishop Zwyer put a finger to his lips. "The truth finally is revealed." He paused. "Love."

"Is love a bad thing?" Evan asked. "You make it sound like the wrong reason. It was the reason my great-grandfather left the Amish. Why can't it be the reason I rejoin the Amish?"

"A valid point, young Kurtz," Bishop Zwyer said. "Have you found if Rachel Graber likes... nay, loves you?"

"I think she does but holds back because I am *Englische* and doesn't want to get hurt. Plus, I think Zeke would have something to say about it with me not being Amish."

"Aye, young Zeke Graber gained much of his distrust of the *Englische* from his Uncle Paul. His sister married *Englische* and then her daughter, Martha, became Amish and married a Daniel Yoder in Centertown."

"I have heard and met them a few weeks ago at the opening of the play. Rachel wanted me to meet her grandfather who taught her to sing."

"I was much younger back then, but I remember Bishop Beiler mentioning his training of Martha Noble in her path to becoming Amish and being baptized so she could marry Daniel Yoder."

"My Grandma Addie told me the tale of Martha Noble and my Grandpa John talking in the front lawn of the farm. He was in college and Grandma Addie and he were dating. Martha and John spoke and she was upset with the wedding or some confusion about it."

Bishop Zwyer nodded. "Yes. There was a lot of confusion. Her father tricked her into an *Englische* wedding to Daniel Yoder. The poor boy had no idea what was happening. She got the marriage annulled and went through the training to become Amish. They married Amish and have been together ever since. Bethany Graber is their daughter and Rachel is their granddaughter."

Evan gulped the last of his water. "This Sunday... church. Where is it?" He leaned back in his chair.

Bishop Zwyer again tugged at his beard. "It will be held at..." He frowned. "Ah, yes, the Beiler farm." He took a deep breath. "If you want to go there on your own, it is about another mile east of here and a mile north." He paused. "If you want to go with the Graber family, I would suggest you be at their house no later than eight on Sunday morning."

"Eight?" Evan exclaimed. "Our church doesn't start until ten-thirty."

"Our service will start at nine and go until noon. Then we will have a lovely meal, visit, update one another of the week, and sometime around two, we all head home."

"So, church is basically an all-day event," Evan said, grimacing. He cocked an eye at Bishop Zwyer. "You do this every Sunday?"

Bishop Zwyer nodded. "Every Sunday. Different homes, though."

"Interesting," Evan said. "I will talk with Zak and see if I can attend with them."

"I think we are done for today, young Kurtz," Bishop Zwyer said. "I am sure you will have many questions next week if you attend church this Sunday."

Evan stood and shook hands with the bishop. "I thank you for the time today."

"It was my pleasure, Evan Kurtz. I look forward to several more of these meetings." He gave a strong grip to the shake. "I think you will be a good Amish man if you decide to become one." He thumped Evan's shirt. "Get with Zak and get the approved suspenders of our community." He shrugged. "We have rules about everything, even our clothing. Zak can help you."

# # #

Sunday, September 1, 2013 7:45 a.m.

Evan rode his bicycle into the Graber front yard and parked it by a tree.

"*gut'n mariye*, (good morning)" Evan said as he approached Zak who waited for him on the back porch.

"You are speaking Amish?" Zak asked.

"I am learning," Evan said. "I know some German, but Amish is a little different."

Zak patted Evan on the back as he came onto the porch. "Still, it sounds good." He opened the door. "Come in. We are about to leave."

Rachel stood by the kitchen table. "Good morning, Evan."

"Thank you," Evan replied, unsure if he should speak Amish to her or not.

Zak elbowed him in the ribs. "Tell her good morning, Evan."

"*gut'n mariye*, (good morning) Rachel," Evan said. "Did I say it right?"

"Close enough," Zeke replied, coming into the room. "I heard you are taking Amish lessons from Bishop Zwyer. Is he teaching you to speak Amish, too?"

Evan shook his head. "No. I am learning it on my own... or, at least, trying to."

"I have heard the *Englische* say that immersion into the language is the best way to learn." Zeke smiled. "Today, you are being tossed into the middle of the lake. You will hear more Amish than you want."

"Hopefully, with what little German I know, I'll be able to follow along," Evan replied.

"We will see," Zeke said and headed out the door.

"Rachel and the three younger siblings will ride with Papa and Mama in the buggy. You, Zeke, Daniel, and I will take the buckboard."

Evan tried not to show his dismay at not being with Rachel, but he nodded approval.

Zak slapped Evan on the back. "Best be going. We do not want to be late for church." He reached over and grabbed a basket and handed it to Evan. "Take this and I will get the other one." He smiled. "It is for our mid-day meal."

Evan took the basket and noticed two pies and something wrapped in a towel.

"Should I have brought something to eat?" Evan asked.

"Nay," Zak replied. "There will be plenty. You are a guest. If you become Amish and get married, you will be expected to bring something, but not now."

They headed out the door and got on the buckboard that Zeke had brought around. At the end of the drive, Evan noticed the buggy getting ready to turn onto the road.

"How long to get there?" Evan asked.

"Not long. It is only a couple of miles away." He pointed. "See? There come the Zook family. We are not late."

As the buckboard turned the corner of the next mile, Evan noticed at least six other buggies approaching from different directions, all heading toward the Beiler farm.

# # #

Bishop Zwyer gathered everyone together to begin the service and opened with a short prayer. Abram Zook, the *Vorsänger* (song leader), began the beginning drone of *O Gott, Vader*.

Zak sat beside Evan and leaned over. "We are singing *O Gott, Vader*."

Evan nodded and mentally translated the song as *Oh God, the Father*. He listened but didn't recognize the words. They were being sung too slowly and with varied notes. He was reminded of Gregorian chanting.

Evan sat listening. The song took almost twenty minutes to sing.

There was a pause and then Abram Zook began to sing another song.

Zak again leaned in. "This is *Das Loblied*," he whispered.

Evan frowned as he struggled to remember his German. The best he could come up with was *Praise Song* which he wasn't sure if it was correct.

Again, Evan listened, hoping to gain a word here and there, but didn't. This time the song only lasted about fifteen minutes.

Evan tried not to fidget on the wooden bench. There was no cushion like at the Shipshewana United Methodist Church. He felt the numbness beginning to set in and he hoped he would be able to stand when the service was finished.

Bishop Zwyer's words came to him. *Until about noon.* He took a deep breath. *Only another two plus hours to go*, he thought then shrugged. *At least there will be food when we finish.*

Suddenly, there were words he recognized.

Unser Vater, der im Himmel ist, geheiligt werde dein Name

It's the Lord Prayer! The words blasted into his brain. He joined with the others reciting the prayer in German as he had learned it.

Zak gazed at Evan and nodded approval.

# # #

"Did you enjoy church today?" Bishop Zwyer asked as he approached Evan who sat with Zak.

"You said I would not know the songs. You were correct, but I did recognize the Lord's Prayer."

"That is well, Evan Kurtz. Be sure to get something to eat and enjoy the community as we enjoy the fellowship."

Bishop Zwyer ambled off toward a group of older gentlemen with graying beards.

Evan frowned. "Why do some men have beards and other don't?"

Zak laughed. "Married men are allowed to grow beards. Single men keep their chins shaved until they marry. None of us have mustaches."

Evan nodded. "When do you plan to grow a beard?"

Zak nodded toward a group of young girls. "See the one in the lavender dress with the white apron? That is Leah Beiler. I am trying to court her, but her father claims she is too young. She is seventeen, a year younger than me. She is the same age as Rachel, a month apart."

Evan's eyes widened. "Rachel could marry?"

"Yes, if she finds an Amish man she likes. So far, none have caught her eye." He gazed at Evan. "Not that the Amish men have not tried to court her."

Evan nodded. *I wanted to wait until I was well established as a dairy farmer,* he thought. *Maybe when I was close to twenty.* He gazed at the group of girls, Rachel was with them. They were looking here and there at the young gathered men.

Will she wait for me? Does she love me? Evan fretted about the situation.

Rachel strolled over to them. "Do you wish I should get you and Evan something to eat?" she asked Zak.

"Nay, Rachel," Zak replied. "Evan and I will go get something shortly. We are young and can wait."

Evan nodded.

Rachel sat down beside Evan.

"Did you enjoy church today?" she asked. "Did you understand any of it?"

"Some," Evan replied. "I understood some of the words." He straightened up tall. "I understood and joined in the Lord's Prayer. That I knew."

Rachel reached for Evan's hand. "That is good. Do you still want to be Amish?"

"Yes," Evan replied. "I am finding it very beneficial."

Rachel frowned. "Beneficial?"

"My anger issues have eased up. I am no longer mad at the world. I find peace and harmony when I am with the Amish."

Rachel nodded. "Do you wish to go get something to eat. We could sit together."

Zak nudged Evan. "Go," he whispered.

"Okay," Evan replied and followed Rachel into the house.

# # #

Rachel laughed at tales Evan told of his days in New York City as they ate sitting across from each other at a table. Zak joined them with Leah Beiler.

Finally, Zak and Leah left, leaving Rachel and Evan alone.

Do I tell her? Evan thought. *Is it too soon?*

"I see you fighting with a question," Rachel said. "Give it time and the answer will become known to you."

She gazed up at the house where her parents stood. They were waiting with Rachel's younger siblings.

"I must go now," Rachel said. "I will see you Tuesday night for the play." She lowered her eyes. "I had an enjoyable time with you." She left.

Zak strolled up and straddled the bench. "Did you and my sister enjoy today?"

Evan nodded.

"Do not be shy, Evan. I know you like her." He paused. "I think she likes you, too." He grinned. "Who did she sit with last night during most of the sing? I do not think she felt obligated because I was with Leah. I have not seen her talk to another Amish man as long as she has talked with you today."

"But, will she wait for me?"

"If you are her chosen, of course, Evan." Zak stood. "Now, I know Zeke is waiting for us. He wishes to get home so he can take the buggy and court Miriam Zook. He does not think I know, but he is my brother, my twin. I know."

Evan laughed and stood and the two of them strolled to the waiting buckboard. Daniel was already sitting up front with Zeke. Zak and Evan jumped into the back and Zeke snapped the reins to get the horse moving.

CHAPTER TWENTY-SIX ~ Growing

Monday, September 2 7:20 p.m.

Evan slid the meatloaf from the oven and stared at his first attempt. He'd followed Grandma Addie's recipe. He shrugged and picked up the special sauce she always put on the top. Slathering it across the top, Evan scraped the last of it from the bowl and then put the meatloaf back in the oven for the five minutes she had scribbled at the bottom of the recipe.

Now for the mashed potatoes, he thought and took the lid off the pot of cut up potatoes. *Hm? Would Dad like mashed or just regular boiled potatoes?* Evan poured the water off and decided if his dad wanted mashed, he could do so with a fork.

Gazing through the glass top, Evan watched the two cobs of corn bob around in the boiling water.

I think Grandma turned off the heat and just let them sit in the hot water, Evan thought and turned the gas off under the pot.

A car pulled into the driveway. Evan waited; it should be his father.

"I'm home," Nathan yelled as he opened the back door and slipped off his shoes. "With it being Labor Day, nobody came to the office and I was able to get a lot of work done." He paused. "What do I smell? Did you cook?" He strolled into the kitchen.

"I made a meatloaf, boiled potatoes and corn on the cob," Evan said. "I'm hoping it tastes okay. I thought we could take a break from constantly eating out at the various restaurants in town." He paused. "I do like going to the 5/20 Country Kitchen, but..." He paused. "Do we always want to eat out the rest of our lives?"

"Interesting question, Evan," Nathan replied. "The rest of our lives. Hm? I graduated from high school, college, got married, had a child, lost a wife and now am working in a little town in the middle of nowhere." He gazed at Evan. "I had a life. I've lived."

"Are you starting the 'go-back-to-school' discussion, again?"

"No," Nathan replied. "What I'm telling you, I lived. You? You're wanting to play Amish... all because of a girl."

Evan opened his mouth to talk. Nathan held up a hand.

"Don't even try, Evan," Nathan said. "You want to get an Amish girl to like you, but you don't even know how to court her." He paused. "How exciting, Evan, riding on the handlebars of your bicycle."

Evan glared at his father.

Nathan thumped at Evan's temple. "Think. Do you have a buggy? Any man who wants to court a young lady knows he has to have the proper set of wheels."

"I have a 1967 red Nova convertible," Evan blurted.

"I'm sure all the Amish girls swoon when you spin tires in their fathers' driveways."

Nathan watched Evan, knowing his son was thinking, mulling over the words. He broke the silence.

"Tomorrow, before you do anything, go visit Zak and make arrangements to get yourself a nice horse and a proper buggy. You want to be Amish, then be Amish. As much as you don't want to do it, sell Grandma Addie's car."

"I can't do that, Dad," Evan said. "I mean, sell the car. I'm giving the car to you. I've already told Bishop Zwyer that fact."

"Me? Why?"

"Because, as Amish, I can't have a car. This is my grandmother's car and I'm not about to have some stranger taking possession of that classic." He took the keys from his pocket and flipped them through the air to his father. "The car is yours, Dad. We can do the legal transfer down the road."

Nathan sat, holding the keys in hand, staring at them. "Thank you," he mumbled, a tear coming to the edge of his eye. "My father loved this car." He inhaled deeply. "At times I thought he loved it more than me." He sighed. "He didn't. Mom assured me that he always put me first, but I didn't see it." He gazed up at Evan. "I was jealous of this car, this inanimate object that I thought took his love of me away."

Evan sat down and stared at his father. "We have a lot of healing to do, yet."

Nathan nodded. "Hm? Do I smell something burning?"

"The meatloaf!" Evan jumped up, grabbed potholders and pulled the dish from the oven. "I think we saved it." He placed the dish on top of the stove. "Supper's ready."

Evan placed a cob of corn on each plate. Nathan scooped some potatoes from the pot, mashed them with his fork, then slathered butter on both the corn and potatoes. Evan sliced the meatloaf, noting a small edge of burn on the bottom. HE offered a slice to his father and then placed a slice on his plate. They went into the dining room. Nathan cut a slice of meatloaf and lifted it to his mouth.

"Wait, Dad," Evan said and bowed his head.

Heavenly Father, we thank you for the food we are about to eat. Let it nourish both our body and soul. We thank you for a beautiful day. Heal our heavy hearts and lift our spirits as we grow and learn to understand one another. In Jesus name, Amen.

Nathan frowned. "When did you learn to pray?"

Evan smiled. "Grandma Addie had me in church the day after you left. She snookered me. I tried to pass and she said we could talk about over the mid-day meal when we got back from church."

Nathan nodded, smiling, remembering. "Yes, my mother knew how to manipulate. I don't even think my father knew it." He gazed at Evan's ears.

"What are you looking at?"

"I figured by the time I came back to take you home; your earlobes would be dangling around your kneecaps." He frowned. "Hm? Did she ever pull on them?"

"Once or twice," Evan said, rubbing his right ear. "She gets her way." He stabbed a piece of meatloaf. "I miss Grandma Addie."

"As do I," Nathan replied.

# # #

Tuesday, September 3   8:15 a.m.

Evan rode his bicycle into the E & S parking lot then around to back loading dock. He placed the bicycle against the wall then raced into the back of the building hoping to find Zak.

Mark and Zak were talking over in the corner.

"Zak!" Evan called. "Can we talk?"

"Aye," Zak said and ambled across the loading dock to Evan. "What is the question?"

"Why do you think it is a question?" Evan frowned.

Zak grinned. "It is always a question."

"Can you help me buy a horse and a buggy?"

"A what?" Zak exclaimed. "Why do you need a horse and buggy?"

Evan cocked an eyebrow. "I am becoming Amish. Do you expect me drive my car? Or worse, ride my bicycle until I die?"

Zak laughed. "We could make you a bicycle for two..." He paused and grinned evilly. "That way you could court."

Evan took a deep breath. "You want me to court your sister but you won't help me pick a horse and buggy?"

"Who said I would not help?" He put an arm over Evan's shoulder. "Come with me and let us talk with Mr. Wyse and see if I can be off a little on Friday so we can go to the horse auction."

"Really?" Evan followed.

"When I get off this afternoon, join me and we will go get your buggy." He stopped and gazed at Evan. "You do know there are rules of what is allowed and not allowed with our buggies." He shrugged. "We are..." He grimaced. "More relaxed. We are allowed a nice black buggy which can be enclosed for foul weather, like rain, snow, or winter."

Evan nodded. "That is good."

Zak snickered. "Rachel will like it."

"Maybe I should buy two horses?"

"If you wish, Evan. Maybe even three. A couple for the buggy and one for working the fields." He hesitated. "Four. Definitely four horses. Two of each."

Zeke came up behind them.

"Why are you here so early?" Zak asked.

"Mama wanted to do some shopping, so I drove her in. I am only about half an hour early. What are you talking about?"

"Evan wants to buy some horses and get a buggy. I am going to ask for Thursday off to help him at the horse auction."

"I can help, too," Zeke said. "Maybe we both can get away."

"Good morning, Evan," Ezra Wyse said. "Why are you two standing here doing nothing? Do I pay you for that?"

"No, sir," Zeke said. "I came in early." He pointed to the clock.

"Fine." Ezra gazed at Zak. "Your excuse?"

"I am coming to ask you if I can have Friday off for a little while to help Evan buy some horses."

Ezra gazed at Evan with a frown. "You don't work here and come in and take my best hired help away?" He smiled. "The auction starts at a little after noon." He grimaced, swiping his hand across his lips and chin. He gazed at the twins. "Both of you?" He eyed Zeke who nodded, along with Zak. "For basically most of the afternoon?"

The twins nodded, again.

"Tell you what," Ezra began. "Both of you come in early that day to help Mark with deliveries and stocking the shelves." He turned to Evan. "And, you, Evan. You also come in to help the twins. At noon, all three of you disappear. Mark can help with checkout and my eldest grandson has been wanting to work so I can throw him into the mix. He can take the groceries to the car for those who want the help." He shook his head. "Fine, you both have Friday afternoon off. Good to see you, Evan. How much longer at the theater?"

"I'm told our last performance will be Thanksgiving weekend."

Ezra smiled. "It will be good to get you back in the store, again."

He walked off mumbling and Evan was sure he heard him fighting with himself as to why he was allowing this on a Friday.

Evan headed back to the dock with the twins.

"I will see you this afternoon," Evan said.

"I get off at two," Zak said. "Remember?"

Evan nodded. "I will be here."

CHAPTER TWENTY-SEVEN ~ The Horse and Buggy

Tuesday, September 3 2:15 p.m.

"Exactly what do I need to do, Zak?" Evan asked as they rode to the buggy shop.

"Just sit back, listen, learn, and pay," Zak said with a grin. "I will make sure you get a good buggy according the *Ordnung* rules of our community."

"How much will this cost?"

"Does it matter? You want a buggy. Yes?"

Evan shrugged. *Zak is right*, he thought. *I have the money; I will buy it and maybe this weekend I can take Rachel to the sing.*

"I know what you are thinking, Evan," Zak said. "It will not be. You will need to train your horse before you can go courting."

Evan tried not to blush but felt the heat come to his cheeks.

Zak slowed and pulled up beside a non-descriptive building. He placed his bicycle to the side of the building and motioned for Evan to follow.

"In ten minutes, you will be the owner of a new buggy," Zak said and opened the door of the building.

Evan frowned. "Ten minutes?"

Zak nodded and was greeted by an older gentleman, Amish by the long, gray beard.

"Ah, Mr. Graber," the man said. "What brings you to my establishment?" He rolled his hands together. "Another buggy?" He smiled. "Are the twins fighting for the family buggy to court?"

Zak shook his head. "Nay, Mr. Wagler. I am here to help my friend purchase his first buggy."

"Aaron Wagler, at your service," the older gentleman said. "You are?"

"Evan Kurtz."

"Kurtz?" He gazed at Zak. "Not the..."

Zak nodded. "Yes. It was his great-grandfather. Evan and the bishop have talked and the elders have agreed. Zak wishes to be Amish." He paused. "The sins of the father are not borne by the offspring."

Aaron Wagler nodded. "Now, to the buggy." He paused. "Graber. Graber. Yes, New Order." He strolled across the open area of the barn-like structure. "Here is a perfect New Order buggy. Standard. No frills. All-weather." He droned on.

Evan listened, amazed the man sounded just like a used-car salesman. He knew his buggies.

"How much?" Zak asked.

"You take it, only six. I deliver, make it six-five."

Evan thought six hundred was quite reasonable.

"Have the buggy delivered to the Kurtz farm to the east. You know where?"

Aaron Wagler nodded. "The Adeline Kurtz farm?"

Zak nodded then turned to Zak. "Pay the man. You just got your first buggy for a mere six thousand five hundred dollars."

Evan tried not to show shock but knew it registered on his face.

"It is a fair price, Evan. Mr. Wagler does honest work and delivers a well-built buggy. It will last for years with proper care." He paused. "I will teach you how to care for it. How to do this is taught to us as small boys." He grinned. "You will be my son I may never have. I will teach you how to be an Amish man."

"Do you take a check?" Evan asked.

"Yes. I may be Amish but I have learned for business to take cash, check, and credit cards."

"When will you deliver?" Evan asked.

"It will be delivered tomorrow morning. Is that acceptable?"

Evan nodded and handed Aaron Wagler the check. "Paid in full."

"Thank you, Evan Kurtz," Aaron Wagler said and shook hands. "It was nice doing business with you and hope to see you, again."

"Perhaps," Evan replied and followed Zak out of the building.

"Now, on Friday, we will get you the horses you need." He paused. "Again, I will teach you how to break the horse, train the horse, bridled and hook the horse to the buggy." Zak frowned. "I did not realize being a father involved so much work."

They laughed.

# # #

Friday, September 6 Noon

Evan sat on the back dock of E & S Grocery. He kicked his legs nervously, waiting for Zak.

Today, I will get horses and become even more Amish, he thought.

His mind wandered to the buggy that arrived on Wednesday. His dad was a bit concerned, but acknowledged the change, especially the car. Evan reminisced his giving the car to his father, watching him sitting behind the steering wheel, hands lightly gliding over its edges.

"You ready?" Zak asked, coming onto the dock.

Evan slipped down to the ground. "Ready."

"We can walk from here," Zak said and pointed to the north. He headed out. Evan followed.

"Is Zak not coming?" Evan asked.

"Nay. He decided to stay and work; it is a busy today."

#

Zak led Evan to the office where they registered and received their auction buyer number.

"Follow me." Zak finagled his way toward the fence, all the while motioning for Evan to keep up.

Zak stood by the fence, arms resting on the top rail. "Great view."

Evan sidled up beside him. "I guess," he said. "Big areana."

"Let the horses come," Zak whispered then leaned in toward Evan. "We will be buying you horses; at least two, maybe more."

"That's a nice one," Evan said, pointing at the buckskin-colored horse with snow-white mane and tail.

Zak shook his head. "Not that one," he said and leaned in to whisper. "Notice the way it favors the right back leg? Not really a limp, but there is or was some damage. Nay, you want a good horse. There will be more." He grinned at Evan.

Evan watched the horses continue to pass, every so often Zak would indicate an interest and Evan would bid. He finally got one, another male buckskin colored horse with a white mane. Evan thought it was even prettier than the first one.

"Next are the ponies," Zak said. "We can watch, but I do not think you will want a pony."

Evan shrugged. "One never knows."

After three ponies, the auctioneer explained the two ponies coming out were twins. They would be sold together, then separately, depending on which way paid the most.

Evan's eyes widened. He fell in love with the two ponies.

"I want them," Evan whispered. "I don't care the cost."

Zak nodded. "They are fine looking ponies, Evan. Are you sure you want them?"

Evan nodded. "I have a purpose." He grinned.

"As you wish," Zak said and raised Evan's hand to get him into the bidding.

Evan got the bid for the twins. Then the auctioneer explained, they would be sold separately, bidding on one pony with the other going for the same price.

Evan listened to the amount increase and he kept track of the figure, doubling it so he knew what the final price would be. He lifted his card and entered the bidding. Evan was not about to lose the ponies.

At one thousand over the original price, he was the proud owner of the twin ponies. He paid more than he should have, but he wanted them and that was all that mattered. He had a plan.

A few more ponies were shown and bought.

Zak leaned in. "Now, we have the work horses. You want to have at least two."

The first horse out was a Belgium. Zak nudged Evan.

"Bid," he whispered. "You want this one."

Evan continued to bid, raising the price. Slowly, other bidders dropped out until there was only him and a gentleman on the other side of the arena.

"How high do I go?" Evan asked as he again raised the bid.

"Until you own that beautiful horse." Zak pointed at the horse. "Look at that stance, those feet. A perfect specimen of a Belgium. I hope we can get a match for it. This is a male; perhaps a female."

The gentleman on the other side of the arena threw up his hands in disgust and stepped away.

"You just got your first working horse. A male. Now we will look for a female." He grinned. "If they breed, you will have more horses."

Two horses later, another Belgium strode into the arena.

"Get this one," Zak whispered. "She is a beauty. Look at those shoulders and flanks. She will be a good breeder and worker."

"I just realized," Evan started. "I have bought five horses and I have no way to get them home."

Zak nodded. "Aye, but I know one of those who work here and he will make a deal to bring your horses to the farm." He shrugged. "Of course, there will be a fee."

Evan grinned "Of course." He frowned, wondering what his father would think and say.

"I will race you to the farm," Zak said. "We need to make sure the barn is ready to accept your horses and that you have a proper paddock." He dashed toward the E & S Grocery.

"To be fair, we need to start at the store," Evan said. "Not here."

Zak stopped and waited for Evan to catch up. "You are right." He placed an arm over Evan's shoulder. "I am enjoying this."

CHAPTER TWENTY-EIGHT ~ Finals

Monday, October 28 3:30 p.m.

The knock on the door startled Evan. He'd not heard anyone pull in the driveway. He was gazing at the paper in his hand; his GED with a ninety-eight per cent. He'd passed. He rushed to the back door.

Rachel and her youngest sister, Elizabeth, stood there.

"Why are you here?" Evan asked.

"I wondered if I could use your phone to call my grandfather in Centertown. I want him to come to the last performance this Saturday."

Evan glanced at Elizabeth.

"She is my chaperon. I must not enter the house alone with you."

Evan opened the door. "Come in. The phone is yours to use. There is one in the kitchen, or one in the living room." He paused. "I would recommend the living room one since we... I mean, you, can sit and talk in comfort. I will wait in the kitchen."

"Nay, Evan," Rachel said. "You may stay in the room."

Evan grinned. "I will sit on the front porch," he said. "That way nobody can say anything. When you finish, you and Elizabeth can join me on the porch for all to see."

Rachel took off her shoes, motioning for Elizabeth to do the same.

"You don't need to do that," Evan said.

"If you do, I do," Rachel said.

Evan led them through the house to the living room and pointed to the phone.

"I will be outside," Evan said and started for the front door.

"Nay, Evan," Rachel said. "It is the end of October and the air is cool. You will remain inside. Elizabeth is with us. None will talk."

"Would you like something to drink, Elizabeth?" Evan asked. "I have some peach-mango drink. Does that sound good?"

Elizabeth nodded. "Very good. I like peach."

"Three glasses of peach-mango coming right up," Evan said and disappeared into the kitchen.

Rachel dialed the office number of the Yoder Farm.

"Yoder U-Pick," Mary said, answering the phone. Her voice was slow and with an edge of cracking.

"Hi, Aunt Mary," Rachel said. "I would like to talk with Grandpa Daniel Yoder."

"I will get him. He is with a customer."

The sound of a 'thunk' let Rachel know Aunt Mary had dropped the phone's handset onto the table. She waited.

"This is Daniel Yoder," Daniel said. "How may I help you?"

"This is Rachel, Grandpa. I wanted to let you know that this Saturday night is the final production of the play. I was hoping you and Grandma could make it."

"Final show?" He frowned. "I thought you said the play would go until near Thanksgiving."

"Mr. Beiler informed us the new play is ready and our last performance will be this coming Saturday. Can you come?"

"Yes, Rachel, we will be there. Is all well?"

"Yes, Grandpa."

"Tell your mother we will come on Thursday."

"I will tell her. Goodbye, Grandpa."

Rachel hung up the phone then took a sip of the peach-mango drink.

"This is good," she said.

"You have not been to my house for quite some time," Evan said. "I would like to show you something out in the barn."

"The barn?" Elizabeth asked. "You have new calves?"

"No," Evan said. He motioned for the two girls to follow. "You will see when we get out there."

The three of them put on their shoes and jackets and headed out to the barn.

Evan opened the door of the barn and guided Rachel and Elizabeth to the stalls holding the horses.

"Zak helped me to buy these horses and I've been learning how to take care of them." He moved to a particular stall. "In here is what I wanted you to see."

Elizabeth climbed up on the gate to look into the stall.

"Ponies!" she exclaimed. "They are beautiful."

"I bought these twin ponies. Zak wasn't sure about it, but I wanted them for a particular reason."

Rachel frowned as she reached out to pet the muzzle.

"They are beautiful, Evan. Both females?"

Evan nodded. "Elizabeth, you can feed them an apple, if you wish."

Elizabeth grabbed a handful of apples and once more mounted the fence to reach into the pen.

Evan led Rachel to the side, away from Elizabeth, but still in sight.

Evan took Rachel's hands in his. "I got these ponies for you, Rachel."

"For me?" Rachel frowned.

"I think you know I love you, Rachel." He watched her for any reaction, but felt her hands clench slightly.

"I know," Rachel whispered. "I love you, too."

"In the *Englische* world, when a boy is in love with a girl, and he wants to show his intentions, he gives her an engagement ring. Amish do not wear jewelry." He paused. "This is awkward. Rachel, I want you to wait for me. I am finishing up my Amish training and will be baptized in the spring. At that time, I want to marry you." Again, he paused. "I don't want you dating any other Amish boy... or *Englische* boy, either."

Rachel gazed over at her sister who was occupied with the ponies.

"I will wait, Evan," she said and leaned up to give him a kiss on the cheek. "Now, as to these ponies. Have you named them?"

"Not really," Evan mumbled. "I just call them 'girl' and they come."

"I have the perfect names," Rachel said, as she moved to the stall with the ponies. "This one, see the small mark here?" She pointed. "This one will be called Jezebel." She grinned. "The other will be named Beauty."

Evan frowned. "Strange names."

"Not really," Rachel said. My great-grandfather, Noah Yoder bought a pony at this auction. He named it Beauty." She grinned. "The pony had a twin which my great-uncle who was adopted and lives in Bird-in-Hand, Pennsylvania bought the other. He named her Jezebel. It was my grandfather who discovered the story."

"Beauty and Jezebel are their names," Evan said.

"You will keep the ponies here," Rachel said. "Papa would not allow me to accept such a gift, even from one who is becoming Amish."

"A gift?" Elizabeth echoed.

"None of your business. You did not hear anything." Rachel glared at her young sibling. "Am I understood?"

"Yes, Rachel," Elizabeth said.

"Since this is the last Saturday of the play, we can start to attend the sings, again." Rachel paused. "Of course..." She gazed at the buggy. "You could come on Sunday to pick me up."

Evan smiled and felt his chest swell.

"I will," he whispered.

# # #

Tuesday, October 29 2 p.m.

"You are doing well, Evan Kurtz," Bishop Zwyer said, lifting the cookie to his mouth. He munched.

"*denki*, (thank you)" Evan replied.

Bishop Zwyer smiled. "And, you are learning the language. That is good. I noticed on Sunday that you were singing *O Gott, Vader* and *Das Loblied*."

Evan nodded. "I found my great-grandfather's *Ausbund* and learned the songs. Maybe I should ask, do you sing every song in the book?"

Bishop Zwyer leaned back and sipped his lemonade. Evan could see him thinking. He watched as Bishop Zwyer mentally went through the songs of the *Ausbund*.

"Yes," Bishop Zwyer said. "We sing each one, some more than others. Does that satisfy the question?"

"The Amish know all the songs of the *Ausbund*?" Evan asked.

Bishop Zwyer nodded. "We know probably sixty to seventy of the songs. If you listen, the *Vorsänger* will announce the song number. Remember it and you can seek it in your great-grandfather's *Ausbund*." He smiled. "I am truly amazed your great-grandfather kept the *Ausbund* after he was ex-communicated from the church."

"I was going through some of Grandma Addie's things and found it. Perhaps he saved it, perhaps Eliza saved it." He shrugged. "It does not matter to me. I have it and that is what is important."

"Bring it with you on Sundays and when the *Vorsänger* announces the hymn number, you can look it up and join in the fellowship of song."

Evan nodded.

"Do you have any questions?" Bishop Zwyer eased back into the chair, all the while watching Evan, knowing there would questions.

"How does an Amish boy marry?"

"I knew you would be asking." The older man snickered. "First, you get the attention of a young girl. If she likes you, then you can ask to court her. If she wishes, you will court. After a proper amount of time, they decide to marry and it is announced. Usually, that would be in the spring before planting, or in the fall, after the harvest." Bishop Zwyer studied Evan. "You have one you wish to court?"

"I wish to marry Rachel Graber," Evan blurted.

"Oh. Marry? Do you not think you should court her first?"

"I am taking her to church on Sunday morning," Evan said.

Bishop Zwyer nodded, knowingly. "I would think it about time. The two of you are together constantly on Sunday."

"The play is coming to an end and then we can, once again, join together at the sings."

Again, Bishop Zwyer nodded.

"Rachel is not baptized. Until she is, she cannot marry." He paused. "She can become *Englische* if she wishes." He cocked an eye at Evan, searching for a reaction. "If she did that, would you still want to be Amish?"

"Rachel is Amish. She will remain Amish. I want to become Amish for two reasons. Yes, Rachel is one reason, but the other is more important. It is the lifestyle. The Amish are a simple people. I am tired of the *Englische* rat-race world."

"I think you are finished with your learning," Bishop Zwyer said. "The next step is to baptized. It is getting late in the season, the water is beginning to chill, but if you wish, we can baptize in the next few days. Otherwise, next spring or summer."

The older man watched Evan.

"I was thinking next spring," Evan started. "But I see no reason to delay. When can I get baptized?"

Bishop Zwyer nodded. "We have church at the Wagler farm. They have a nice pond we can use." He shivered. "I do hope the water is still somewhat warm."

"May my father attend?" Evan asked.

"If he wishes," Bishop Zwyer replied. "I will see if any others wish to be baptized." He stood.

Evan realized the meeting was over. He stood. "*gut'n daag.* (good day)"

Bishop Zwyer smiled. "*gut'n daag,* (good day) Evan Kurtz."

# # #

Saturday, November 2 6:30 p.m.

Evan and Rachel sat on the ladder. The lights were off and they held hands under the shimmering fabric.

The light turned on and the music began. Rachel waited and then began to sing. Again, Evan joined in on the second verse.

This is the last time, Evan thought. *The last show.*

Evan stared out at the audience. He'd only done that a few times, preferring to stare off into the dark distance and ignore them. He saw his father at one table. He sighed.

I wish Grandma Addie was here for tonight and especially for tomorrow, he thought.

At the table next to his father, a group of six Amish sat. He recognized them immediately: Jeremiah, Bethany, Ezekiel, and Isaac Graber. Two older people also were at the table. Daniel and Martha Yoder.

Before Evan realized, the last song was ringing through the audience.

The play was over. Done.

"Tomorrow, I get baptized," Evan said as he gazed at Rachel while taking their bows.

"I know," Rachel whispered. "You are picking me up tomorrow?"

Evan nodded. "Indeed, I am."

"I heard Liam Beiler will be baptized, also."

"At least I won't be alone," Evan said with a smile.

"No, you will not be alone," Rachel repeated.

Nathan jumped on stage. "Congratulations, Evan. A play well done over the weeks. What is your ambition now?"

"To be a good Amish dairy farmer," Evan replied.

"So, you're going to go through with the baptism tomorrow?"

"Yes, Dad." He stared at his father, eye-to-eye. "Tomorrow I will be Amish and a member of the Amish community."

"If that is what you wish," Nathan said, his voice filled with resignation. "Will you be removing the electricity from the house?"

"I asked Bishop Zwyer if I needed to do that. He said I could leave it in until you moved out."

"Move out?" Nathan asked, his eyes wide. "I am to move out?"

"I plan to marry, Dad," Evan said. "If you wish to live with us, that is fine, but it will be an Amish lifestyle."

"Married, eh?" Nathan glanced over at Rachel who spoke with her family.

Evan nodded.

"I may have to consider an apartment." He paused. "One with a garage for the car." He grinned. "I'm not about to have it sit outside in the weather."

Evan grinned. "Well, Dad, we could consider an *Englische* version of a *Dawdi* Haus."

Nathan frowned.

"A small place for you to live and still be a part of the family, but at the same time, have your own place. Of course, it would have electricity and plumbing, plus you could keep the car in the garage." Evan paused. "Or, I can use the garage for the buggy and build you a small garage by the *Dawdi Haus*."

Nathan stuck out a hand. "Shake, son. This is something I can deal with. My own place with my grandchildren next door. What man can resist that offer?"

Evan excused himself from his father and walked over to Rachel.

"I will see you tomorrow morning for church," Evan said.

"Yes," Rachel replied. "Be sure to bring a change of clothes. You do not want to be in wet clothes all day."

Evan nodded.

"Ah, young Evan Kurtz," Daniel Yoder said. "I heard you bought a set of twin ponies and Rachel named them Beauty and Jezebel."

Evan nodded.

"May I see them tomorrow?" Daniel asked.

"Yes, sir," Evan replied. "Zak said they are American Saddlebreds. They are a beautiful pure black."

"I will see you tomorrow at church," Daniel said. "We will eat and then, if you would, show me these ponies."

Evan nodded. "I will see you tomorrow morning, Rachel." He excused himself and left.

# # #

Sunday, November 3 8:20 a.m.

Evan steered the buggy into the Graber driveway. Rachel stepped from the house and headed down the steps toward him. Elizabeth walked with her.

The chaperon, Evan thought. Zeke followed. Evan frowned.

Jumping from the buggy, Evan walked with Rachel to the opposite side and helped Elizabeth into the back of the buggy and then Rachel into the front seat of the buggy.

Zeke walked with Evan to the other side of the buggy. He leaned in. "You are becoming Amish today. This is my sister. She seems to have picked you." He paused and took a deep breath. "Treat her with the proper respect."

Evan placed a hand on Zeke's right shoulder. "I respect your sister. She has chosen me. I have chosen her. I think of you and Zak as brothers I never had. I..."

Zeke nodded. "See you at church. I need to pick up Miriam Zook." He walked away to a waiting buggy.

Evan jumped into the buggy and snapped the reins.

"What did you name this horse?" Rachel asked, all the while staring forward.

"His name is Merlin," Evan said. "He is a great horse. Zak and I had him broken and ready for the buggy on the first day. It was like magic."

Soon they were pulling into the Wagler driveway. Other buggies were there and young Amos Wagler was working to put the horses to pasture and line up the buggies.

Evan helped Rachel from the buggy and then assisted young Elizabeth as she jumped out. She waved at friends and disappeared.

Bishop Zwyer stepped on the porch, gazing about. He waved at a young man.

"Liam Beiler!" he yelled.

He gazed at Evan and Rachel. "Come!" he ordered.

Liam ran to the porch. Evan and Rachel walked to the porch.

"Please, come in. We will discuss the process of the baptisms." Bishop Zwyer turned and entered the house.

Evan frowned as Rachel continued into the house.

Bishop Zwyer sat and motioned for them to sit.

"With three baptisms, I will make it Rachel first, Liam next, and finally, our newest member, Evan."

Evan frowned and gazed at Rachel. "You are being baptized?"

Rachel nodded. "It is time." She leaned in and whispered. "If the man I wish to marry is baptized, I must also be baptized to marry him." She shrugged. "It is the Amish way."

Bishop Zwyer asked them the last few questions of their confirmation, affirming they truly were ready to join the church.

"Let us begin church," Bishop Zwyer said and led the group out of the house.

Nathan drove into the driveway. Everyone stared at the bright red vehicle. He pulled it to the side and jumped out.

Evan waved and Nathan joined his son as the group came down the steps of the porch.

"I probably should have asked," Nathan said. "How long will this event take?"

"With the meal, we should be finished by two this afternoon," Evan replied and guided his father to a bench to sit beside him.

Nathan's eyes widened. "Two?" He hesitated. "This afternoon?"

"Trust me, Dad. The food is worth it."

Nathan nodded and shrugged. "Okay."

# # #

"Mr. Kurtz," Daniel Yoder said as he approached. "Are you available to show me these ponies you purchased?"

"Aye, Mr. Yoder," Evan said. "We have two modes of transportation. We can use my buggy, or my dad can drive us in his car."

Daniel gazed over at the red Nova. "Much too flashy for an old Amish man," Daniel said. "We can take the buggy, but to get the horse and buggy, hitch it..." Once more he gazed at the Nova. "Perhaps the car is a better choice." He grinned and walked toward the car.

"Dad? Can you drive us to the farm?" Evan asked.

"Certainly," Nathan replied and excused himself from the group.

"It's beautiful day, Mr. Yoder," Nathan said as he approached the car. "Would you like the top down?"

Daniel placed a hand atop his hat. "That would be nice, I think." He grinned. "It has been a long time since I rode in a convertible since my friend, Jason, finally grew up and started buying adult vehicles."

Nathan put the top down and carefully pulled out of the Wagler driveway and made the trip to the farm in mere minutes.

"This way, Mr. Yoder," Evan said, leading the two men toward the barn. "The ponies are out in the paddock but they will come into the barn when I call." He opened the barn door.

"Jezebel! Beauty!" Evan called.

Two black ponies trotted into the barn stall.

Daniel leaned against the gate and stroked the muzzle of Beauty. "She does remind me of my father's horse." He nodded and stroked the muzzle of Jezebel. "Yes. If I did not know better, I would swear they are the off-spring." He turned to Evan. "Did I understand correctly? You gave these ponies to my granddaughter, Rachel?"

Evan nodded. "Sort of a promise from me to her that I love her and want to marry her."

Daniel grinned. "You *Englische* need to promise with worldly things. We Amish speak with our hearts and words. If she has chosen you..." He shrugged. "There will be none other."

"I know, Mr. Yoder. I love your granddaughter and I bought these for her... and only her."

"Has she mentioned when... I mean, if she wishes to marry?" Daniel stroked the mane on Beauty. Jezebel nuzzled his hand for attention.

Evan shrugged. "We mentioned it and I think we were going to wait until next spring. It seems a little late."

"Nonsense," Daniel blurted. "If you wish to marry; then marry."

"I will be taking Rachel home. I will ask her."

"If I know my granddaughter, do not force her." Daniel smiled. "Now, I should be headed back so I can get a ride to Centertown."

"If... I mean, when we marry, Mr. Yoder, you will be in attendance?"

Daniel nodded. "Evan Kurtz, you are a good man. She has chosen well. I will be at the wedding."

# # #

Evan glanced back at Elizabeth who sat quietly as they rode back to the Graber farm in the buggy.

"I spoke with your grandfather," Evan said. "He liked the ponies."

Rachel nodded. "He spoke with me, also."

"Oh?" Evan raised a questioning eyebrow.

"I was thinking of a spring wedding, if you wanted to marry me," Rachel said.

"Marriage?" Elizabeth squealed.

"Hush, Elizabeth," Rachel said. "You are a chaperon. You hear nothing." Rachel turned and glared at her younger sister. "Am I understood?"

"Is it too late to marry this year?" Evan asked.

Rachel shook her head. "Nay. We could marry the first weekend in December, if you wished. Or, we could wait until spring."

Evan took a deep breath. "I would marry you tomorrow if you wished."

"I would prefer to wait for spring. The trees will be in bloom and..."

"I can wait," Evan said.

"Darn!" Elizabeth muttered.

CHAPTER TWENTY-NINE ~ End of the Year

Monday, November 4 7:45 a.m.

Evan walked with Zak into E & S Grocery.

"Guess I should go speak with Mr. Wyse to make sure he still wants me to work here," Evan said.

"Do not worry, Evan," Zak replied. "He told me Friday to make sure you came in today." He grinned. "Mr. Wyse is waiting for you."

Evan strolled the store to the front, not seeing Mr. Wyse. Seeing Mary, he asked. She pointed at the office. Evan hustled up the steps and knocked on the door.

"Come in," Ezra Wyse replied.

"Reporting for work," Evan said, stepping into the office.

Ezra stood and shook hands. "I'm sorry about your grandmother. Adeline was a wonderful woman; a true blessing to this community."

"Thank you," Evan replied.

Ezra sat and picked up a pencil. "So, you're ready to come back to work. Did you enjoy your time at the theater?" He gazed at Evan, noting the new Amish look. He frowned.

"I am now Amish," Evan said. "I was baptized into the church yesterday. I have the start of a dairy farm. I plan to be a dairy farmer like my great-grandfather was."

Ezra frowned. "Do you plan to continue to work here?"

"At least until the end of the year, if that is okay. I can only work part-time." He shrugged. "I have a barn full of cows and horses and they need my attention. I milk the cows in the morning, feed and water them and the horses." He paused. "Still, there is more for me to do and the days are getting shorter and I don't work by lantern in the barn at night."

Ezra nodded. "How about coming in at ten in the morning and working until two in the afternoon. That way you can get your farm chores done, work here, and get home to finish the remainder of chores?"

"We could try that," Evan said. "At least until the end of the year."

"What will you do next year?" Ezra asked.

"I plan to buy more dairy cows in the next week or two," Evan said. "I hope to have at least thirty by spring."

Ezra nodded. "I think you will need a source of income until you are a full-fledged dairy farm." He gazed about the room. "Working at this store will give you the extra income you might need."

"Actually, Mr. Wyse, I received a tidy inheritance from Grandma Addie. I do not actually need to work, but I do not want to just sit at home all day."

Ezra nodded. "I see." He paused. "So, I have you until the end of the year." He stood and clapped his hands. "Okay. Let's get you down to Zak and I hope you remember most of what you learned before becoming a big theater star." He grinned and led Evan out of the office.

# # #

Wednesday, December 25, 2013 9:30 a.m.

The lingering scent of fried bacon filled the room. Breakfast was a memory as Nathan and Evan strolled into the living room.

"I am glad Bishop Zwyer allowed you to have the electricity on for me to celebrate Christmas one last time in my mother's home," Nathan said.

"Dad!" Evan exclaimed. "You will spend many Christmas's in this house over the next years. Of course, there will not be electricity, but, you will always be welcome here. Besides, when your grandchildren come along, will you be able to sit in your *Dawdi Haus* and be alone?"

Nathan grinned. "No, I guess not." He reached under the tree. "I had to think hard of what to get my son, an Amish man, for Christmas." He held out the narrow rectangular box wrapped in red. "I hope you like it."

Evan opened the package and lifted the lid on the box.

"Suspenders!" Evan yelled. "Wonderful!" He lifted the suspenders from the box. "An Amish man can never have too many suspenders."

Nathan gazed at the other two red packages under the tree. "I think you can guess what these other two presents are."

Evan laughed. "First, I want you to open your present." He reached under the tree and pulled a long tube out. "This is for you. I hope you like it."

Nathan ripped the shiny blue paper from the tube, frowning, wondering what it could be. Removing the metal screw cap, he pulled the rolled-up paper from the tube. Nathan opened it out and stared at the blueprint.

"A house?" Nathan asked and scrutinized Evan.

"Look closer," Evan said.

Nathan moved to the dining room table and spread the blueprint out for a better look.

"Two bedrooms. A bathroom." Nathan ran his fingers across the layout, checking each room. "A small kitchenette. A living room." He smiled. "A front porch? Really? A front porch with access to an attached garage?" He gazed up at Evan. "Where is this?"

"Outside, Dad," Evan replied. "I had the lumber company deliver the wood and store it in the bar where I knew you would not see it." He took a deep breath. "You will have your own house, a *Dawdi Haus,* by the end of the tomorrow, or pretty close to it."

"With electricity and running water?" Nathan asked.

"Of course, Dad," Evan replied. "You're *Englische* and I don't expect you to live the Amish lifestyle."

"Tomorrow?" Nathan repeated.

"I have the crew coming in at eight in the morning. The ladies will be making a lunchtime meal and the men will have the house up before you can count to ten."

"Who is doing the electricity and plumbing?"

"My Amish crew, Dad. Just because we don't use it, doesn't mean we don't know how to install it."

Nathan, again, turned his attention to the spread out blueprint.

"Hm? A thirty-by-thirty house with a fifteen-by-thirty attached garage. Rather large garage, isn't it, Evan?"

"I had the garage made large so you would have storage." He paused. "Like adding a freezer, toolbox... stuff like that."

Nathan nodded.

"Also, I considered solar but decided against it because I know you. Dad, you will be up practically all night working on a project. I figure you'd suck all the solar power out and be in the dark by nine at night." He laughed.

Nathan nodded. "You're right."

Again, he slid his fingers across the blueprints. "Can I make a couple of adjustments?"

"Changes?" Evan asked.

"If I can," Nathan said while nodding. "I would like to move the front door from the middle to about here." He pointed at second window in the kitchen area. "And, the roof ridge is from side to side versus front to back. I would like to add a dormer over the door area to drain the water away from the front steps. Can that be done?"

"Whatever you want, Dad. This is your Christmas present from me. I will tell the crew tomorrow and I am sure they can make the adjustments."

Nathan smiled. "The Amish are excellent carpenters. My new house will be great."

# # #

Thursday, December 26 8:15 a.m.

Nathan stood at the big window in the living room watching the line of Amish buggies and buckboards coming in the drive. Evan stood at the edge of the driveway directing the buggies to one side where Zak and his younger brother, Peter, unhitched the horses from the buggies after lining them up. A few feet beyond Evan was Zeke who directed the men in the buckboards to the location of the new *Dawdi Haus*. Rachel stood at the front door and helped the women bring in the food.

I guess I'd best get out there and see what I can do to help, Nathan said, noting the growing number of women in the house.

"Hi, Dad," Evan said. "The crew is here and assignments are about to begin."

Nathan frowned.

"This is like a barn raising," Evan said. "They will break into groups and start assembly.

A horn blasted and coming down the driveway was a small bulldozer with a backhoe attached. Tobias Snyder waved and drove the vehicle toward the men.

"Where do you want the foundation?" Tobias yelled at Evan.

The men parted and Evan pointed at the stakes in the ground indicating the foundation's outline.

"Let me at it," Tobias yelled over the noise of the bulldozer. "I'll have a hole dug in no time and they can start to build the foundation." He put the bulldozer in gear and moved to the first of the stakes.

Jeremiah Graber got the attention of the men as Tobias worked.

"We have walls for the house, garage, rafters, and joists to build. Four walls of the house, three for the garage. There is a few last minute adjustments, but we can incorporate them as we go. I need at least four to six men on each wall. Break into groups and we'll begin.

Bishop Zwyer moved forward. "Before we begin; a prayer."

Lord, keep our hands and minds dutiful to our work. Let no harm come to those who work here today. Bless this endeavor and may the Lord reside within this residence until the walls tumble of their own accord. Bless the hands that work not only on this residence, but also those who are preparing the food. In Jesus name, Amen.

Nathan mumbled 'Amen' with the others. He still wasn't sure about the religious aspect of his son's newfound Amish lifestyle. When he left home, and after the argument with his father, Nathan had allowed religion to be a word to be bandied about; not something to live. He saw the change in his son.

Perhaps I should attend the United Methodist Church of Shipshewana like I did when I was a kid, he thought, and sighed deeply. *Mom would like that and...* He let the thought dwindle away as Jeremiah Graber slapped him on the back.

"Join me, Mr. Kurtz," Jeremiah said. "We will begin the front wall with four others. I understand you want to move the front door to the left. Is that correct?"

Nathan nodded and followed Jeremiah.

# # #

Evan stood beside his father. The sun was beginning to touch the horizon.

"It is a good house," Evan said.

Nathan nodded. "I still can't believe there was nothing here this morning, and now, my house."

"Just a few finishing touches, and the *Dawdi Haus* will be ready for you to move into." Evan paused. "Do you like it?"

Nathan watched the last two men scramble from the roof. "Yes. It is the best Christmas present any father would love."

"The ladies have left us some food for our evening meal," Evan said. "When we finish, I will take care of the livestock; milk and feed them."

"Can I help?" Nathan asked. "Or, is there more in the barn I should not see?"

Evan laughed. "Nay, Dad. Nothing to hide. You can help. I spoke with Aaron Stoltz and I will be buying another ten milking cows from his after the first of the year. By next Christmas, I should have a nice herd of dairy cows and be ready to be a full-fledged dairy farmer."

"A married farmer," Nathan whispered. "Am I not correct?"

"Aye," Evan mumbled.

CHAPTER THIRTY ~ A Spring Wedding

Sunday, March 30, 2014 8:30 a.m.

Evan pulled the buggy into the Graber driveway. Rachel stood on the back porch with her younger sister, Elizabeth. They were waiting. In the distance, Evan saw Zeke and Zak headed out in separate buggies. Zak waved. Evan returned the wave.

Jeremiah Graber stepped onto the porch. "Come along, Bethany," he said. "We do not wish to be late for church today. It is announcement day."

Evan frowned. He remembered the day he approached Jeremiah to seek Rachel's hand. He wasn't sure of the proper Amish method, but decided to just 'go for it' and see what happened. Jeremiah surprised him as he remembered the incident.

"I had wondered how long before you came to ask for my daughter's hand," Jeremiah said. "You have been courting her all winter." His lips curled in an evil grin. "I think you have been courting her since last summer, too." He watched Evan squirm. "If my daughter has chosen you, I give you my blessing."

Evan sighed, remembering how relieved he felt at that moment.

Rachel and Elizabeth approached the buggy. Evan jumped down and helped Elizabeth into the back of the buggy. Then he assisted Rachel get in the front where she slid over to the opposite side. She smiled at Evan as he got up into the buggy.

"Today is a special day, Evan." She patted his hand. "Bishop Zwyer is announcing our marriage."

Evan gripped the reins and snapped them, easing Beauty and Jezebel into a trot.

#

Evan sat with Zak and Zeke at church, watching Rachel on the opposite side. He smiled.

Bishop Zwyer stepped forward and began his sermon, opening with a prayer. Forty minutes later, he finished.

"Today, I have four announcements for the community. Sarah Stoltz has chosen Joshua Yoder to marry. They have chosen Tuesday, April 8 as their wedding day."

Peter Stoltz, Sarah's father, stood. "I invite the community to share in their happy day."

"Also, Miriam Zook has chosen Ezekiel Graber. They have decided on a wedding Thursday, April 10."

Evan nudged Zeke in the ribs and whispered, "I did not know you were getting married."

Zeke grinned.

Adam Zook stood. "You are all invited to this joyous event. Please come."

"Next, Rachel Graber has chosen Evan Kurtz. They will be married on Thursday, April 17."

At that moment, Evan realized and thought, *Rachel is marrying me. Me, Evan Kurtz.*

Jeremiah Graber stood. "Join us at our farm. The whole community is invited."

"Finally, Leah Beiler has chosen Isaac Graber to marry on Tuesday, April 22."

Evan elbowed Zak who sat on the other side of him. "Why did you not say something?" he whispered.

Zak shrugged and grinned.

Amos Beiler stood. "Need it be repeated?" He paused. "Again? All are invited to the wedding."

A few snickers could be heard from the congregation.

"We have truly been blessed this coming month," Bishop Zwyer said. "We have four weddings." He took a deep breath. "I cannot remember a time with that many weddings. Let us pray." He bowed his head and a silent prayer ensued.

# # #

Thursday, April 17, 2014 8:30 a.m.

Evan pulled the buggy into the Graber driveway. Nathan sat beside him.

My son is getting married today, Nathan thought. *His mother, Barb, would be so proud of the young man he has grown to be.* He took a deep breath and sighed. *Not because of me.* He gazed to Heaven. *Thank you, Mom. You did what I couldn't. Love you. Miss you.*

"Did you say something?" Evan asked.

"No," Nathan replied. "I see Bishop Zwyer standing on the porch. Is he waving for you to get up there?"

Evan gazed at the porch. "I believe he is." He handed the reins to Nathan. "Take the buggy to Peter or Adam."

Nathan frowned.

Evan pointed at the two young boys. "Those are Rachel's younger brothers. They will unhitch the horses and make sure the buggy is off to the side and the horses are able to get food and water."

Nathan nodded as Evan jumped from the buggy and raced up the steps of the porch.

"Come inside, young Kurtz," Bishop Zwyer said. "We will get Rachel and I will talk with the two of you." He grinned. "Just to make sure you truly wish to get married."

As they walked through the kitchen, Evan noticed Daniel Yoder.

"*gut'n mariye* (good morning), Mr. Yoder," Evan said as he passed.

"*gut'n mariye* (good morning), Mr. Kurtz," Daniel replied. "You may call me Grandfather Daniel or Grandpa Yoder. We are almost family." Daniel grinned. "By the time we eat, we will be family." He reached out and grabbed Evan's hand. "Welcome to the family, Evan Kurtz. Rachel has chosen wisely."

"Thank you, Mr. Yo... I mean, Grandpa Yoder," Evan replied.

Rachel joined them and Bishop Zwyer ushered them into the main room where they talked.

Evan walked behind Rachel. He gazed at her blue dress; the color almost matched his blue shirt. *She is most beautiful woman*, he thought.

#

Evan sat with Rachel at the *Eck* (wedding) table. He was happy. He was married.

Nathan came to the table. "I'm not sure what to do at an Amish wedding," he said. "But, Mrs. Kurtz, welcome to the family." He reached across and hugged her. A tear ran down his cheek. "That was from me, Grandma Addie, and Barb, Evan's mother."

Rachel hugged Nathan back. "*denki*, (thank you) Dad," she whispered into his ear.

Nathan wiped his cheek and moved along, getting a plate of food and then finding a seat beside Jeremiah Graber.

"Being Amish has been a true blessing for my son," Nathan said. "I wasn't sure, but his Grandma Addie straightened him out during last summer before she passed." He took a deep breath. "Rachel has been by his side all this time. She is the perfect one for my son."

"I was not sure about your son, Mr. Kurtz," Jeremiah said. "He was *Englische,* but when he came to visit to buy the cows with your mother, I realized he was a young man to be reckoned with." He grinned. "My daughter seemed distant when other Amish boys showed an interest. Your son caught my daughter's heart and there was nothing I could do but to accept the fact she would marry him, *Englische* or Amish." He slapped Nathan on back. "I am glad he is Amish. A fine young man."

Daniel Yoder joined the two men. Martha was with him.

"You have a great son, Mr. Kurtz," Daniel said, grabbing the chicken leg. "I love my fried chicken." He bit into the meat and gave a soft sigh.

"Honestly, Daniel Yoder," Martha said. "I am amazed you haven't grown feathers and become a chicken yourself."

"We were discussing Evan," Daniel chastised. "Not me becoming a chicken." He pointed at the field. "If you look at the field, you will see Evan's twin horses; Beauty and Jezebel."

Martha's head snapped up to gaze out the field. "Twins? Beauty and Jezebel?" She giggled. "Where have I heard those names before?" She paused. "Oh, yes. Your father and my uncle in Bird-in-Hand."

Daniel nodded while Nathan frowned. Seeing the frown, Daniel felt obligated to explain.

Nathan laughed after the explanation. "I wondered where Evan had gotten those two names." He nodded. "Rachel named them." He turned to Daniel.

"How long will you be staying in Shipshewana, Mr. Yoder?" Nathan asked.

"We will be headed home tomorrow," Daniel said. "Our driver, Jason, my best friend from school, will pick us up after lunch in the afternoon."

"May I offer you accommodations at my place?" Nathan asked. "That way we could talk more and learn about each other."

"I do not think my granddaughter would enjoy the fact I am staying at the house on their wedding night."

"Oh, no!" Nathan said. "I have a... a..."

"*Dawdi Haus*," Jeremiah said. "Mr. Kurtz has his own fully electric home. Evan has made the Kurtz family home into a typical Amish home."

"Your offer is kind, Mr. Kurtz," Daniel said. "We will stay here tonight so our driver will know where to pick us up."

"It was an offer," Nathan said. "I understand."

Aaron and Mary Graber strolled to the table. "Hello, Papa," Aaron said to Jeremiah. "Have you seen Jacob? He was running with the other children."

"This is Nathan Kurtz," Jeremiah said. "Nathan, this is my eldest son, Aaron and his wife, Mary." Jeremiah pointed at a group of young boys chasing chickens. "I think Jacob is over there terrorizing my chickens with the other boys."

Aaron sighed. "I will get him." He left.

"How many grandchildren do you have," Nathan asked Jeremiah.

"Five at the current time," Jeremiah replied. "Now, with three more children married, I am sure there will be more." He grinned. "Are you ready to become a grandfather?"

Nathan sighed. "I hadn't considered that." He shrugged. "We talked about grandchildren when the *Dawdi Haus* was being built with the front porch." He took a deep breath. "But the reality is hitting now." He paused. "Me. A grandfather," he mumbled. "I think I like it."

CHAPTER THIRTY-ONE ~ Death

Thursday, April 17, 2014 5:35 p.m.

Daniel waved at Jason and Patty as they left the driveway. He felt the weight of age and weariness settle heavily upon his shoulders as he slowly ascended the familiar steps leading to his humble home. The sun was beginning to set, mere inches from the horizon, casting a golden hue across the fields that surrounded his dwelling.

Gazing to the area behind the barn, Daniel could see the U-Pick farm and the fruit trees in bloom. The cherry trees with their pink blossoms filled the air with a heavenly scent. In the distance, the different apple trees filled their branches with blossoms.

Daniel continued up the stairs. Each step was an effort, a reminder of the passage of time and the toil of a long, fulfilling life. It had been a long and arduous trip to Shipshewana. Still, he had seen his granddaughter get married to a wonderful, young Amish man. He smiled as he remembered how she gazed at Evan Kurtz, the *Englische* boy who had caught her heart while they performed at the Blue Gate Theater.

For some reason, the steps seemed higher and the porch appeared even wider than normal. He grabbed the handrail and held tightly to it. A shortness of breath filled his chest. He reached the top of the stairs and felt a sudden dizziness wash over him. He grasped the railing, his weathered hands trembling. His heart labored, as if carrying the burdens of a lifetime in those final moments. Daniel took a deep breath, feeling the cool spring air fill his lungs, and he closed his eyes.

Martha reached down to help him as he sprawled at the top of the front porch steps.

As the world around him seemed to fade into a soft, ethereal light, he felt a profound peace wash over him. He heard whispers, voices of loved ones long gone, calling to him from the beyond. Opening his eyes, he was met with a breathtaking sight.

"Let me help you." Dressed in a glowing white gown, Adam Brown stooped down to grab Daniel's hand and help him up. "How you doing, mate?"

Daniel frowned, but it was good to see his old Australian friend. He nodded.

"I..." He shook his head. "I feel really good." He clutched his chest. "The shortness of breath is gone." He frowned. "But, Adam, you are dead. How are you here?"

"C'mon, mate," Adam said. "They're all inside, waiting."

Daniel grimaced in a frown. *Who is waiting?* he thought.

Adam opened the door and Daniel looked back at the steps. He saw himself stretched across them with Martha sitting beside him, crying.

Why is she crying? Daniel thought, but followed Adam into the house.

Daniel gazed at the group - his father and mother, Antonio Cardivale, Bishop Schmucker, Julia Bronson Jones, and Jonathan Bell. Adam Brown joined the group. They were bathed in a gentle, warm light, their faces radiant with love and serenity. Daniel's heart overflowed with joy at the sight of them.

"Our *Vorsänger* (song leader) has arrived," the group said in unison.

"Sing for us," Antonio bellowed and waved his Italian hands in the air. "Lead us. Sing."

"You are our *Vorsänger* (song leader), young Daniel," Bishop Schmucker said, and nodded in agreement. "Sing."

Julia Jones stood behind Bishop Schmucker and his father. She motioned for him to stand straight, and to lift his head.

"What song do you want me to sing," Daniel asked, noticing the walls of the house shimmering, becoming translucent. He squinted, watching the walls disappear. Clouds filled the area. Big, white clouds floated in the clear, cerulean blue sky.

Daniel stood and began to sing the only song he knew they all had heard - Where're You Walk.

The group joined him and they sang parts. *Parts!* he thought. *Harmony.* He felt his heart lift and a glow of happiness envelope him.

Daniel gazed one last time down at Martha. She still hugged his body, rocking and crying.

The Amish Singer's voice was silent.

THE END

Series History

The Secret Voice.

Originally the novel was written more as a memoir of my days in high school from 1961 through 1965. My writing mentor enjoyed the story but told me it lacked a 'hook' to make it interesting. In other words, it was a nice story, but boring.

I gave it some thought and noticed the Amish who live near me. I changed the story to be about a young Amish boy wanting to go to high school and learn.

There are many facts in the story. The school district had just consolidated a few years earlier, combining four separate schools into one new school district.

In 1961, when I started high school, we had a black chorus teacher. She was the only black person in the area for approximately fifty miles - in other words, Toledo or Fort Wayne.

She taught me to sing light opera. Entering my freshman year, my singing voice was meek, at best. By the end of the first year, I had grown the confidence to sing without fear of others listening. By the end of my sophomore year, I had entered area competition and did well, but not well enough. It was during my junior year in high school that I competed well enough locally to continue on to state competition. I scored well at both levels.

As to the trip to Fort Wayne for the presentation of *The Messiah*, that also is a real experience. There were five students and our teacher. There was a small contingent of rioters and our teacher knew exactly what to do.

Yes, the chorus teacher lived in a trailer and was watched constantly. Some of the lines in the story are real comments by people who didn't know I was near enough to hear.

My English teacher read the rough of the book. She recognized the school, the classes, the hallways, everything. She was point on as to who Jason was, a colorful combination of two of my best friends during high school.

As you will discover, all my books have facts and *blue sky*; it is up to the reader to figure out which is which.

Originally, this was to be a single book. I was wrong.

The New York Voice

After being 'harassed' by the ladies of my church as to 'what happens next' this novel came to be.

Again, like my first book, it is based on facts from my life, woven with fiction.

A Navy buddy of mine with whom I shared an apartment for several month, decided to move to New York City with another friend. That friend was in a play and the lead, who he was backup to, was killed.

It only took a little bit to change the characters to work with my Amish character of Daniel.

To be honest, I don't truly know the outcome of the murder or how it was resolved. So, yes, my final of the story is all *blue sky*.

Back to the facts, the gentleman murdered, I don't remember his name, so I made that up. He was English, but I decided Australian was more interesting. Yes, he did have a play. Was it good? I have no idea.

Using the character of Cardinale from *The Secret Voice*, I continued with him in the *New York Voice*. With a little research, I was able to find a location with both a dry cleaners and restaurant on the Internet that worked for my story. I had a true visual to work from.

The day in the park, basically, that is true.

I, with another friend, and our girlfriends at the time, went to New York to visit my Navy buddy. We spent time sight-seeing and there was all sorts of things happening in Central Park.

My first time going to New York, I ended up in the bus terminal and was 'friended' by a young hippie. Basically, that scene is all true.

The trip to Bird-in-Hand was my memories of a one-day trip there.

Other items described about New York City were enhanced by quips from my minister who I think he said was a cabbie in NYC back in the day.

The Amish Voice

Again, pressured by the ladies of the church when they finished *The New York Voice,* I needed something to finish the series. Thus sprung *The Amish Voice* which I felt would finish the series. I was wrong, but more on that later.

This book is probably one of the more 'fictitious' of the series. Yes, there are facts in the book, but they are subtle.

When I was a young boy, in our town, Bryan aka DeMotte, there was a department store named *The Charles Company*. I loved that store, it was fascinating. There was a fabric area in the basement and on the main floor, a central checkout which had a tube which connected with the office upstairs. Sales slips and invoices were slipped into small tubes, placed into the 'magic'aka pneumatic tube and it was sent automatically up to the next floor. Remember, this was really back in the mid-1950s. I was only ten. At the time, the technology fascinated me.

The town of Bryan has a wonderful 'castle' courthouse. Today, my grandchildren, and great-grandchildren, enjoy going uptown to walk around the central block with the courthouse at the center. They love the fantasy.

It was at this point I had conflicts that maybe I should have not used fictitious names for the communities and locations. Especially, after using Shipshewana in this book.

In other words, the communities and locales were:

Centertown: Farmer
DeMotte: Bryan
Lyons: Ney
Myersville: Mark Center
Hayton: Williams Center
Madison: Montpelier
Frontier: Pioneer
Lake Hakihet: Lake Seneca

I did an immense amount of research about Amish weddings, courtship, etc. I spoke with the Amish constantly to make sure that I was portraying the Amish in the correct light, not some glorious dream world many consider.

Now, as to thinking this was the last book. When I finished it, I handed the rough draft to my wife to read. She finished it and the first words from her were... NOT it was a great book, an enjoyable read, I enjoyed it. NO!! The first words were what I had come to dread: What happens next?

What happened next? I got COVID. The doctors didn't expect me to survive.

I spent the next two plus years struggling to write the next book. I was working on The Family Voice but kept being slammed against the wall with time issues. Things weren't working. Finally, I got it figured out and book 4 came to be.

The Vietnam Voice

Book four in the series, this was one that caused me to step back and review the overall timeline of the series.

I was working on The Family Voice but kept having issues. The book would cover the years 1965/66 through 2013. Hm? That wasn't going to work. Book 5 was scheduled to be The Vietnam Voice but that meant doing The Family Voice and bringing you up to 2013 and then taking you back to 1965/66. Even worse? Book 6, *The Englische Voice* would jump back to 2013.

No! No! No! That wasn't going to work.

Hence, book four became *The Vietnam Voice* so it would agree and work within the timeline I was creating.

As to what is fact and what is fiction.

I was in the Navy. I was trained to speak, read, and write Russian. During the time I was at the Language School in Monterey, CA, I leaned a smidgen of several other languages including Vietnamese, Chinese Cantonese and Mandarin, Swahili, Turkish, Japanese, and a few others. Oh, yes, I learned Russian, too, and had to relearn to speak English. As the cab driver told us, picking up students from the language school, you listen to them and try to guess the location they want. Without realizing it, I had asked to go to the craft store at the corner of third and main. Yes, I had slipped between English and Russian so he knew it was a 'craft' 'corner' and 'main' but had no idea what the words were for 'store at the' and 'of third.' In fact, my banker spoke Russian, and we did all my transactions in Russian, but I digress.

I had a church member who was stationed in Vietnam make sure that most of my story-telling of Vietnam rang close to the truth without being too depressing. He was Army and was a great reference. He was the one to tell me about how the different locales had different smells to them.

It is amazing the amount of research one must do to write. I learned more about burns than most average people know about. For me, it was like two hours of searching and learning, ten minutes of writing. The hard part was not going down a bunch of rabbit holes on other stuff while researching.

I used a lot of my COVID time at the hospital in the story. I was isolated and not allowed visitors. In fact, my two-week stay probably had less than ten hours of social interaction and most of that (over half) happened on the day I was released.

Again, I did a lot of research with the Amish about baptism, marriage, etc. I want my books to ring as true as they can about the Amish lifestyle.

Again, this book came to be because of the church ladies' mantra: What happens next.

This one took some finagling to write. I had to cover almost fifty years so the final book in the series could be written.

Yes, I could have expanded on stories and created another three or four books, but I felt it was time to finish the series.

The Family Voice as one reader put it... sure has a lot of babies.

Well, family is about... parents, grandparents, children, grandchildren. It's about those who come in contact with you, one way or another.

This novel includes the creation of Lake Hakihet aka Lake Seneca. I fictionalized the tale, but the bottom line, the real lake was created.

Another aspect, the family farm. Again, fictionalize, but based on a friend of mine who lives in another state whose parents decided to go out on a limb and create a U-pick operation that actually did expand to include growing produce for a local grocery. Again, facts blurred with fiction.

A fan asked me how I kept all the names, dates, families straight in my head. I didn't. I created a chart that listed my characters and their interaction with one another. I had created it with book three, expanded it with book four, and was so happy to have it with book five.

Elsewhere in the book, you will find what I call my 'family trees' that I had all on one chart connecting them between each other and also into which books the characters were introduced and used.

I used a wonderful program for my writing - Scrivener - which allowed me to keep all my chapters, characters, locations, research, and anything else, all in one place. If I found an article on the Internet, I was able to print it as a PDF and store it within my novel and be able to read it anytime I wanted.

Why do I mention this? Years ago, one of the stories I was writing, I found some interesting research. I printed it out, lost the printout, and when I went to find it again, it was gone, no longer available. The whole story line was based on this one article and it was gone. That story never was written.

Again, there was a lot of research for this novel because I had to discover what land cost at that period of time, what vegetables and fruits were priced, and anything else to make the story ring true.

The Englische Voice

Before the mantra even started, I let my fans know ahead of time, this is the LAST book in the series. There is no 'what happens next.'

I thought I had it under control. Again, I was wrong. The next question was: What is the next series? What Amish story do you have planned?

To those questions - I have a couple of possibilities up my sleeve.

One is an Amish tale of young boy on *Rumschpringe* in New York City. The year? 2001. The date? September 11th. Current working title: *Amish 9-11*.

The other is a light horror read. Working title: *The Amish Hunter*. It involves Amish, *Rumschpringe,* and vampires. So, sue me. It will be a dark tale but not a lot of blood, guts and gore. I prefer to grab your brain, take it out, play with it, and put it back with minimal damage.

About this book, *The Englische Voice*. This one involves more romance and the Amish angst, but in an opposite situation. Rather than a young Amish girl having inner fights of being Amish or becoming *Englische*, it is about an *Englische* boy deciding if he wants to be Amish or not.

Of course, it involves singing. My main character, Daniel Yoder, is up in his years, in fact, he's almost sixty-seven.

What is fact? Location. Location. Location.

This story is 95% fiction. Of course, I still had to do a lot of research. TB, tuberculosis, isn't something on the tip of everyone's tongue now-a-days. Again, what is the current price of cattle, calves, birthing processes, etc. in 2013? Those are the truths.

But, the rest of the story is mainly the creation of my mind.

I hope you enjoyed the series.

Be sure to check my website - www.bobnailor.com - for new books and series. I am constantly writing. As my one friend said, and I agree, I will write until they yank my keyboard from my rigor-mortised hands when I die.

Thanks for reading this series.

Bob Nailor, Author.

Family Trees

Benjamin Yoder Family Tree

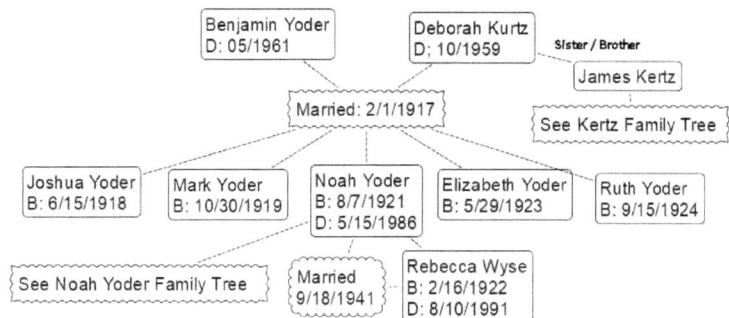

Noah Yoder Family Tree Page 1

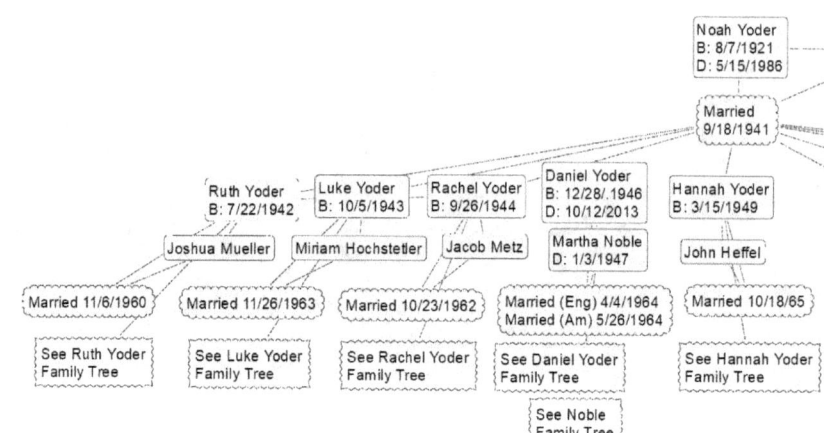

Noah Yoder
B: 8/7/1921
D: 5/15/1986

Married
9/18/1941

Ruth Yoder
B: 7/22/1942

Luke Yoder
B: 10/5/1943

Rachel Yoder
B: 9/26/1944

Daniel Yoder
B: 12/28/.1946
D: 10/12/2013

Hannah Yoder
B: 3/15/1949

Joshua Mueller

Miriam Hochstetler

Jacob Metz

Martha Noble
D: 1/3/1947

John Heffel

Married 11/6/1960

Married 11/26/1963

Married 10/23/1962

Married (Eng) 4/4/1964
Married (Am) 5/26/1964

Married 10/18/65

See Ruth Yoder
Family Tree

See Luke Yoder
Family Tree

See Rachel Yoder
Family Tree

See Daniel Yoder
Family Tree

See Hannah Yoder
Family Tree

See Noble
Family Tree

Noah Yoder Family Tree Page 2

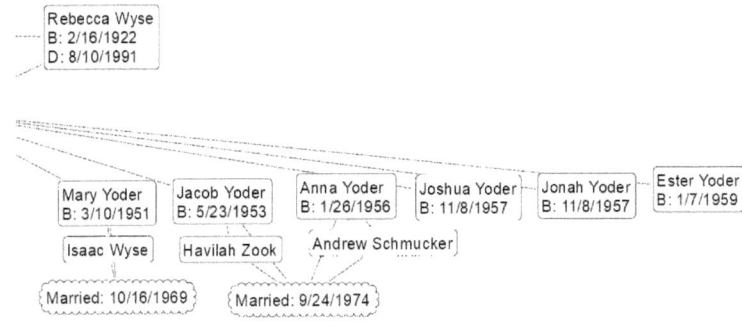

Rebecca Wyse
B: 2/16/1922
D: 8/10/1991

Mary Yoder
B: 3/10/1951

Jacob Yoder
B: 5/23/1953

Anna Yoder
B: 1/26/1956

Joshua Yoder
B: 11/8/1957

Jonah Yoder
B: 11/8/1957

Ester Yoder
B: 1/7/1959

Isaac Wyse

Havilah Zook

Andrew Schmucker

Married: 10/16/1969

Married: 9/24/1974

Ruth Yoder Family Tree

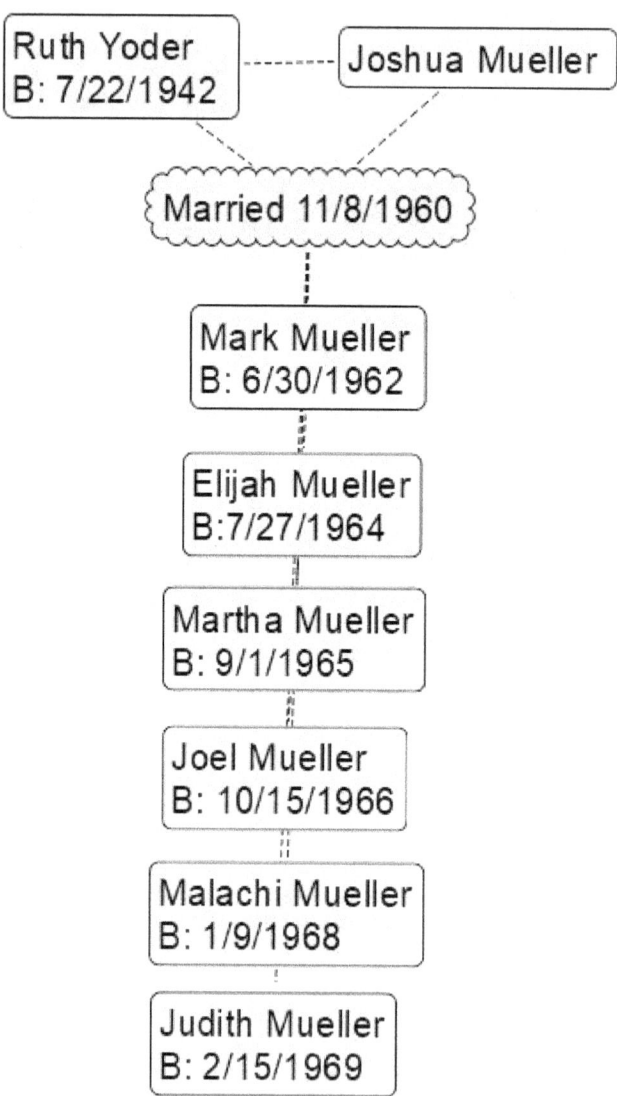

Luke Yoder Family Tree

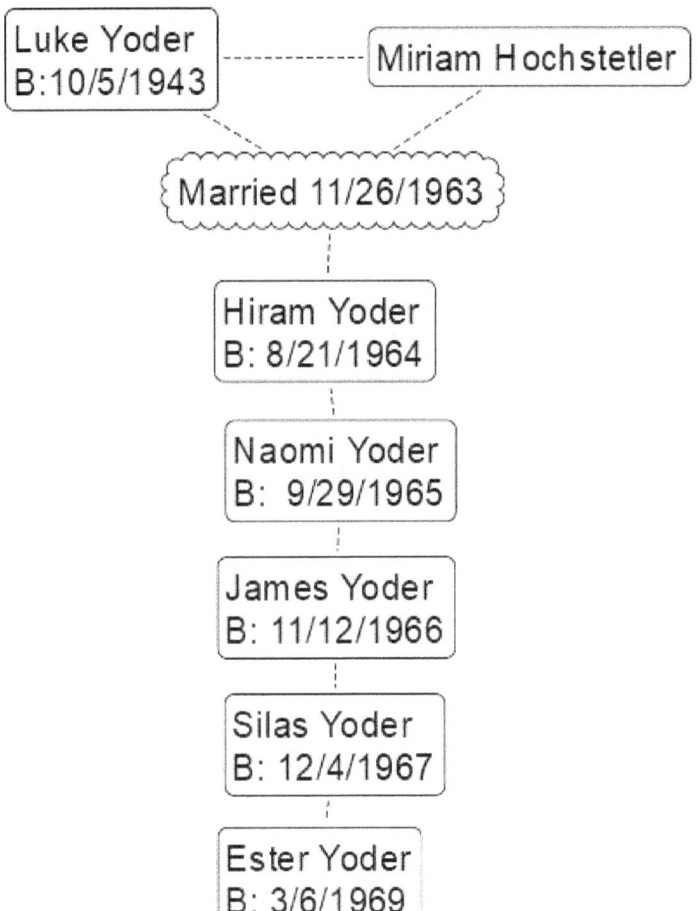

Rachel Yoder Family Tree

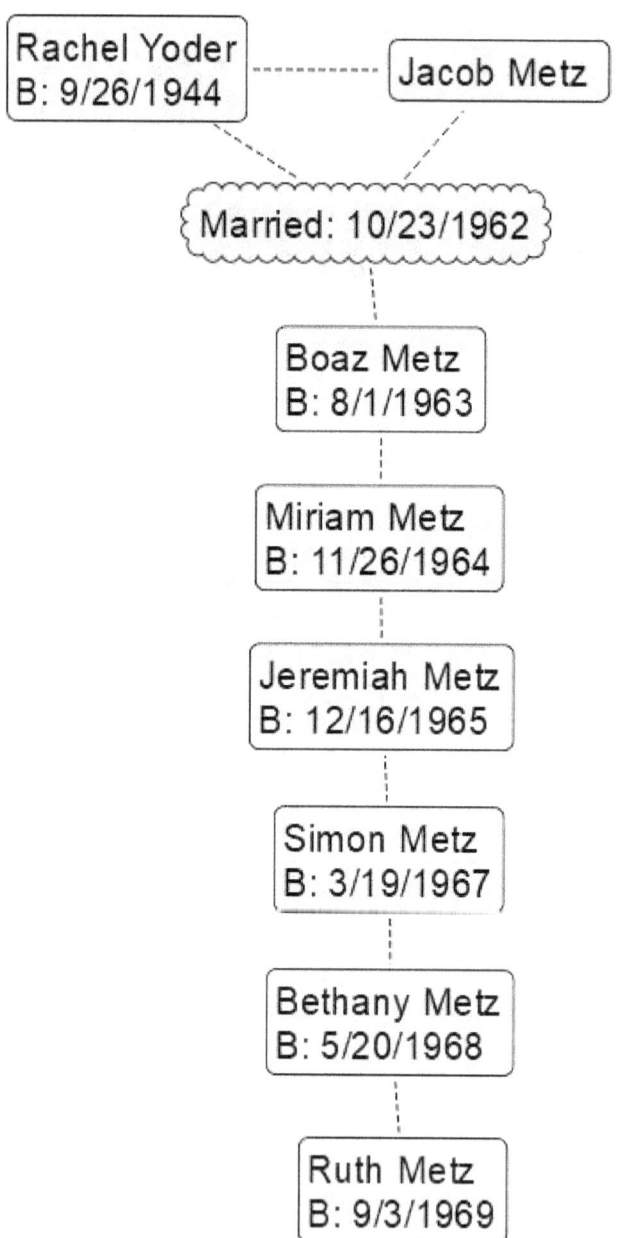

Daniel Yoder Family Tree

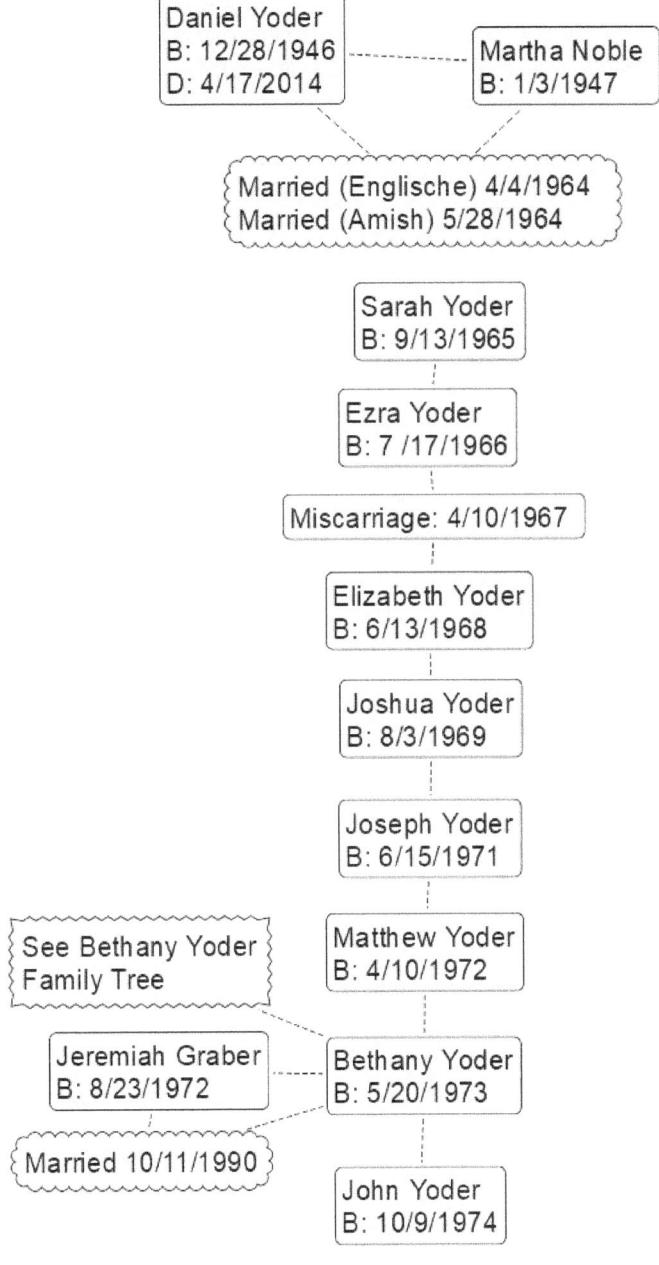

Hannah Yoder Family Tree

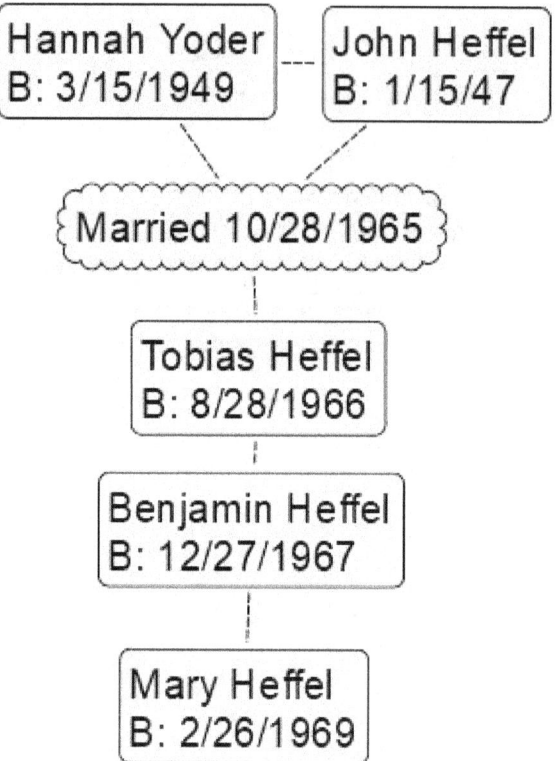

Bethany Yoder Family Tree

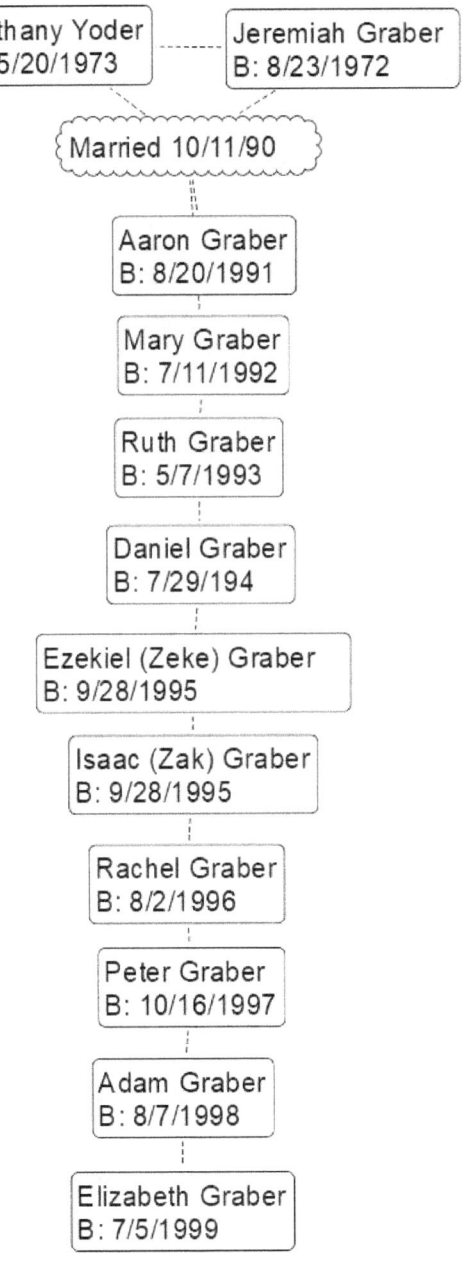

Kurtz Family Tree

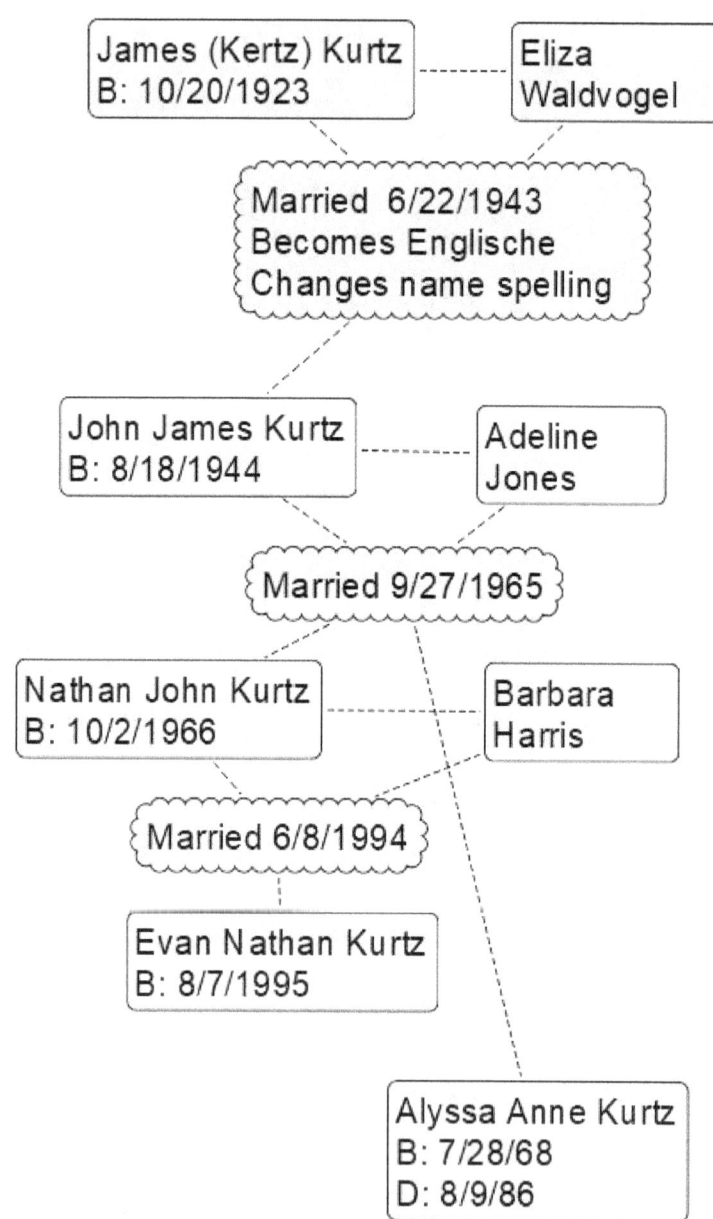

James (Kertz) Kurtz
B: 10/20/1923

Eliza
Waldvogel

Married 6/22/1943
Becomes Englische
Changes name spelling

John James Kurtz
B: 8/18/1944

Adeline
Jones

Married 9/27/1965

Nathan John Kurtz
B: 10/2/1966

Barbara
Harris

Married 6/8/1994

Evan Nathan Kurtz
B: 8/7/1995

Alyssa Anne Kurtz
B: 7/28/68
D: 8/9/86

Noble Family Tree

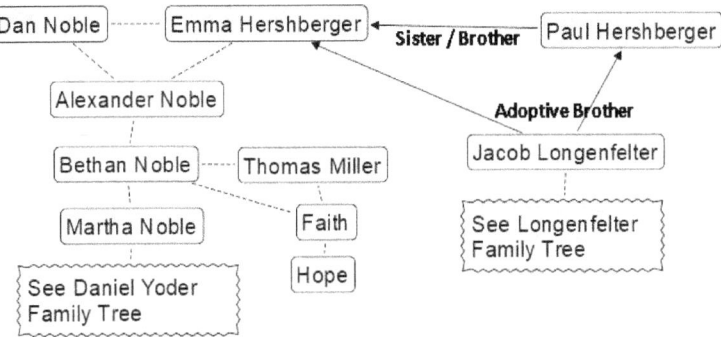

Bell Family Tree

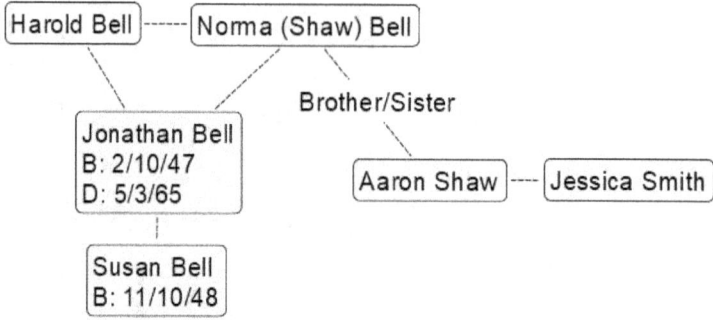

Muirs Family Tree

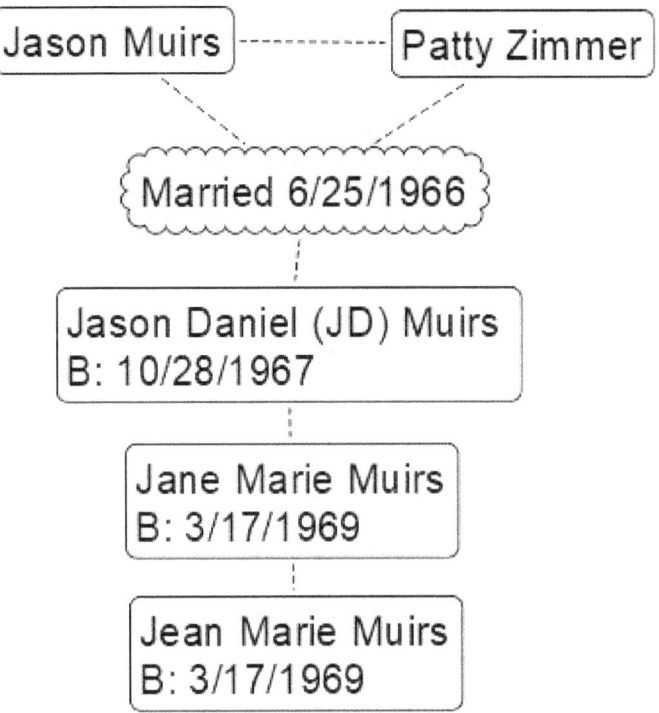

Longenfelter Family Tree

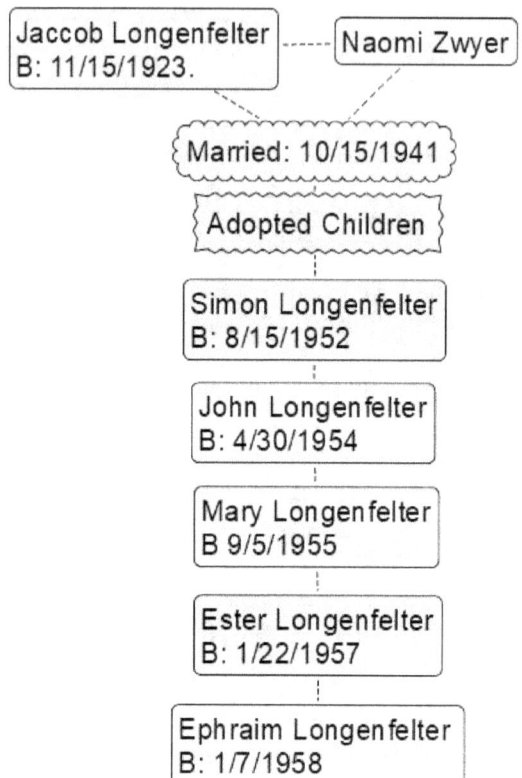

About the Author

My name is Robert S. Nailor but most people call me Bob.

I'm retired from the federal government. I was a computer geek and still do some programming yet today. One would think I should have plenty of time to write, but I actually seem to have less now. So, to make sure that things work out correctly, I force myself to sit down and write. That doesn't always work. Today, writing is fun and I find it relaxing. I get to visit those fantastic and strange places within my mind and well, if I don't come back right away, there is no longer somebody behind me writing on a pink sheet of paper.

I live with my wife, Violet, in a ranch home snuggled into a small wooded acre in NW Ohio. I was born in Sioux City, Iowa but my parents moved to Ohio in 1953. I have four sons and currently have ten grandchildren - 7 granddaughters and 3 grandsons. Plus, I have 11 great-grandchildren — 5 great-granddaughters and 6 great-grandsons.

My interests are camping (have RV, will travel), gardening, music, cooking and reading. So where do I travel? I've been in 46 of the 50 states and strangely, Hawaii is one of the states I've visited (U.S. Navy) but not Alaska. I have also visited two of our territories - Puerto Rico and the Virgin Islands. Traveling allows me to add the ambiance to my stories and also to some of the characters. Gardening is a bit gamey since we live in the country and have the wildlife visiting us constantly — deer, rabbits, raccoon, birds, squirrels plus many others. So, vegetables don't always make it to harvest, but what does is more than tasty.

There are flowers, sometimes too many, to keep me busy. Music? I love New Age music and my favorite group is Mannheim Steamroller... and not just because of their fabulous Christmas albums; I was hooked on them before that. I also have created some of my own electronic music which I've been told is pretty good. Should I mention cooking? I love to cook and do gourmet cooking. Having worked with Boy Scouts for several years, I have taught many boys the basics of cooking beyond hot dogs and beans. I have won quite a few contests. As to what I read; well, obviously a lot of science fiction, fantasy and some Christian. Horror, romance, adventure and other genres are also great reads when they catch my attention with an intriguing tag line or cover.

Bibliography

Novels:
The Secret Voice ~ Book 1 in The Amish Singer series
The New York Voice ~ Book 2 in The Amish Singer series
The Amish Voice ~ Book 3 in The Amish Singer series
The Vietnam Voice ~ Book 4 in The Amish Singer series
The Family Voice ~ Book 5 in The Amish Singer series
Eternal Blood ~ Book 1 in the Barry Hargrove detective mysteries
The Babbling Sphinx ~ Book 2 in the Barry Hargrove detective mysteries
Dragon Feast ~ Book 3 in the Barry Hargrove detective mysteries
Pangaea, Eden Lost ~ a Barclay Havens, relic hunter mis-adventure
Three Steps: The Journeys of Ayrold ~ an Irish fantasy for today
2012 Timeline Apocalypse ~ the Mayan calendar comes to an end
At Death's Door ~ a collection of "light" horror stories about death
The Emerald ~ Book 1 in The Shiyula Realm series

Coming Soon...
The Topaz ~ book 2 in The Shiyula Realm series
Mommy Missing ~ book 4 in the Barry Hargrove mystery series
Fire Life ~ a fire-cat fantasy series

Anthologies I Am In:
52 Weeks of Writing Tips ~ tips to improve one's writing ability
Telling Tales of Terror ~ essays on how to write horror and dark fiction
Mother Goose Is Dead ~ a collection of favorite fairy tales, fractured
Dead Set: A Zombie Anthology ~ a collection of unusual zombie tales
The Complete Guide to Writing Paranormal-Vol 1 ~ various essays
Nights of Blood 2 ~ different takes on the vampire story
Guide to Writing Science Fiction ~ essays on writing science fiction
Firestorm of Dragons ~ an eclectic collection of dragon stories
Fantasy Writer's Companion ~ essays on writing fantasy
13 Night of Blood ~ 13 amazing vampire tales
Spirits of Blue & Gray ~ a collection of Civil War ghost stories

PLUS more at www.bobnailor.com

www.ingramcontent.com/pod-product-compliance
Lightning Source LLC
Chambersburg PA
CBHW070921260626
47162CB00007B/2754